WITHDRAWN

STIR UP THE DUST

**Center Point
Large Print**

**This Large Print Book carries the
Seal of Approval of N.A.V.H.**

STIR UP THE DUST

WILLIAM COLT MACDONALD

CENTER POINT PUBLISHING
THORNDIKE, MAINE

This Center Point Large Print edition
is published in the year 2004 by arrangement with
Golden West Literary Agency.

The text of this Large Print edition is unabridged. In other
aspects, this book may vary from the original edition. Printed in
Thailand. Set in 16-point Times New Roman type.

ISBN 1-58547-461-4

Library of Congress Cataloging-in-Publication Data

MacDonald, William Colt, 1891-1968.
    Stir up the dust / William Colt MacDonald.--Center Point large print ed.
        p. cm.
    ISBN 1-58547-461-4 (lib. bdg. : alk. paper)
        1. Large type books. I. Title.

PS3525.A2122S75 2004
813'.52--dc22

2004001605

For
Elizabeth and Wallace

PART ONE

JENNIFER

1

FOR SEVERAL DAYS AND NIGHTS THE GUNS HAD BEEN silent. The heavy detonations had already commenced to slacken when the intermittent rains, suddenly changed to violent, unabated fury, burst forth to compete with the pounding of heavy artillery, until the cannon, as though vanquished by the thundering storm, finally ceased, and the rain, triumphant, settled to a steady downpour that churned the Carolina soil to gumbo. Remained now only the continual dripping from pines and from the eaves of a cabin where lay Major Darius Urquhart, C.S.A., moving feverishly on a built-in bunk, his delirious mind still roaring with a confused cannonading of guns and downpour.

The afternoon waned; the wind rose, tossing tree limbs and laying flat the patches of wiregrass surrounding the cabin. Within the log structure, a girl rose from her seat and placed fresh fuel on the dying embers in the fireplace. It was growing dark, and after crossing the room to gaze at the sleeper on the bunkbed, the girl picked up a splinter of pine, stuck into a molded chunk of baked clay. Lighting one end of the slim torch, she returned to the table, oily smoke spiraling in a thin ribbon from the small light which threw into pale relief the girl's high cheekbones, the faintly hollow cheeks and the twin braids of thick blue-black hair. Wider through the shoulders than is general in women, her frame was sapling-slim, almost angular. The nose was high-arched; thin features with a not small mouth were enhanced by unbelievably long-lashed eyes the color of blue gentians veiled through grey smoke. Her breasts were high and small beneath the worn dress clinging to her legs in cotton stockings; her feet were long and narrow, and shod with well-worn moccasins which reached above the ankles. The girl wasn't more than seventeen or eighteen years old.

The tiny torch combined with the fireplace to illuminate the single room with its animal skins spread on plank flooring. Rain traced channels down window panes. Planed oaken planks made a closed door at the front; similar planks formed a heavy table, with a bench at either side. The fireplace was flanked by bookshelves loaded with worn volumes. Two straight-backed chairs and a low rocker completed the furniture.

A pot on a swinging crane in the fireplace next occupied the girl. Procuring a small bowl from a cupboard, she ladled out a thin gruel for the sick man. At her voice he ceased his delirious mutterings and accepted automatically the food she fed him. It was pitch dark without, now; again the girl busied herself with the invalid, pouring a whitish powder into a cup and filling it from a bucket. This liquid the invalid accepted not so easily: a delirious protest filled the cabin; one wasted hand moved feebly to push the cup away.

The girl spoke firmly, "Major Urquhart, drink of this

8

you must." She slipped one arm beneath his shoulders, raising him. There didn't seem much weight to the man. Some of the liquid spilled, but he swallowed most of the cup's contents before she again lowered him. A certain righteous indignation entered his tones. "Bitter," he mumbled, "bitter as defeat . . ."

Not once had he opened his eyes. The girl stood a moment gazing down on his tangled hair, the color of dark rust, and the matted beard. With a bandanna she wiped at his cotton nightgown where some of the liquid had splashed, and the touch of her hand brought a plaintive query to the man's lips: "Where's . . . Dix?"

"The sergeant's not far off, Major. Likely carrying out your last order, he is."

The white mask above the whiskers, eyes still closed, gathered in a frown. Memory's fingers probed through a labyrinth of delirium. What order? Had he given an order? The pale brow gradually smoothed out. Whatever it was, Dix would handle it. The invalid relaxed for a moment. Abruptly, his voice rose clear and shrill: "Forward, Rangers! Front into line! Charge the Yank blue-bellies!" He started up from his pillow, one arm waving.

The girl pressed him back. "Hush, Major. That's all over now, and the war's . . ."

"Of course it's over," the sick man stated querulously, eyes still closed, voice carrying contempt. ". . . those Fed cannon . . . no match for Terry's Rangers . . ." His voice ceased and he commenced to breathe deeply. Sleep again came and the deranged mutterings dwindled.

The girl made a second trip to the pot, adding to her

9

meal a chunk of corncake, dusty from the ashes of the fireplace, and from a coffee-pot a concoction composed of boiled water and roasted acorns. After eating, she seated herself in the rocker and fell asleep.

The pine splinter burned lower. A gust of wind shook the cabin. The girl sat erect, listening. There were horse sounds without, a certain scrabbling of hoofs in wet gumbo, and a man's irritated oath. The girl recognized the voice and relaxed, waiting. Minutes passed. A foot struck the door and it was flung wide to admit a tall individual with something of the quality of sinew sheathed in rawhide. A wet gust swept through the cabin and the man slammed the door at his back. The girl rose.

The man was swarthy, unshaven, in his late thirties, with hair as black as the girl's, and wide cheekbones and mouth, and keen eyes beneath heavy brows. Water dripped from his battered grey flop-brimmed hat. His stained blouse was that of the Eighth Texas Cavalry. There was a rent in one sleeve; most of the sergeant's insignia on the other sleeve was missing. His patched, faded blue trousers, with wide yellow stripes along the seams, were, or had been at one time, those of a Federal cavalryman. One boot was in fair condition; the sole of its mate was held in place with knotted rawhide. "I just couldn't make to get back no sooner," he said. "How's the Major doin'?"

"The fever is down, I'm thinking. He's been sleeping for probably two hours. I fell asleep myself."

Dixon Corbillat crossed the floor to place a hand on the invalid's forehead. Some trace of light entered his saturnine features. "He's sweatin'. That's good, ain't it?"

"It is a very good sign," the girl replied quietly. She commenced placing on the table—such food as there was.

Corbillat said, "Wait! I can do better than that." He left the house and re-entered minutes later carrying a slab of bacon and a burlap sack from which he produced various small bundles. "There's bacon and corn-flour and real coffee, Miss Jen. I even got some candles—"

"Wherever in the world would you be getting all this?"

"Over to'rd Bentonville. The place is lousy with Yanks. I didn't go clear into town. Where there's Yanks, there's fodder. I cotched me a freighter haulin' rations. He objected some . . ."

"You didn't kill him?" The girl's eyes were wide.

"Not less'n he died of fright. There's more fodder out back in the lean-to."

The girl's eyes showed how much she wanted food, real food. "I'll fix supper in a minute. Meanwhile . . ." She went to a closet in one corner and returned with clothing of rusty-black. "My father's," she explained. "Get your wet clothing off."

Dix Corbillat protested. "This ain't the first time I've been wet, Miss Jen."

"It could be the last time, Sergeant. One sick man here is enough." Corbillat meekly accepted the clothing and started toward the door, but the girl stopped him. "You'll change here." The man flushed

11

under the swarthy skin; he made further protestations. "You're just making fool man-talk," the girl said impatiently. "With real food to prepare, would I be wasting time looking at you?" With no further words she busied herself over the sacks on the table. Still blushing furiously, Corbillat retreated near the door, whisked off his sodden clothing and frantically thrust his lean frame into the trousers and coat. By the time he'd returned to the fireplace, salt pork was sizzling in a spider and the fragrance of coffee was filling the cabin.

They ate hungrily, in silence, Corbillat wolfing down the food, thinking: *This is the first real meal in—how long?* Until now, lack of food had pushed from his mind nearly all resentment of Union victory; suddenly he found his thoughts returning to the defeat the South had suffered. He scowled at the girl, but at her querying look, said only, "We want to put some beans to soakin', tonight."

Later, after another look at the sleeping man in the bunk, the girl crossed to the other bunk, slipped in on a corn-husk-filled mattress, and undressed beneath the blankets. "Wake me, if anything is wanted."

"I'll 'tend anythin' that's needful, if the Major rouses." Corbillat put out the light, found a blanket in which he rolled himself on the floor, and closed his eyes against the flickering from the fireplace. Without, the wind died away, and only the steady dripping from the eaves and trees broke the nocturnal silence.

2

THERE HAD ALWAYS BEEN AN URQUHART, EITHER through duty, or a liking for adventure, somewhere in the vanguard of American events, and to this rule, Darius Urquhart was no exception. Darius was the son of Diomedes Urquhart, a widower and veteran of the Mexican War, who had erected some twenty miles from San Antonio, Texas, a great house with portico and tall white pillars, which it had pleased him to name Urquhart Oaks. Here he had concentrated on the breeding of horses and cattle and cotton. His wife's death had left him a lonely man, and when the clouds of approaching war commenced lifting black thunderheads, in the east, Diomedes Urquhart almost welcomed the inevitable clash between North and South. Perhaps he sensed, even before John Brown's ill-starred attempt at Harper's Ferry, that war would bring him a certain surcease from his loneliness.

True, Urquhart supported Sam Houston's losing fight against secession (neither man had ever believed in slavery, and Houston was to be ousted as Governor of Texas for his own unyielding stand) but when he learned that Texas had left the Union, Urquhart immediately recalled his sons, Darius and Douglas, from Virginia Military Institute, and took steps to ensure the serving of all three Urquharts in the Wax between the States. Urquhart did not believe in war, but he was a son of Texas: his destiny lay with his state. It was now he remembered an idea spoken of by a blond giant of a man, Benjamin Franklin Terry whom he'd met at the Secession Convention at Austin, some months previously. Terry had spoken of organizing a cavalry regiment of mounted Texans, for the Confederacy.

Urquhart wrote to Terry, but by that time Terry had been commissioned a major with orders to proceed to Brownsville and rout out a Federal garrison stationed at Fort Brown. It proved a bloodless victory for Terry, and he was rewarded with a commission to raise the regiment, later to become famous as Terry's Rangers. Terry's reply to Urquhart's letter was to the point: "Come to Houston and answer the call for mounted rangers."

Urquhart journeyed to Houston, taking his two sons, Douglas and Darius, as well as Dixon Corbillat who had been for many years past, Urquhart's major-domo in stock raising. Through Frank Terry, now a colonel, Urquhart received a captain's commission and was ordered to "enroll a full company to consist of one captain, two lieutenants, four sergeants, eight corporals, one blacksmith, two musicians and seventy-five to a hundred mounted privates, each man to furnish equipment for one horse and to arm himself." Though Urquhart asked no favors, Terry arranged that Darius and Douglas were made lieutenants. Corbillat entered as a corporal and was later raised to a sergeantcy.

In less than thirty days nearly a dozen companies of rangers had been organized. They were mustered into service as the Eighth Texas Cavalry, though the regiment was considered an independent command and was better known as Terry's Texas Rangers. From the first, the Rangers bore a well-earned reputation as a body of mad-riding, fire-eating knight-errants, half centaur and half daredevil, men who raided towns, destroyed Union railroad bridges, and captured Federal bases of supplies, always striking where least expected, caring little for life, so long as death served better the cause of Southern Glory.

Colonel Terry was killed in the first skirmish he entered, near Woodsonville, Kentucky, in December of '61, leading a relatively small force of Rangers—seventy-five cavalrymen—against three hundred Union fighters. A few months later, his brother, Clinton, died at Shiloh. It was at Shiloh, too, the first of the Urquharts met his end: Douglas Urquhart was swept from his saddle, a Minié ball through his chest.

Casualties and, consequently, promotions came rapidly in Terry's Rangers. Opposed always against odds, the Rangers carried more than their share of fighting. Old records show that from their enlistment to the very end, Terry's Rangers maintained themselves at their own, and the enemy's expense. At Beardstown, Kentucky, when they should have been in full retreat, they charged suddenly and, with six-shooters, won victory against a superior force equipped with cannon. It was Terry's Rangers who protected General Longstreet's rear in Tennessee. Rangers covered Johnston's retreat at Corinth.

It was at Chickamauga, in September of '63, that Diomedes Urquhart, now a colonel, made his last charge before being mowed down by Federal bullets, leaving Darius the sole survivor to carry on the

15

Urquhart name. By this time, there was little with which to carry on, where the war was concerned; the conflict long since had taken an ominous toll of the Rangers. They were gaunt, ragged, hungry, almost exhausted, depending for supplies, clothing and mounts on whatever might be captured from the enemy. Following the death of his father, Darius Urquhart was wounded during the fighting near Missionary Ridge, but later rejoined his men in what he suspected were futile efforts. The following year, the Rangers made daily harrying skirmishes against Sherman in his march through Georgia.

Urquhart, now elevated to the rank of Major, had realized the Confederate cause was lost when the Rangers were ordered into action, in March of '65, near Bentonville, North Carolina, in what was to prove their final engagement of the war. Charge followed fruitless charge, from which, of a force of two thousand Rangers, participating, only one hundred and fifty emerged. Even before the final sacrificial attack had begun Urquhart had taken a chunk of lead in his left shoulder and had been ordered to the rear in charge of Sergeant Corbillat, himself wounded, though not seriously.

Protesting, half-crazed with pain, Urquhart swayed in the saddle, the bridle reins of his mount in the hands of Corbillat. It commenced to drizzle; clouds hung low in a fog of rain and powdersmoke. Rocking blasts from big guns shook the earth; balls and canister screamed through the murky atmosphere, lighted vividly at times by blinding flashes of cannonading. Now Corbillat's one thought was to get his major to safety. Dix knew inexorably that there'd be no reforming of ranks this day. The grey lines were pressed back under the Federal onslaught until a retreat was ordered. What started as an orderly withdrawal was turned into a rout, with the Union forces scattering the worn-out Confederates, as tumbleweeds are scattered before the blast of a Texas norther.

Urquhart, only half conscious, allowed his horse to be led by the mounted Corbillat toward the shelter of young pines. The horses panted up the slope. Corbillat paused to look back over the smoke-drifted terrain. Big guns were chanting their lethal litany, but Corbillat noted that all the firing seemed to be coming from the Union lines. A rattling far-off noise sounded through the sulphuric grey mist. Here and there, mounted Federal cavalrymen pursued running figures in tattered grey. There were sharp flashes of crimson fire, or a dull gleaming of steel sabers, and the grey-clad figures seemed to melt into the sodden earth.

Corbillat muttered, "Christ . . ." and urged the horses over the crest of the hill and down a long slope between pine trunks. Rain fell in slanting arrows to seep through the shabby uniforms of the two men. Urquhart was slumped down, eyes wide but unseeing, bloodless fingers clinging to the saddle. Rain, low clouds were blotting out the light by the time the riders reached shelter provided by a clump of cedars beaded with moisture. They paused to rest the horses, then continued the descent. The drumming of guns was farther off now.

They should have stopped. To leave the timber meant, likely, an encounter with a Federal patrol. That might be worth while, the sergeant considered, if it would bring Urquhart aid, but the major wouldn't want to surrender, not now after four years of fighting. Besides you couldn't trust those Yank bastards; they might not accept a surrender, or even give a man time to tell he wanted to surrender. It would be best to keep going, even though (Corbillat was at last inclined to believe) they were headed in the wrong direction, away from, rather than toward the Confederate forces.

The long wet day passed. It must have been close to five in the evening, when Corbillat spied a small clearing planted with orderly rows of sprouting corn, surrounded by a rail fence, though few rails remained in place. Then, as Corbillat and the major emerged into the open, the sergeant saw at the far side of the clearing a cabin of chinked logs. Blue smoke, scarcely discernible against the grey atmosphere, rose from a stone chimney; beyond the cabin a body of twenty horsemen, in rag-tag outfits of blue and grey, were just riding off. Three more saddled, but riderless, horses waited by the cabin door which stood open.

By then, it was too late to turn back. Corbillat felt his horse rear even before the report of the rifle blended with the animal's agonized scream, and a voice yelled frantically, "Confeds coming!" There came a sudden rush of galloping hoofs as the mounted riders fled.

As his mount crashed down, Corbillat loosened his feet from stirrups and threw himself wide, beyond the thrashing hoofs of the stricken beast, eyes already probing through the grey light for the source of the bullet. Then Corbillat saw him. The Yank was already firing a second shot, intended for Urquhart, though the leaden missile succeeded only in clipping through the pine needles, a yard above the major's head. Whether the report of the first shot shocked Urquhart to a momentary sanity, they never knew. Even as Corbillat was struggling up from wet earth, he felt the reins of the major's horse jerked from his fingers. Urquhart spurred toward the cabin, a wild Rebel yell rasping from his throat. It was this sudden movement that had caused the Yank to miss his second shot.

A tall man with heavy black whiskers, wearing a captain's blue uniform, emerged from the doorway of the pine structure, leaped into the saddle of one of the waiting horses and disappeared abruptly around the corner of the cabin, where the sounds of his horse's hoofs blended instantly with those made by the other departing riders.

Corbillat was running now, one hand tugging at his cap-and-ball pistol. He got the whole picture as Urquhart closed in, saw the Yank rifleman drop to one knee to take careful aim. There came the bright slithering gleam of Urquhart's saber as it was whipped from scabbard, and again that wild Rebel yell as the major charged the kneeling Federal cavalryman.

Corbillat fired, missed, but the shot was close enough to make the man in blue hesitate a moment. And in that moment, Urquhart swept down on him, saber swinging in a wide glittering arc. The Yank collapsed like a limp sack of old clothing. Urquhart was out of the saddle now, half-running, half-staggering toward the open doorway of the cabin. Panting, sobbing curses, Corbillat forced his stiff legs to carry him on. He heard a woman's scream, just as Urquhart disappeared within the structure, and then the short sharp report of a gun.

A second man came plunging from the cabin, a heavy-bodied man in a blue uniform. He saw Corbillat approaching, hesitated as though to return to his cabin, then made a scrambling dash for the nearest horse. This time the sergeant didn't miss his aim.

Still running, Corbillat stepped over the twitching form and on through the doorway. Within, he paused to accustom his eyes to the light, or lack of light. A table was overturned, and beyond stood a white-faced girl, eyes wide with terror, the back of one hand pressed against her open mouth as though to suppress further screams.

None of the furniture in the room was upright. Near the fireplace a grey-haired man lay face down in a pool of blood. Just within the doorway, almost at Corbillat's feet, was sprawled the grey-clad form of Major Urquhart, one side of his face smeared with something dark and wet. There was no sign of life in the major's ashen features when Corbillat stooped at his side. "I allowed we'd get somewheres, tonight," the sergeant spoke dully. "I might've knowed it wouldn't be any place good."

3

THE DAYS WERE INTO EARLY MAY, AND THE AIR FULL OF the moist spring fragrance of growing things. Darius Urquhart, swathed in blankets, sat in a rocking chair outside the open doorway of the cabin, the bright morning sun warm on his gaunt features. There was a certain healing quality in the piney-scented atmosphere. The new life it carried was not confined alone to Urquhart: a dogwood tree near one corner of the cabin had exploded in a riot of starry blossoms. Yesterday, the girl had brought in a great armful of tiny purple wild iris. Fleecy clouds pursued each other across the blue expanse of sky.

Each day's exposure to sun and pine-fragrant air had brought fresh strength to Urquhart's bony frame and renewed life to his thick, dark rust-red hair and beard. He raised long restless fingers and probed at his chin; that beard should have come off long since. When Dix returned, something would have to be done about it. Urquhart lounged there, a long lean man with a sardonic face in which was a touch of weary arrogance. He'd been looking through a book of poems, but the flashing red flight of a cardinal grosbeak had distracted the perusal. Now he just sat, a meditative look in his grey eyes, turning idly on one finger a heavy silver ring set with a carnelian intaglio.

One hand strayed unconsciously to his left shoulder: at least he had regained some use of the arm. He bent his head once more to the leather-bound volume. A triangle of dark rust-red hair fell across his forehead and he brushed it back, as he'd been doing most of his life, only to have it fall into place once more. He turned idly the pages, but the rhymed verses failed to hold his interest. Again he raised his head and gazed meditatively at the pines ringing the cabin clearing. And so, at long last (if the girl were to be believed) the war was over. With Lee surrendered, the end must be approaching with incredible speed. It was no more than Darius Urquhart had been expecting for some time.

The words came, half-aloud, "The war is over." It seemed incredible. A man doesn't readily relinquish an idea to which he has clung for four long years. The girl had seemed to know what she was talking about, though Urquhart reminded himself he wasn't at all sure just where she'd procured such information. So far as he knew, she'd seen no one except those two old Indians who came occasionally to the cabin to hoe the cornfield, the elderly man and woman with faces like black wrinkled walnuts, each looking like a discarded scarecrow, and little to indicate any difference in their sex.

The girl herself puzzled Urquhart. Quiet, rarely speaking unless spoken to and generally replying with a simple yes or no. Was she shy? That had been Urquhart's first impression. But there was nothing shy about the manner in which she attended his wounds each day with the deft touch of one who knows what she is about. No, it wasn't shyness; rather a reticence born of good breeding, Urquhart concluded. Breeding, she certainly possessed; whence else could come that finely chiseled nose, the level gaze from eyes like smoke-dusted gentians, the serene composure. And no one except a lady born and bred ever had such skin, somewhere between rich cream and ivory, with a healthy, dusky quality pulsating beneath the surface. He judged her not more than eighteen, though she owned the poise of one more mature.

Queerest of all had been her talking to those old Indians in their own language. Wherever in the world had a girl picked that up? Queer, that's what it was, a girl as pretty as—no, pretty wasn't quite the word. Something beyond that, something (the girl and this cabin and the old Indians), Urquhart couldn't quite dovetail in his mind. The whole business evaded classification.

He turned to see the girl emerging through the encircling trees. Urquhart guessed her father's grave was somewhere in that direction. He watched her approach, appreciating the long-limbed, even pace in the worn moccasins, the proud carriage and the clinging shabby calico taut against small high breasts. When she was closer he noted that her bare arms and legs (browner than the skin of her face with its darkly red mouth, beneath the wide-brimmed straw hat), looked scratched from contact with sharp grass. Thick braids of midnight hair hung over either shoulder.

She stopped a few feet from Urquhart, the gentian eyes questioning. "You're all right?" Urquhart replied, naturally, he was all right. Why shouldn't he be? When would the doctor come again?

The girl surveyed him from beneath the lovely long black lashes. "Doctor?"

"The doctor to check on my wounds." Urquhart's voice, like that of most Texans, carried a drawling quality.

"Oh, it's the doctor you're asking about." She paused. "I do not think it will be necessary for a doctor to come. You are healing nicely. Rest and food will do what is needed." Again she started toward the cabin doorway.

Urquhart twisted to look over one shoulder. "Just where did you hear the war had ended? It was such a surprise and . . ."

"My grandparents told me. They'd been to Bentonville . . ."

"Grandparents—?"

"The old couple, Tom and Mary Událi, who were here early this morning."

"Grandparents? They're Indians."

"Of the Cherokee Tribe," the girl assented, evenvoiced. Her already straight back stiffened.

Urquhart found comprehension difficult. Grandparents? That ancient crone and the man, withered, toothless . . . "But—I understood your name is Keating—Jennifer Keating. Keating—an Irish name, I believe—"

"My father married a Cherokee," the girl explained.

Outraged indignation was slowly replaced by amazement in Urquhart's thoughts, though his feelings showed but momentarily in his face. "Ah, I understand, now," he said quietly, but the girl had already noted that first instant resentment in his grey eyes, and

24

had passed on, into the cabin before he spoke.

A long breath escaped slowly from Urquhart's lips as he leaned back in the chair. Certain qualities were now explained, made clearer: the thick blue-black hair, the lovely wide cheekbones and generous mouth; the faint touch of the oblique in the delicate eyebrows, the thinly-chiseled high-arched nose; erect back and easy clean-limbed walk—all traits of the Indian. "No, by God," Urquhart whispered stubbornly. "No. It's too much for a man to take in! She's as white—whiter than I am."

4

URQUHART, MOVING WITH THE CAREFUL GAIT COMMON to convalescents, had made his way back to the rocking chair before the cabin, when he caught the sound of hoof-beats through the pine trees. He heard the horse stop near the lean-to, at the rear of the cabin, and within a few minutes Dixon Corbillat rounded the building, carrying heavily-laden burlap sacks. The sergeant's saturnine features brightened when his black eyes spied Urquhart.

"I'll be dawg-swiped! Major, you're gettin' along, sure enough. When I left, it was 'bout all you could do to make to get on your feet." His voice, too, carried the soft Texas drawl, as his lean fingers closed tightly on Urquhart's right hand.

"It's good to see you back, Dix. Nearly three weeks you've been gone, excepting that one night when you brought supplies and lighted right out again before I knew you'd been here. Oh, I've progressed, no doubt about it."

Corbillat said, "I'll be back immediate," and carried the two sacks to the cabin. Urquhart heard him greeting the girl and her low-voiced reply. When the sergeant returned, he brought a chair and placed it beside Urquhart's. He didn't speak at once. One hand shoved the battered grey hat to the back of his coarse black hair, while the fingers of the other groped in a pocket of the shabby pants and produced a cornhusk and tobacco, which were slowly manufactured into a cigarette which he offered to Urquhart. Urquhart refused with thanks. Corbillat, still not speaking, searched out a sulphur match, lit and inhaled meditatively. He said harshly, "You know somethin', Major? Them Yank bastuds have give up. We just given 'em a belly-full and they quit cold. I knowed they couldn't stick it much longer."

Urquhart thought: He doesn't know I've heard the war is ended. He's trying to spare my feelings. Aloud, he said gravely, "Taking a rather optimistic view of matters, aren't you, Dix?"

"You heard about it?" Corbillat's surprise showed in his dark eyes. He jerked one thumb toward the cabin. "I reckon she told you." Urquhart nodded. Corbillat said, "Surrenderin' don't mean anythin'. Christ A'mighty! Ain't no man goin' to accept no surrender when he's winnin'. No-siree! He's a-goin' to keep stompin' until you're dead. General Johnston done the same thing as Lee over near Durham's Station—"

"I hadn't heard about Johnston—"

"Do you know somethin' else? Lincoln's dead, so probably Grant won't tell him, and we can start fighting again. What you think?"

"Abe Lincoln dead?" Urquhart evinced interest. "What did he die of?"

"Lead-poisonin'. Some actor shot him at the opera house. And a friend of the actor's busted into Secretary Seward's house and did a heap of stabbin'. I reckon he knifed nigh everybody in Seward's household. Major, we've made those Yank bastuds sick of war. So anybody figures we're whupped . . ." Corbillat indulged in another tirade, Urquhart only half listening. Lincoln dead; the Confederacy surrendered. Peace had come at last.

"I've always considered Abe Lincoln was the victim of bad advice," Urquhart said. "I never could hold with folks who made him out to be some sort of fiend. Trouble was, he got in over his depth and had to back up his political party."

"Ain't no Rangers surrendered," Corbillat continued, stubbornly. "Colonel Harrison, of Terry's Rangers, wounded bad like he was—on crutches they tell me— has already sent orders none of Terry's Rangers is to surrender. *Texans don't surrender!* Them's his exact words. He sent word to us to come out and not get tangled in no surrender orders."

Urquhart asked curiously, "Just where did you hear all this?"

"I've covered country the past three weeks. Been clear down to the South Car'lina line and over towards Tennessee. Entered Bentonville three times. Last time

I almost had a mite of disturbance. Some fool Yank insisted on seein' my pay-role paper, when, naturally, I ain't got no pay-role paper—"

"Parole paper? What sort of parole paper?"

"It's a writin' that was distributed when General Johnston surren—when Johnston agreed to let up on the Feds. Seems like this paper set down terms allowin' cavalry to keep hawsses and side-arms, if we went straight on home. Would them Yanks agreed to that if they'd whupped us? And what use it is for us to go home, I don't know, what with Colonel 'Medes dead, and Doug dead, and Urquhart Oaks burned to the ground—" He paused, contrite at the look that had come into Urquhart's face. "I'm sure regretful, Major."

"It's all right, Dix. And just forget that 'Major.' Call me by my first name, as you used to do, before—before—"

"But, Major—"

"It's an order, Dix. The war's over. And now, this parole paper. What happened when you didn't have one to show?"

"No trouble to fret about. Says he, 'Where's your pay-role paper, Johnnie Reb.' Says I, 'In my gun-holster. It's writ in lead. You want to see it, Yank?' With that he beat a retreat. Figurin' he's aimin' to bring up a platoon to look at one Texan's paper, I took up a rear position in the direction I'd advanced from, the same bein' a clump of hawss-chestnut where I'd left my mount. I'd been aimin' to leave, anyhow, not bein' able to learn anythin' new—"

"What information were you seeking?"

"Me, I've been cravin' to hear someplace where we could get outfitted again and the regiment re-formed, but I ain't found a man I know. Our outfit is scattered from hell to breakfast. It's taken time to pick up rations too. Them damnyanks keep a close guard on supplies. But once we get organized again, I cal'clate we can take up where the shootin' left off—"

"The war's over, Dix. Get that through your head."

Corbillat snorted. "You don't really believe that, Maj—'Rius? Look at the facts. Texans whupped Mexico. I don't figure these Yanks are tougher, particular when we got other southern states to help us. The Yanks are already squawking for us to let up—"

"The Confederacy is done for, Dix. That's the fact you and I have to face, right now. From what you say, Terry's Rangers are considerably dispersed. I can't see a chance for us to get organized again."

Corbillat collapsed like a punctured balloon. "I reckon you're right," he conceded dismally. "I feared you'd figure we was done." His dark stubbly chin came up again. "But we ain't whupped."

"I don't think you and I are whipped," Urquhart said, soberly. "All I know, the war's ended, and we are going home. I don't understand how we hung on so long. Fighting to perpetuate slavery, and not more than two men out of ten who fought ever owned slaves. What in God's name was the majority fighting for? You, for instance?"

"Me? Hell, that's easy. I been fightin' for you and Colonel 'Medes and Urquhart Oaks—and—and, well,

I'm from Texas." This last seemed to explain everything to Dix.

Urquhart sighed. "I guess we just got into a rut of fighting and didn't know what else to do. Now we can find something more productive to occupy us. Dix, this parole paper—what happens to a man if he doesn't have one?"

"According to terms of surrender, anybody caught without a pay-role will be treated as a guerrilla, and get shot instanter," bitterly. "Guerrillas, murderin' sons-a-bitches, looting both sides when an army has passed, wearin' the uniforms of Feds and Confeds both. Like them sons-a-bitches we routed when we come here, that day. Only a Yank could stomach such bastuds."

Urquhart said slowly, "I seem to remember a number of the same breed followed our forces, too."

"Not none from Texas," stubbornly.

"Speaking of guerrillas, it's not been clear in my mind what happened that day. You mentioned it a couple of times, but I wasn't capable of taking it in. I have a vague memory of men in blue—"

"Which uniforms they prob'ly stole," Corbillat growled. There must've been twenty of the skunks, altogether. They didn't wait to see was there more than just us two. We come ridin' in, with you outten your head, and one son-of-a-bitch commenced shakin' lead outten his Spencer. Dropped my hawss first shot. Say, did you ever have occasion to bury a hawss? You ain't no idea what diggin' is until you excavate a hole big enough to cover up a rottin' hawss—"

"I have a vague recollection," Urquhart cut in

placidly, "of riding down a man. But after that—"

"Ridin' him down! You nigh decapitated his head off with your saber, and then lit, runnin', and headed into the house. One blue-belly in a captain's uniform had already come outten the cabin and made a getaway. A tall feller with wide shoulders and heavy whiskers. But there was that other one, inside the cabin, waitin' for you to come in. He was standin' inside the doorway, and he thrun down on you with his pistol, when you showed up. His slug taken you across the side of your head, but it wa'n't serious. Just a furrow ploughed up, about like that wound I taken in the Bentonville fight."

"Let's forget Bentonville, Dix. I want to get things clear. After that jayhawker had shot me, what?"

"I shot him, when he came scurryin' out, makin' for his hawss. A big bastud he was and a good mark for my Colt. There'd been more of 'em here—don't know how they found the place less'n they just stumbled on it. It's off the roads,—"

"You said there were about twenty of them here," Urquhart hinted patiently, "led by a big-bodied hairy man with black whiskers, in a Federal captain's uniform. What became of them?"

"I already told you about the one with whiskers gettin' away. Then there was the two we dropped, and why they couldn't have left us better hawsses, I don't know. Just crowbaits—"

"I'm still wondering," Urquhart said wearily, "what that bunch was doing here. Please, Dix, try to stick to your story."

Corbillat looked blank. "I thought you understood

31

those bastuds come here to steal, like guerrillas been doin' every place else. They turned the house inside out, hopin' to find money, which I guess there wa'n't none. Then they raided the provisions and murdered Miss Jen's paw when he objected. It was the one who made his getaway that shot him—but maybe she told you that part."

"I knew her father had been killed, but I've hesitated to ask for details. I've been expecting you each day—now, I'm doing the interrupting. What became of the remainder of the guerrilla band?"

Corbillat swore. "The big bastud and the tall one with whiskers had ideas—none of their ideas nice. They'd already ordered the gang to wait for 'em in the woods, after they done the murderin' and stole two hawsses and a pair of mules. So there was nobody at the cabin except them two and the cavalryman outside, when we showed up. Maybe he was to keep watch. Him's the one you cut down, after Black Whiskers hightailed it. When the one that shot you come runnin' out, it was my bullet that finished him. So there was two bodies to plant besides my hawss."

"Did you say besides, or *beside?*"

"Catch me diggin' three holes when one will do," scornfully. "I did make another grave for the girl's father; buried him in the woods, near her mother's grave. I don't know why them other jayhawkers didn't stay for the fightin' except they mistooken us for a whole regiment of Terry Rangers. But I didn't plant nary a body until I'd seen to you. For a spell it didn't look like I'd be seein' you much longer. It was that

bullet in your shoulder that raised all the hell. It was —
this is Miss Jen's word—suppuratin', and turnin'
purple and green. And Miss Jen allowed you'd die if
that bullet didn't come out. So, we got 'er out. You
wouldn't remember that, naturally, bein' ravin'
delirious. From your talk, you was fightin' the artillery
down in Aiken, again. And me holdin' you down and
Miss Jen—"

"Just a minute. Where did you get the doctor?"

"What doctor?" Corbillat looked puzzled.

"The one who removed the bullet. I've been
expecting him to call—"

"The doctor who removed the bullet?" Corbillat
looked exasperated. "I'll be God damned! You don't
know yet! Ain't Miss Jen said anythin'?"

"Concerning what? I've talked to her very little. She
seems shy."

"Shy!" Corbillat exploded. "And you haven't talked
to her? I know! All you done was eat and sleep and
bury your nose in book-readin'. And you call Miss Jen
shy! Don't you know nothin' about her a-tall?"

"Is there somethin' in particular I should know about
her?"

Sarcastically. "Her and all women! Ain't you ever
goin' to realize they're human, same as you and me,
with the same appetites and the same needs—?"

"I'm still trying to learn what you know that I don't
know. I supposed you've talked to her quite a bit."

"Considerable, while we were waitin' for you to get
back your sanity. At first she was plumb quiet, but the
time come when there was nothin' else to do, and we

habla-ed a-plenty. Maybe it was because I knew her language—" He broke off. "Say, I bet you didn't even know she was a half-breed Cherokee."

"That, I learned today. To my surprise, I'll admit."

"I never guessed it myself, until one day her grand-parents came here and I heard them talkin' the language. Then I sort of edged myself into the conversation. I was mighty rusty, at first, then the right words started comin' back to me. What? Sure I could understand 'em. Has it slipped your mind, Rius, that I'm a quarter-breed?"

Urquhart frowned. "Now you mention it, I remember my father dropping something to that effect once."

"Sure, Colonel 'Medes knew it. My grandpap was French, and he married one of 'em—my grandmother. When I was a button, playin' with Cherokee kids so much, got me sort of adopted into the tribe. But my parents moved to San Antonio—"

"Dix, you are the damnedest man to get off the trail. I'm trying to learn something about a girl and a bullet that was in my shoulder." Impatiently, he fidgeted with the carnelian ring on his finger.

"Don't bunch me; I'm gettin' to it. First off, I'll tell you what she told me about her father. He was from Ireland, but he'd gone to school in Edinburgh—"

"Edinburgh, in Scotland? There's a university there."

"That's where he learned to be a doctor, Doctor Leinster Keating. But after he came back to Dublin the trouble started. Maybe for an Irishman it wasn't what you'd call trouble. Maybe it had been going on all the time, only this Leinster Keating had his eyes opened

34

after he became a doctor. It could be, like a lot of Irishmen, he just liked a fight. But it was the English rule and the poverty in Ireland he couldn't stand, so he revolted against the British queen—"

"Revolted?" Urquhart questioned.

"Something the way the Yanks revolted against Texas, only Keating never had a hound-dawg's chance. The girl he'd intended to marry, returned his ring, and his family sided against him. So, with what money he had and some books and his bag of surgery tools, he lit a shuck outten Ireland and landed in Ca'lina. I reckon his family was glad to get shet of him, and the feelin' was mutual with the Doc."

"I suppose this Doctor Keating had an idea of retiring from the world when he arrived in the States."

"Rius, you've hit the nail on the head," Corbillat drawled. "Keating gets himself a section of holdin's, back here in the timber far off from everythin', exceptin' the Cherokees scattered through these woods and he builds a cabin. He's through with women and don't aim to push his nose into other troubles. The first thing he knows, he's hearin' of miseries among the Cherokees and doctorin' 'em becomes a habit. They're sod-busters and hunters, but they get sick like anybody else. By the time he learns the language, he's like one of 'em. And there's one Cherokee girl special, it ain't needin' no language in particular to tell her what he's got in mind. So he marries this squaw. I suppose he got woman-hungry just like everybody."

"So he married this Cherokee girl and they had a child?"

35

"The same bein' Miss Jennifer. I thought you understood that. But Doc Keating, when a smallpox epidemic broke out, he's so busy ministerin' to the wants of the Cherokees, he don't realize his own wife has got the disease until too late, and she dies and he's got this year-old baby on his hands. You know somethin'?"

Urquhart breathed a long sigh. "I'm waiting to hear."

"He takes on the job of raisin' this baby *hisself!* 'Course, bein' a doctor, it was maybe easy for him. So he took on not only the rearin' of her body but of her mind too. Educated her with books. She's even read Shakespeare. Never knew anybody, 'ceptin' you and Colonel 'Medes done that. On top of it all, she learns Cherokee language and customs. When she got older she used to help him with his patients."

"You mean, Dix, he educated her in medicine and surgery?"

"No, not that." Corbillat shook his head. "Just the givin' of medicine and the bandagin'. None of the cutting with the sharp surgery tools. She never done that. And that's what makes it surprisin', her takin' out the bullet. It was the first time she ever—"

"Wait a minute, Dix." Bewilderment entered Urquhart's eyes. He half-raised one hand in protest. "What bullet are you talking about?"

"Ain't you listenin'? The bullet that was cached in your shoulder and was turnin' everythin' bad until it had started to smell—"

"Are you telling me, Dix, that girl, Miss Jennifer, removed the bullet from my—"

"What else could she do?" Corbillat demanded

36

earnestly. "She said that herself, and I hadn't been able to find any doctor to come here, less'n I run the risk of havin' you taken to a Yank prison. She said you'd just get worse until that bullet come out and we'd have to face it. Then she heats some water and gets the doctor's bag and there was a mite of morphine there, but not enough, and me holdin' you down on that oak table, and you doin' the finest cursin' of Yank sons-a-bitches I ever heard from you, and her workin' steady all the time, not sayin'a word while she plied them bright cuttin'-tools, though by this time they wa'n't bright no more, and her hands was the same color, but just as steady as when she'd started, despite, *de*spite I tell you, all the thrashin' about you was doin' like a bronc with a cactus needle under his saddle, and me sweatin' and holdin' you back from whatever your crazy mind—"

"Lord God Almighty!"

"—and even when she'd probed it out, you kept on while she was snippin' away edges and cleanin' and patchin' that hole. And there was three things which could have give up, but only two of 'em did—my strength and your vocabulary. But not her, 'cause by that time she was through and just lookin' sort of white and sayin' in that slow husky voice of hers, 'I think we've managed it, sergeant.' That was all, 'cepting for the business of tryin' to persuade your fever to come down and that not easy, because there wasn't enough quinine in that medicine bag, only maybe there was enough because about the time it run out, you'd started to get rational again—"

"Lord God Almighty," Urquhart repeated in awed tones. "And I thought she was shy. She didn't talk to any extent . . ." His words dwindled off.

"Shy?" Corbillat spat disgustedly and busied his fingers with the making of another cigarette. "You know somethin', Rius? It just sudden occurred to me. Here's Cherokees in the Ca'linas, and there's Cherokees in Texas, which is natural country for only Comanches, Apaches, Lipans and such, but not Cherokees. How come Cherokees to be way off there in Texas, so far from their natural stampin' grounds?"

With an effort Urquhart brought his mind back to Corbillat's question. "Dix, you'd better ask Miss Jennifer. She seems to have answers to things I don't know."

5

SILENCE CAME OVER THE TWO MEN WHILE THE SUN swung to the west. A feeling of humility had come over Urquhart. Before, he'd been scarcely aware of the girl, thanking her for food and certain attentions to his wounds and various other things, as he might have a servant. A servant, say, like one of the many who had attended his requirements during the old days at Urquhart Oaks. Though not quite the same, Urquhart reminded himself. There'd been a certain condescension in all his contacts with the girl; that thought struck him with a shaming impact, bringing a flow of color to his gaunt cheeks.

It came to him now, thinking back over certain incidents, that he had (unconsciously, it is true) been "looking down" upon Jennifer Keating. That, definitely, had been an error. Leinster Keating's blood, undoubtedly, was as good as the Urquharts'. Certainly (Urquhart found himself insisting on this, over and over, and still without being convinced) the Cherokee blood had in no way contaminated the Keating strain, so far as was discernible. What difference, after all, did it make? In the final analysis it was the manner in which a man, or a woman, reacted to adverse circumstances, that rendered the final, indisputable judgment.

A feeling of annoyance at dwelling too long on things that, as he insisted on maintaining, couldn't matter in the slightest, commenced to possess him, a part of that annoyance being due to the manner in which Jennifer Keating was assuming too great a portion of his conscious thought. My God, he told himself angrily, you'd think he was falling in love with this half-breed Cherokee. The idea brought a slight curving to his lips. Whatever would the neighboring ranchers near Urquhart Oaks think, were he to return home with a half-Indian bride?

He checked the thought suddenly. God above! What was he thinking of? Most of the neighbors had been killed during the war, according to letters he'd received from Texas. Urquhart Oaks, itself, no longer existed. That last letter he had from Gault Madison (how long ago was it, two years back?) had brought the news that the big white house that stood for Urquhart Oaks was no more. There had been raiding by Comanches. The house had been burned to the ground. I keep forgetting that, Urquhart brooded. I continue to think there'll be a return to the old life which is now forever gone. Has this long war, this four years of bloodshed and starving, taught me nothing at all? The whole South had vanished in a gigantic cloud of powdersmoke. There was nothing left at Urquhart Oaks, Gault Madison had written, except the earth and a mound of ashes. The few slaves Diomedes Urquhart had retained at the beginning of the war, had left on news of the owner's death. Things could never again be the same. It wasn't that Urquhart knew this, nor believed it; he just sensed it, sensed it against his willingness to accept such inevitability. At least he would rebuild the great white house some day. Mentally, he cursed the Comanches. Damned red devils. A new thought intruded: in what way did the Comanches differ so greatly from the Cherokee tribe?

Maybe, Urquhart chuckled grimly, I'd better ask her about that. His thoughts returned to Jennifer Keating. Shy? No, that wasn't the reason for her reserve. Rather, she probably knew, sensed with no word from me, or maybe it was my lack of words, that I was placing her on some inferior social level. He thought wearily, what does it matter? Before long Dix and I will be traveling the long way to Texas. It occurred to him he'd given little thought to the means necessary for that journey. Dix would take care of things, as Dix had for years managed affairs for Diomedes Urquhart. Darius Urquhart said suddenly, "It's about time, Dix, I shouldered the burden myself."

"You're sayin' which, Maj—er—Rius?"

Urquhart spoke slowly. "For four years, you've taken care of my father or my brother or me. You saw to our mounts; when there was food you saw that we got it. You—"

"Christ A'mighty! You done the fightin' didn't you?"

"I seem to remember you did your share of that too. I've taken much for granted from you for a good number of years—even before the war, you—"

"Colonel 'Medes wanted things that way," Corbillat spoke with deliberation. "My education has been with hawsses and cows, but Colonel has had me keepin' a weather eye on you since you were a button. I reckon it become a habit, watchin' out for you—" He changed the subject. "A spell back, you allowed we'd be headin' for home soon. You calc'latin' to rebuild Urquhart Oaks house?"

"With what?" Urquhart asked bitterly. "I've no money, Dix, except what is in my pocket. Perhaps, thirty or forty dollars, Confederate."

"They don't call that money in Bentonville," Corbillat grunted. "But we'll make to get home, Rius."

"There's nothing left but the land."

"The land is always good. With land, a man has a chance. We'll make out."

"We'll make out," Urquhart repeated. "It will be good to have a destination after four years of getting no place in particular. A poem I read today, said something I liked." He tried to explain the poem to Corbillat, but found his companion's attention wandering, and gave up.

Later, back in the cabin, with candles burning and a blaze of pine knots helping illuminate the room, Urquhart tried to thank the girl for what she'd done. Corbillat was sitting on Urquhart's bunk, mending his broken boot-sole. The girl was placing dishes on the table. Urquhart stopped her near the table, his words coming awkwardly: ". . . you see, I didn't know who had removed the bullet from my shoulder. I'd taken it for granted it had all been the business of some doctor. I didn't even learn, until today, it was you." His voice dwindled before her level, grave-eyed glance. Unsmiling she waited for him to continue, then blew a trace of wood-ash from the corn-bread she held, walked past him and set the pan on the table. For a second, Urquhart thought she intended to ignore his words, or at least utter a trite "it was nothing." Instead she spoke over one shoulder, still unsmiling: "I was very frightened," she said in even tones. "I'd done nothing before like that. I'm not sure I want to have the doing of it a second time . . ."

"Yet you went through with it," he said.

She answered quietly, "There was nothing else to do."

He felt suddenly humble, meeting the calm scrutiny of her eyes, and managed, "You saved my life."

"That is a thing of which neither you nor I can ever be certain, nor does it amount now to any importance."

"My life?" He endeavored to inject a jocular strain into the conversation.

Still she did not smile. "I'm thinking, Major Urquhart, you know I didn't mean that."

"My attempt at humor wasn't—" He stopped. "I apologize, Miss Jennifer."

"That is unnecessary. I'm thinking a little humor would be brightening the world for all of us." This time she smiled, and Urquhart felt himself grow warm all over. There didn't seem anything else to say. The girl was once more busying herself between table and cooking utensils.

Urquhart wandered over to the bookshelves. His eyes ran along certain titles and names on the worn bindings: Coleridge, Pope, Byron, Shakespeare, Scott, Dumas, Voltaire, Rabelais, Villon (the latter three in the original) and a host of other names; certain shelves held medical books, a dictionary, almanac, Holy Bible, old newspapers and magazines; there were several volumes devoted to European history. Leinster Keating had, apparently, been a well-read man. Urquhart speculated as to the degree of knowledge the doctor had passed on to his daughter.

He lifted from an upper shelf a slim volume bound in half-calf, now browned darkly with the years, its leather edges scuffed. He opened the book and gazed idly at the title page with its simple POEMS, *by Prescott Deveraux*. Further information near the bottom of the page: *Printed for J. Smithburne, and Fold and Bound by Thos. Longmuir in Scalding Alley, near Stationers-Hall, London, 1792*. Urquhart fingered through the foxed pages, then crossed the floor to Corbillat.

"Here, Dix, is that poem *Lines to the Defeated* I mentioned to you."

Corbillat glanced up. "You know, Major, I never

taken much to poetry, but if it says what you want it to say, and you can savvy it, why then—"

"Listen, see what you think." Urquhart read in measured tones:

Stir up the dust!
Sweep cobwebbed dreams from out your moulding skull.
Scour clean the rust
From dulling, sanguined swords and then strike out;
And when you've slain each cursed obstacle
And vanquished every fearful, chilling doubt,
Stir up the dust!
Carve bright new roads into a stronger world.
Brave, when you must,
Adversity; spur charger straight and true,
With all defiant banners proud, unfurled,
Until you're one with Fortune's retinue.
Stir up the Dust!

Corbillat squinted his black eyes. "I don't know as I understand all of it, Rius," he confessed. "Still and all, what I got, I liked fine. I figure that Deveraux would do to ride the river with."

"That," Urquhart began, "is the reason—" He broke off at an exclamation from the girl, standing just beyond the table. "You said something, Miss Jennifer?"

"Would you be having any reason for picking out those particular lines?" Her smoky-gentian eyes were wide.

"No special reason," Urquhart replied. "I like it. Why?"

44

"It was a favorite of my father's. He always read that poem when he felt discouraged. It is a book he brought from Ireland."

Urquhart smiled. "I didn't think the Irish were ever discouraged."

"The Irish," the girl said quietly, "are always discouraged, though they never let themselves, or anyone else, know of it."

"And do you often find yourself discouraged?"

"You're forgetting," she replied, "I'm but half Irish."

For some reason it irritated Urquhart to be reminded of the fact. He nodded, "It had slipped my mind, Miss Jennifer."

Corbillat took the opportunity to observe, "That side-meat sizzlin' in the skillet sure smells elegant."

The girl acknowledged the remark with one of her rare smiles. "I'm thinking, Sergeant, you have your own ideas of what constitutes poetry. The fragrance of the coffee is a sonnet in itself. Come—everything's on."

It occurred to Urquhart, later, that for two or three hours now, his thoughts had not once turned toward the war. Toward home, toward Urquhart Oaks, yes; but for the first time in years the guns, the hunger, the blood and burnt powder that had so long permeated his system were vanquished. Corbillat was again working over the worn boot. Urquhart sat in the rocker watching the girl, her head bent over Corbillat's cavalry jacket, sewing a rent in one shoulder. On the table, a tallowdip burned in a brass holder, its light making sharp glints on the needle as it flashed through stained cloth.

Abruptly, Corbillat tossed down the boot, rose from the bunk and approached the fireplace. "Miss Jen, I was wonderin' howcome there to be Cherokees here and Cherokees way out in Texas. Did the original tribe split up?"

The girl's head lifted. "The tribe has been split and re-split and re-split," she replied. "I know something of it. It's a pity you could not have talked to my father. He was greatly interested in the Cherokee Tribe and uncovered every possible fact about it. Shall I tell you what I know?"

Urquhart said, "Please do," before Corbillat could reply. The girl took a few more stitches in the jacket, then commenced: Originally the Cherokees had come of Iroquoian stock and had held a territory of some forty thousand miles lying within an area that comprised Virginia, Tennessee, the Carolinas, Georgia and Alabama. They hunted and farmed, and the tribe had once been composed of nearly twenty thousand persons, but smallpox brought in by slave-ships had wiped out about half the tribe. There was considerable intermarrying, from time to time, with Scot-Irish and English colonists, the white blood bringing to the males a greater stature than the true-blooded Cherokee possessed.

". . . but even before the arrival of the colonists," Jennifer was saying, "there may have been marrying with whites. An old legend claims that when the Cherokees first came here—I don't know from where—they found a tribe of whites. Father deduced these whites were some sort of albino."

"That could account," Urquhart put in, "for many Cherokees having much lighter skins, and perhaps other qualities . . ."

"It could," Jennifer agreed. "Father always said I was a throw-back. Back in 1819 and 1820, more than a hundred Cherokees emigrated to land given them by the Spanish, on the Sabine and Neches Rivers—"

Corbillat broke in, "So that's how they got into Texas."

"Some of them," Jennifer nodded. "My grandparents have told me they have distant relatives, there. Father thought the Cherokees had first settled in Arkansas Territory. The Cherokees' big trouble arose when gold was discovered on their land in eastern United States. The white men wanted that gold; a scheme was put afoot. Government men met with a small group of chiefs, and in return for some millions of dollars, and territory west of the Mississippi River, those chiefs agreed to surrender to the government their last remaining lands. Other chiefs who had not been consulted, repudiated the treaty and refused to leave their lands. In that decision, they had most of our people with them. An appeal was made to the Supreme Court which rendered a decision in favor of the Cherokees—"

"Good!" Corbillat ejaculated. "For once the Indian beats the white man."

"You're jumping to conclusions, Sergeant," the girl said. "Andrew Jackson did not agree with the court. He had his mind made up, the Cherokees should be removed from their lands. It wasn't long afterward that

47

President Van Buren sent General Winfield Scott with soldiers to round up the Cherokees and move them west. Our people were driven into stockades and forts at the point of the bayonet. When they were forced from their homes, other men, following the army, raided the houses and stole stock—"

"Them Yanks!" Corbillat disgustedly shook his head. "What skulduggery don't they think of?"

"Once rounded up," Jennifer continued, "the Cherokees were started on the long march west to Texas and Indian and Arkansas Territories. They traveled on foot; they were not given proper food or medical attention. Thirteen thousand started; nearly a quarter died on that long journey."

Urquhart said, "I'd never given much thought to, white men's atrocities before this war. I guess they've been going on always. Perhaps, Miss Jennifer, you Indians have a right to hate the white man." He checked himself. "It is difficult to think of you as—"

"I'm but half Indian," the girl said quietly. She turned to Corbillat. "There you have the story, Sergeant, as much of it as I know."

Corbillat said, "But all the Cherokees were not driven west. Your people—"

"Many escaped being rounded up and remained hidden until the time became peaceful; they are known as the Eastern Band of the Cherokee Nation. Of all Indian tribes, I think the Cherokee have reached the highest level of education. A great Chief, Sequoyah, once ruled the Cherokees. Sequoyah was a mixture of Cherokee and German. He realized the advantage the

48

whites held in their ability to read and write, so he invented an alphabet for the Cherokees. Many of my people became literate. Forty years ago, the Cherokees had a newspaper. Some of the wealthier Cherokees were slave owners. Does that astonish you, Major Urquhart?"

Urquhart looked gravely at her. "I do not think, after today, Miss Jennifer, that anything can astonish me again. I've found a new respect for your people." He nearly added, "For you as well," but checked the words. The heightened flush died from the girl's cheeks. Her hands reached again to the threaded needle and torn jacket.

That night, Urquhart lay in his bunk and considered the information he'd gathered. The contrast between Cherokee and Irish bloods was more than he wanted to accept. One or the other, he speculated fiercely, must eventually dominate. At present, white blood seemed in the ascendancy, but who could say what development future years might bring? Jennifer might become like her grandparents. Urquhart wasn't certain, exactly, what it was he objected to in the old Cherokees, beyond the squalor and state of ignorance in which he imagined they lived. He cursed himself for a fool. Were Jennifer Keating greasy, uncultured, like the majority of squaws, would he be so concerned? Immediately he told himself he would not, that he wouldn't give a damn. His thoughts were overly occupied with the age-old conflict of white blood and dark, he reminded himself, his whole heritage affronted by any mixture of two strains.

And yet, this hadn't been true of Jennifer Keating. In the proper environment she could be nothing less than a lady. Urquhart had known girls in Texas and Virginia with far less to offer. But exactly what was the proper environment for this girl? Should she leave this cabin and take up residence with white people? Or would some greasy buck Cherokee mate with her, and produce on that slim white body a multitude of squalling papooses, while the cape-jasmine skin turned quickly to brown wrinkled flesh, and the straight back grew bent under the labor common to Indian women?

Something like a groan escaped involuntarily from Urquhart's lips. Corbillat twisted his dark head under the blanket. "You all right, Rius? Want anythin'?"

"No," Urquhart whispered back. "No, I'm all right. I just yawned, I guess. I—I—" He fell silent a moment, then, "I've been wondering if you could cut my beard tomorrow. These whiskers have reached the itching stage."

Corbillat replied, "I'll sure enough have a try at it."

The girl spoke drowsily from her bunk. "Use my father's razors. He always said there was no better steel than that of England. I'm sure you'd be pleased with English steel, Major Urquhart."

He said, "Thank you, Miss Jennifer. I'm sorry if I awakened you two."

Neither Corbillat nor the girl answered. The light from the fireplace was nearly gone now. Urquhart turned on his side. Had there been any special meaning behind the girl's reference to English steel? Was she

50

accentuating a thought that only English steel forged by white men, would be sufficient for his needs? Or was he, Urquhart irritably asked himself, lending an undue importance to her words?

6

THE DAYS WERE BUILDING UP TOWARD JUNE, AND DARIUS Urquhart was almost whole again. Occasionally, a slight twinge in the left shoulder reminded him of the wound, but dressings were no longer necessary. The scar was forming cleanly, Urquhart had practically regained the use of the arm. He found a certain regret that the girl's ministrations had been discontinued. They had brought a daily contact with Jennifer, affording an excuse for his continued presence. Now he felt like an interloper, though in no way had the girl's words led to such belief.

Now that he was virtually recovered, the propriety of the situation bothered him. Corbillat's being away so often, left Urquhart and the girl sharing the cabin alone, except when her Indian grandparents came, which wasn't often. Urquhart had endeavoured to express his feelings realizing even while he talked that the words sounded gauche. A hitherto unsuspected fire had leaped in the smoky-gentian eyes; her voice had been cold: "Is it yourself, or me, you are thinking of protecting, Major Urquhart?" The words were direct, leaving nothing to the imagination.

"Please, Miss Jennifer—" His features crimsoned.

"You believe because I am a Cherokee, I have no—"

"Miss Jennifer," he said stiffly, "that thought was far-thest from my mind. It was merely—" Words deserted him before her scorn that made him feel like a whipped school-boy. Tiny spots of scarlet burned in Jennifer's cheeks. It was unnecessary to say more.

Nor did Urquhart pursue the subject, though that night he carried his blankets outside to the lean-to at the rear of the cabin. The girl watched his departure in silence, only a heightened color giving any indication she was aware of his leaving. Stubbornly, Urquhart had spread his blankets on the floor of the lean-to. There weren't any walls; just the floor and the slanting roof. Except for the wall of the cabin, the sides were open to the night. Urquhart stretched out angrily. Could any man alive understand women, he asked himself. He'd been considering only her reputation, and she had chosen to misunderstand . . . He found eventually a sort of angry slumber.

Half an hour later, what had been a soft night breeze changed to a gale, bringing with it a deluge of rain. Thunder rolled heavily in the mountains and there were brief flashes of lightning. The first drops brought Urquhart to a sitting position. He moved the blankets nearer the cabin wall, but such small shelter was unavailing. Torrential gusts brought drenching sweeps of rain to soak through his blanket. Urquhart consid-ered taking the tarpaulin that covered the supplies. That, naturally, would leave the supplies unprotected. He decided he could tough out the storm, and huddled closer to the log wall. Common sense ordered a return to the cabin, but Urquhart, perversely, refused. The rain would be over shortly; these spring rains never lasted long.

He didn't hear the girl until he felt her touch on his shoulder. Then he squirmed around and in a flare of light from the sky, saw her standing tall and dark beside him, a blanket encasing her slim form. Urquhart stared. "I beg your pardon?" he said inanely.

The girl said cuttingly. "Am I going to have to nurse you back to life a second time? Come back into the cabin. Now!" There was furious rage in the tones. She turned and made her way through the mud to the doorway. Meekly, shivering, Urquhart rose and followed her. The girl was in her bunk when he entered. Nothing more was said but from then on Urquhart remained in the cabin at night.

He spoke to Corbillat when next the sergeant returned. Corbillat scowled. "You made a mistake, Rius, just in hintin' that anythin' could happen between you two, because you're alone here."

"But I wasn't hinting," Urquhart persisted. "It was on her account. What would people say—?"

"What people?" Corbillat asked bluntly. "Exceptin' for her kin-folks, nobody knows you're here. What you don't understand, Rius, is Miss Jen's got a core of steel inside that soft manner. Make no mistake, there ain't no man goin' to have that girl unless'n she wants him."

"But I keep telling you, Dix," Urquhart said desperately, "I had nothing of the sort in mind."

"The very fact you brought it up," Corbillat pointed out, "shows it wa'n't far from mind. Ain't no healthy young buck goin' to neglect his tomcattin', when the time's right. Now don't misunderstand me," as Urquhart started a protest—"I'm not accusing you of evil thoughts. I just know you're an Urquhart, and a friend once told me no Urquhart ever had trouble attractin' women. To the contrary. There's always a woman in the life of every Urquhart—bolstering him up when he's in need. And you're an Urquhart. And you can't tell me that even four years of whippin' Yanks ain't left room for other ideas."

"We'd better forget the subject," Urquhart said coldly.

"I didn't bring it up, Rius," Corbillat replied.

"When do you think we can get started for Texas?" Urquhart asked shortly.

"That depends on when you're in shape to travel. I don't think it will be long. There's one or two more things I want to see to, before we pull up stakes."

Now, Corbillat was gone again. Since the morning he had shaved Urquhart's beard, leaving only a narrow moustache on the upper lip, the sergeant had made three trips away from the cabin. The first time he had returned with two superb saddle horses, each of which carried a *U.S.* brand on the left hip. Urquhart had never demanded details regarding the horses; the sergeant had explained he had "emancipated 'em" from the Yanks. That seemed substantially to cover the question. As to the *U.S.* brand marks: with the aid of a hot cinch-ring and a section of wet blanket, the *U.S.* brand had been quickly converted into an 08 marking, which Corbillat insisted stood for Backward-80, "in case some nosey Yank bastud should ever ask questions."

In the creek bottom, a short distance from the cabin, Corbillat had thrown up a small corral of stripped saplings, and there, screened in a jungle of brush the horses were hidden, Urquhart, in the sergeant's absence, walking there each day to see to the animals. He was sufficiently strong for that now. He had saddled one of the horses, two days ago, and made a ride through the pines, only to discover that neighbors weren't as distant as he had imagined. True, the neighbors were Cherokees; scattered through the forest were small clearings and cabins and tiny fields, tilled and planted. He had returned from his ride in the afternoon. It had been good to ride again, though his saddle muscles ached from unaccustomed use.

Nearing the cabin he saw the grandparents were there again, both of them plying hoes industriously in Jennifer's small cornfield. The corn was knee-high, green blades waving in the breeze. The mule belonging to the grandparents (on which both the ancient Indians rode, tandem-fashion) was drinking water from a bucket which Jennifer had brought it, and flopping lazy ears in the afternoon sunlight, not far from the cabin. Jennifer set down the bucket as Urquhart approached. "You've been riding," she said.

Urquhart removed his grey felt hat and wiped his forehead. His shirt was stained with perspiration; there was dust on his worn boots. "How did you know?" Urquhart asked.

"You left early this morning and,"—the girl was unsmiling—"your walk told me you'd been in the saddle."

55

Urquhart hadn't suspected that aching saddle muscles had affected his gait. "You've sharp eyes, Miss Jennifer." She didn't reply, but took up the mule's bridle and led it around the corner of the cabin. Urquhart realized he'd been hoping the girl would show some concern for his condition, but she hadn't. When she again appeared, "I suppose it was all right for me to ride. I had to learn what shape I was in."

"There's no reason you shouldn't ride, Major Urquhart. You're well enough entirely, I'm thinking."

Urquhart bowed. "In that event, and with my doctor's permission, we'll be leaving before long."

"In nothing I've said do I intend to hurry you," the girl said quietly. "The time of departure is your concern." Urquhart thanked her. She continued, "You missed your dinner, I'll get something for you now."

"Please don't bother," Urquhart said, but the girl had already vanished within the cabin doorway. Urquhart strolled over to a section of broken-down fence and stood watching the old Indians hoeing the cornfield. It was, he considered, amazing to find two old people still wresting a living from the soil; they not only managed their own small place, a few miles off, but also possessed the energy to work Jennifer's field. They toiled on either side of a row of waving green, pausing now and then to ease aching backs. Once, old Tom Událi saw Urquhart and gave him a slow, toothless grin. Urquhart nodded stiffly, but when Tom's wife, Mary, glanced around, Urquhart courteously lifted his weathered grey hat. Mary and Tom grinned simultaneously and ducked their heads in a series of bobbing bows. "Like a couple of slaves in a cotton-patch when the master rides past," Urquhart chuckled. "Or maybe I've been accepted into the family. They've scarcely noticed me before." He turned and started toward the cabin, as Jennifer called to him from the doorway.

7

THE GRANDPARENTS WERE THERE AGAIN, TWO DAYS later, when Corbillat returned in mid-afternoon, bringing this time something more than supplies: trailing his horse was a light spring wagon equipped with rolled leather curtains and drawn by a pair of small dun mules with black stripes down their chunky backs, driven by (at least he was perched on the driver's seat) an emaciated undersized Negro in a rusty-green frock coat, with red flannel shirt beneath, a battered infantry kepi on the woolly head, and worn cavalry boots with spurs, sizes too large for him. The baggy, once-red pants might originally have belonged to a soldier of one of the showy zouave regiments, but that was uncertain, so patched and three-quarters hidden were they by the oversize boots. Urquhart gained an impression of an ebony skeleton detained on its way to a carnival.

Jennifer emerged from the cabin and the two old Cherokees came to inspect the wagon and its occupant. Corbillat swung from his saddle. He sized up briefly Urquhart's condition and was satisfied with what he saw. "The Negro's name," he said, "is White,"— looking at Urquhart as though daring him to doubt it.

57

Urquhart shifted his glance to the figure on the driver's seat. The Negro met his look with anxious eyes as though uncertain of welcome. "Of the Tainnessee Whites, suh. Albumen White, suh, body suhvent to the late, lay-mented Cunnel Bu'lette White, of Ve'de Groves Plantation and the Foath Tainnessee Cavalry. Wheah y'all want dese mules dis-hitched, suh?"

"Just a minute." Urquhart looked inquiringly at Corbillat.

Corbillat shifted uneasily. "We got that little old spring wagon loaded with supplies, Rius, and I got somethin' to show you. Somethin' we been needin'."

Urquhart said, "What's the Negro want?"

Corbillat turned to the Negro. "All right, get them mules outten harness." The Negro moved with alacrity. Urquhart saw he scarcely came to the nearest mule's head, his thin wiry form (one scrawny hand continually clutching at the slipping trousers to keep them above invisible hips) skirting around the mules with a proficiency that could have come only from habitual practice. Urquhart walked to the rear of the wagon and glanced at the provisions the sergeant had gathered. His eyes widened. He came back to Corbillat and, with twitching lips, said, referring to the mules, "More Backward-80 stock, I presume."

"I figured somethin' of the sort. No brands to change though. These are Tennessee mules."

"And the nigger hasn't a brand to change, has he?" Corbillat didn't reply. Urquhart continued gravely, "You might tell him that he could use *both* hands and

58

work twice as fast, if he'd get a length of rope around his waist to keep those pants above his hips. Or maybe he hasn't any hips. Now I come to think of it, I don't think he has any brand either, because where in God's name would you find a wide enough section of hide to put an iron on?"

If Corbillat knew, he didn't say. Or his resentment at Urquhart's humor may have prevented his answering. The mules, droop-eared, sleepy-eyed, stood free of the wagon now. Corbillat stripped off his saddle and handed it to the Negro, then taking his horse's bridle reins, the sergeant said, "Walk down to the creek bottom with me, Rius." He spoke to the mules; the Negro squealed some sort of additional order at them. Corbillat started off, Urquhart pacing slowly at the sergeant's side. Yards away, Corbillat paused and called over his shoulder, "Miss Jen, you tell the Negro what's needed—water, kindlin'. He'll rustle for you." He started on, talking to Urquhart. They were nearing the pines at the edge of the clearing before the sergeant paused.

Urquhart said, "I've wondered how you could get so much food from time to time. So it was him, this Albumen White, who helped you."

"Not the first couple of times. I made out alone. But later, he stopped me one time, outside of Bentonville—you see, it was like he'd met a friend, seein' my Confed uniform. Albumen, he don't want to be emancipated nohow. He's a good Negro, Rius. We can use him—"

"You say these supplies have been coming from that

Yank depot, near Bentonville. And him, this Albumen White, sneaking into the depot every day and waiting until night to let you in, while the Yank sentry was asleep. You say he was able to hide there each day—?"

"And that wasn't hard, either," Corbillat explained. "It was dark in that depot, with that crushed-down cap to cover his woolly head and him black enough to go to a funeral nekkid. He didn't know until afterward that all the Negroes had run off when Lincoln done his emancipatin'. That was after this Colonel Burlette White, of the 4th Tennessee's had been killed at Shiloh, and his son, Tom, captured. He—Albumen White—had druv that little old goddam wagon clear all over the South, trying to catch up with the son that was carted off by the Yanks. By the time he'd found the son, the son had died of wounds. So then the Negro starts back to this Verde Groves Plantation, and when he gets there Colonel White's wife had died and the Negroes had left, and there was nothin' but ruin at the plantation. But by this time he'd got a line on his Dicey Nell, and he heads out for up North again, and still drivin' that damned little wagon with the little old trunk—"

"Dicey Nell? Trunk? You mean that small leather box I saw in the wagon?"

"What else?" Corbillat said impatiently. "It's got a complete uniform, gauntlets, and yellow sash and ostrich plume for the hat. I judge from lookin' at it, it would fit you perfect, and we could take off Colonel White's rank-markin's and put on your major's insignia and—"

"In God's name, Dix, what would I be doing in a dead man's uniform?"

"You can't return to Urquhart Oaks lookin' like a tramp."

Urquhart was commencing to absorb the idea. "And the body-servant goes along with the uniform, I suppose," he said caustically.

"That's the general idea," Corbillat admitted, abashed. "He's a good Negro. He cooked and shaved and sewed for Colonel White, when the colonel was alive, and was aimin' to do the same for the son that died, could he ever have cotched up with him—"

"Damn it, Dix," Urquhart said irritably, "nothing in my present circumstances allows the expense of a body-servant. The Negroes are free, now. Can't you understand that?"

"Albumen don't cater to no freedom. He don't aim to be emancipated. He's got no white folks any more. He—he just sort of adopted us—"

"Or vice-versa," drily, "and speaking just for yourself, Dix. Texas is a great way off. The Negro doesn't realize that."

"I've told him. More'n once," Corbillat insisted earnestly. They were nearing the corral in the creek bottom, and Urquhart could see within the bars the heads of the horses. They crossed a plank bridge over a swampy slough and reached the corral. Removing the entrance bars, the sergeant stripped off bridle and turned his horse and the two mules in with the other animals, then replaced the bars. He and Urquhart started the return trip, pushing their way through a jungle of willow and scrubby turkey-oak. "I've told him," Corbillat said again, "and he allows he don't care how far Texas is. He don't ask for pay—just rations while he makes the trip. He says if Dicey Nell can go that far to Texas, he cal'clates it ain't too far for him."

"You mentioned that name, before," Urquhart reminded, "but it's not all clear yet."

Corbillat sighed deeply. "Like I already told you, the Negro had run off from Verde Groves, and Dicey Nell White was one of 'em that Albumen trailed clear up through the Yank-lines. When he did catch news of her, some Negro told him she'd lit out for Texas. So he aims to follow her."

"Who is this Dicey Nell White?"

"His daughter—Negro gal around twenty years. He wants to find her, though lookin' for one Negro gal in all Texas seems like a job. Anyway, I promised him—" Corbillat checked himself suddenly.

"Promised?" Urquhart frowned. "You promised we'd take that Negro—a free Negro—back to Texas?"

"That was part of the bargain, the supplies and all that," Corbillat said sulkily. "Damn it, Rius, you and Miss Jen had to have food. I had to have his help."

Urquhart drew a long breath. "All right, so you promised the fellow—"

"It was only *my* promise. *You* ain't promised anythin'. We could tell him the deal's off, though I don't like—"

"You promised him. Negro or no Negro. But will you tell me, Dix, what in hell we're going to do with that damned little spring wagon trailing us all the way to Texas? At best I figure we'll be more than three months on the journey, and with his blasted wagon bogging down in mud every so often, it will require longer."

"The reason I wanted the wagon was in case you found yourself ailin'. You could ride—"

"I'll hold up. I could start now. I tried out that black gelding, yesterday."

"You did?" Corbillat brightened. "You made out all right?" Urquhart assured him his body was in complete commission. "Good enough!" Corbillat exclaimed. "We'll be stirrin' up some dust like that poet said, right soon."

They recrossed the bridge, ascended a rise between trees, and strode on. Corbillat mentioned the Negro. Urquhart said, "What about him? So far as I know, it's settled. We've promised. But we don't take the wagon. Just the mules. He can ride one and pack on the other."

Corbillat produced from one pocket two folded sheets of paper. "Here's what I mentioned I aimed to show you."

Urquhart slowed pace, unfolded the papers, read them, glanced sharply at Corbillat. "Dix! Where did you get these paroles made out in our names?"

"The Negro got the papers for me. You see, he was working, runnin' errands and so on, for a damnyank captain over there, and had his freedom around the quarters. He got me some ink and pen. I copied these from one a feller had—"

"What fellow?"

"Don't remember his name; trooper from a Mississippi regiment. He had his parole and I just copied it, same as his, except for changing our names and ranks. I signed the name of that Yank captain—"

"Just a minute," Urquhart's eyes narrowed. "You're telling me you forged these?"

"We ain't surrendered, have we?" Urquhart conceded they hadn't surrendered, nor, he stated, at Corbillat's next question, did he have any intention of surrendering. "All right," Corbillat continued, "And you don't want to take no oath of allegiance to the damnyanks, and you neither don't want to be shot as a guerrilla. So you got to have a paper, or we get stopped before we get to Texas."

Urquhart considered, thoughtfully twisting the ring on his finger. "I don't like forgery," he frowned at last.

"Don't you go gettin' a rush of Sunday-school to the head. This is what you call an ex-speed-yuncy. These ain't the first paroles what been forged. There's plenty fellers doin' it."

Irritably, Urquhart extended the papers. The sergeant accepted them, handed one back. "You'd best keep yours." Urquhart reluctantly placed it in his pocket. By this time the cabin was in view. The two old Cherokees were seated near the doorway. Jennifer wasn't in sight. The small wagon had been moved to the rear of the cabin. The Negro had finished unloading. A sizeable pile of supplies rested beneath the lean-to roof. The Negro was inside the wagon, arranging blankets in the vehicle. Hearing Urquhart and Corbillat approach, he twisted around on skinny haunches. "Ah's jist mekkin' down mah pallet, suhs," he informed them. "Ah shuah aims to rest peaceful, now Ah knows Ah's goin' to Taixus—"

"Just a moment, Albumen," Urquhart said testily. "Why do you have to go to Texas with us? I understand you did very well driving your wagon all through the war. Why can't you get to Texas the same way?"

"Well, now, suh, thass a question Ah's pow'ful pleased you brung up." The Negro twisted around and backed from the wagon, one skinny hand clutching the slipping trousers. "Hit's dis way, Majuh Ukhart, suh. Foah long time Ah ain't had no white folks up ontil de present, and Ah'm almahty dawggone tahd of bein' a free man. When Ah's a slave, iff'n Ah gets fotched a kick by a mule, of Cunnel White picks me up and sets me to heal. But when Ah's 'mancipated, iff'n dat mule fotches me a blow from he hoofs, all dem white Yan-kees jist laughs dey heads off, and says, 'Hit's only a Negro. Maybe now he larn stay cleah of de mule's hin'quartehs.' 'Preciate de diffurunce, suh?"

Urquhart nodded. "Make sure you stay clear of the hindquarters on the way to Texas. We'll not be taking the wagon."

Albumen's eyes rolled whitely. "Y'all says Ah'm ridin' fork-style all that way to Taixus?"

"Fork-style's the only way you'll come with us."

"Well"—uncertainly—"iff'n y'all says so, Ah does hit. Iff'n Sodom and Gomo'ah kin stands hit—"

"Sodom and Gomorrah? You mean those mules?"

"Yassuh, Majuh, suh. Most 'propriate names foah

65

dem mules when dey young. Pow'ful wicked, de both of dem, fist like dem evil cities de good Lawd puts He cuss on. But dis Confed'rat wah, done soften dey, ontil now dey tractable lak two kitten-pussies, from all de weahin' dawn dey cotched haulin' dis wagon up mountings and 'cross rivers," He paused. "Iff'n y'all excuses me now, suh, Ah promises Miss Jennifuh Ah gits she some split-wood." At Urquhart's nod, the Negro made a ducking bow and started toward a pile of chopped kindling beyond the cabin.

Rounding the building, Urquhart saw Corbillat in conversation with the two old Indians. The three were speaking in Cherokee and the talk was apparently serious. Corbillat looked concerned. The Indians spoke again, their syllables touched slightly with a guttural accent. Corbillat swung around at Urquhart's step. His voice sounded bitter: "Maybe we'd best take the wagon, after all. I'll be damn-blasted if I can see your objections to one Negro and that wagon. What you aimin' to do if these old folks gets sick on the way—?"

"What in the devil are you referring to?" Urquhart asked.

"Did you, or did you not tell these old folks you'd take them to Texas with us?"

Urquhart's jaw sagged. "No! Whatever gave you that idea?"

"Nobody gave *me* the idea. They say they go where Miss Jen goes—"

"What did you say? But, look here, Dix—I don't know what—"

Corbillat breathed easier. "Maybe this is a surprise to

66

you. You didn't"—looking narrowly at Urquhart—"promise to take the girl with us?"

"Definitely not! I'll swear I didn't. I—"

"All right," Corbillat nodded, satisfied. "It's all sort of mixed up—but, well, you have been living in her cabin. These old people got some sort of idea because she saved your life, you belong to her, or she belongs to you. If I knew the language better, I could get things clear. It's just a mistake, I reckon."

Urquhart mopped perspiration from his forehead. Corbillat swung back to the old couple and spoke slowly in Cherokee. When he had finished they digested Corbillat's information, then, without speaking, moved toward their mule a few yards away. The old man mounted first, then the woman got on, clutching her spouse with both arms around the middle. The mule swung about and started toward the pine trees. Urquhart looked after them, then turned to Corbillat, "Thank God, we got that cleared up."

At that moment, Albumen came scuffling around the corner of the cabin, one arm loaded with firewood, the other hand supporting his baggy pants, the loose wide seat of which hung nearly to boot tops. A feeling of irritation still fraying Urquhart's thoughts, his gaze followed the Negro's progress until a second movement at the cabin doorway, as Jennifer stood aside to let the Negro enter, diverted his attention. A slow flush traveled up Urquhart's features, as he realized the girl had been standing there, listening to the conversation with the grandparents. Even as she withdrew within the cabin, Urquhart thought her face assumed a sudden, rosy hue. Irritability swept through Urquhart, he spoke loudly, "You, Albumen! I told you to get a rope for those pants. The minute you get that wood delivered, you attend to it.". He didn't wait to finish all he'd intended, but strode in perturbation away from the cabin. Corbillat followed and caught up to hear Urquhart swearing savagely. The sergeant waited until Urquhart paused for breath, then inquired, "You really didn't say anythin' to her, about takin' her to Texas, did you, Rius?"

"Do you think I'm an unmitigated fool?" Urquhart demanded.

Corbillat considered. His eyes strayed toward pines where the old Cherokees were just disappearing. Jennifer appeared at the cabin doorway and announced that supper would be ready shortly. The sergeant shifted his inspection to the slim form of the girl silhouetted against the cabin doorway. He turned back to Urquhart, "Yes, Rius," he said dryly, "sometimes I think you are."

8

THAT EVENING PASSED WITH URQUHART RARELY meeting the girl's eyes. No one spoke to any extent, and when Corbillat tried to make conversation he received only monosyllables in reply. Finally when he produced a weather-stained map, Corbillat got Urquhart's attention. Together they studied the printed rectangle of paper, planning the route that would return them to Texas: straight through the heart of South Carolina and across Sherman-ravaged Georgia; then into Alabama, traveling south of Montgomery, original capital of the Confederacy. With Alabama at their backs, there remained only a relatively short stretch across Mississippi, then the Mississippi River and Louisiana to be crossed before an entry into Texas could be effected. How they would live on the way, what difficulties would arise, were obstacles Urquhart and Corbillat decided could best be met as the occasion arose.

Even after they'd set foot on Texas soil, they'd still be approximately two hundred miles from Urquhart Oaks. From her bunk, Jennifer offered a suggestion: it was possible to head directly west across Tennessee, make their way to the Mississippi River via the town of Memphis, then cross the river into Arkansas, or catch passage on some vessel down the river to Vicksburg and make a crossing at that point.

Corbillat admitted he had given consideration to the plan she offered, but the mountains barring the approach to Tennessee might mean delay; as for taking ship down the Mississippi, Jennifer was reminded finances were low and ship passage ran high. A direct route to Louisiana appeared safer. Most Texans were returning home that way. The girl didn't press the subject. When next Urquhart glanced in her direction, he judged by the even rise and fall of the blanket across her breast that she had fallen asleep.

The following morning the girl mentioned the subject her grandparents had brought up the previous day: "It was really my fault," she said directly, as though sensing the subject had been on his mind as well as her own continually since the previous day. Urquhart replied, a bit lamely, he didn't understand the fault, if any, was to be placed at her door. She explained, "I'd already told my grandparents, that when you left, I hoped it might be possible for you to take me with you. They took too much for granted."

"But why?" Urquhart frowned. "I've said no words to lead you—"

"I know," she interposed swiftly. "It is not a thing of your doing, Major Urquhart. It was in my own mind— a hope, I suppose, that somehow—"

He interrupted, "But why should you wish to leave here?"

"Could you be naming me a reason for staying?"

He considered the question and found no reasonable reply. "Your people," he ventured finally, "live in this forest. I don't just mean your grandparents—" He fumbled for words.

"You mean the Indians. My people? I am of them, yet not of them. True, half my blood is theirs. But do you, Major, really think of me as a Cherokee?" The calm eyes demanded an honest answer. Urquhart replied instantly it was something he found extremely difficult of belief. She made it clear to him she maintained no Cherokee customs, had no contacts with Indians, save her grandparents.

"But what of them?" Urquhart asked.

"Ah, there's the rub," she conceded ruefully. "I don't know. I'm fond of them. They realize I am different. I do not believe I owe them anything; on the contrary. They have their land; they are capable. The war has

70

scarcely touched the people in this forest."

"And yet," Urquhart put in, "you hesitate to leave, even when there's little you can do for them."

"They are old," the girl said quietly. "I'm not sure what I should do—except that I want to leave here." Urquhart frowned, considering her slim form and the young swelling breasts beneath the calico. Sunlight, through an east window, made highlights in the thick braids. While he groped for words Jennifer continued, "You've said, yourself, I should learn more of the world. It was always father's plan that we'd travel one day, when I was older. And then the war came . . ." Her words ceased and her long fingers made a gesture of futility, then she became direct: "You'd not be taking me with you, I suppose, even if I asked you?"

"Good Lord, no!" Urquhart looked startled. "You don't realize what you're asking. It's a long way to Texas, a difficult ride for a girl. We may encounter hardships—"

"I could ride as soon as I could walk," the girl broke in. "Do you think me incapable of endurance, or that I'd become a burden on you? I'm sure I could make myself useful on the way. I'd not be delaying you in the slightest. I must get away from here—"

"Why go to Texas? There are places closer at hand." Urquhart could feel his forehead growing damp.

"Where I go makes little difference. Here, there is nothing but a continual reminder of father."

This was understandable. Neither of them spoke for a few minutes. Finally he said, his words as gentle as possible, "I don't think, Miss Jennifer, you quite

71

understand. There are not only the hardships of such a journey, but dangers as well. Neither Dix nor I have surrendered. We could encounter trouble. Where trouble exists there could be shooting. I couldn't accept the responsibility of taking you into danger."

"I'm having no fear of that." There was scorn in the girl's face. "Nor do I think that your true reason, Major."

Urquhart's cheeks grew warm. Nervously, he twisted the ring on his finger. "Look here," he burst out, "there are certain things you do not understand. We just couldn't do it—I mean, take you with us. How would it look, you—a young girl—with two white men, day after day, night after night. There are people who would believe—well—"

"Do you think I'd be caring what anyone believed? I'm no longer a child."

"You certainly aren't," he snapped irritably. "You're a very lovely young lady—" He checked himself and added roughly, "It just wouldn't do, that's all. You'd best stay here and look after your grandparents."

"You're not believing that, either," the girl accused, angry spots of color in her cheeks. "I'll ask you for the last time: would you be taking me with you when you leave?"

He said again, still avoiding her eyes as he hurried out to find Corbillat, "I couldn't accept the responsibility." He fancied he heard a taunt of "Coward!" hurled after him, as he made long strides toward the trees beyond the clearing. He found Corbillat at the corral in the creek bottom. The sun's rays filtering

72

through the brush and tree-tops formed dappled shadows on the horses and mules. A few yards away, running water gurgled through the pondweed. The piney fragrance was heavy in the warm air. Corbillat straightened up from an inspection of a horse's hind hoofs. "These Backward-80 critters are in good shape for the ride," he commenced.

Urquhart snorted violently. "To hell with your critters. The sooner we start riding, the better." Corbillat asked what had gone wrong. He studied Urquhart's face, then listened in silence while Urquhart relayed his conversation with Jennifer. ". . . but why," Urquhart demanded, "with other places to go, must she choose Texas?"

"We—ell," Corbillat spoke deliberately, "maybe she figures she wants to be with her friends. That's natural."

"What friends?" Urquhart looked blank.

"You. Me. She's never known anybody but her paw and us and some Indians. Aren't we friends of hers?"

"Oh, yes, of course we are—"

"Rius?" Corbillat looked sharply at his companion. "You ain't let it go any deeper?" His jaw dropped at another thought. "Or maybe you couldn't prevent it, if it has."

"That's ridiculous," Urquhart insisted angrily.

"I don't know if it is. You might have trouble with her yet, though I ain't sayin' it would be exactly trouble. No, that's not the word for it—"

"God damn it, Dix! What are you hinting at?"

Corbillat's eyes narrowly scrutinized Urquhart. "You

73

made it clear to her? That she couldn't go with us? Definite?"

Urquhart sounded wrathful. "There's not a doubt," he snapped. "Do you take me for a fool?"

"There you go again with that same question," Corbillat said wearily. "I already answered that. Yesterday."

9

THREE MORE DAYS BROUGHT TO COMPLETION THE preparation for the journey. Albumen, with a pair of tattered blankets, a leather strap and lengths of baling wire, had contrived a sort of saddle and stirrups, with which to ride his mules; more wire had gone into the fashioning of a strange device which the Negro insisted was a bridle.

The night before the departure, Urquhart was awakened by rain. Across the darkened room he could hear the girl breathing easily. He wondered if she, too, was awake, and he visualized her slim, clean-limbed form beneath the blankets, the placid rise and fall of smooth white breasts, the blue-black cloud of tousled hair massed about her head and spread widely on the pillow. He'd seen her sleeping those nights when he and Corbillat had talked late; he remembered in particular one disturbing night when Jennifer's midnight hair had formed a transparent webbing across one uncovered shoulder.

He turned restlessly on his bunk. A faint snoring came from near the fireplace where Corbillat lay. The other bunk creaked slightly in the dark room, and Urquhart's thoughts winged back to Jennifer. Not once had the girl again alluded to her request to accompany them to Texas, for which Urquhart couldn't determine whether or not to be thankful. Nor had there been the slightest sign of reproach in the smoky-gentian eyes. It was as though her request had never been voiced. Now that departure was at hand, Urquhart found himself wishing it were farther off. And on this thought Urquhart fell asleep. At the same moment the rain ceased. The skies began to clear.

Before dawn, while the two men slept, Jennifer arose and by the light of a tallow dip, busied herself with their clothing. When they awoke, sunlight was slipping through the east window. Their clothing lay in neat piles. Urquhart found a clean shirt, his mended uniform with its tarnished braid, and long officer's cloak of threadbare but well-brushed weathered grey, with its black lining. Just before the two men left the cabin to wash, Jennifer entered and, with a quiet "Good-morning," started preparing breakfast. It was now that certain tweakings of Urquhart's conscience were intensified.

Breakfast was consumed in silence. The sun climbed higher, cutting a sharp swath of light near the open doorway. Urquhart and Corbillat rose, Urquhart pausing to get Leinster Keating's razors before leaving the cabin. With the aid of a cracked mirror, he shaved slowly, listening to the conversation of Corbillat and the Negro, as they packed their belongings.

"No, don't wrap them guns," Corbillat was saying.

"The Major and I will be packin' them." Somewhere in his travels the sergeant had picked up two Federal repeating rifles, a Spencer and a Henry, with several rounds of ammunition. "We might be needin' those guns to kill us a Yank bastud."

"Yassuh," Albumen agreed. His eyes rolled whitely toward Urquhart. "Ah 'spects, sahgent, Ah'd betteh tek over de shavin' foah de Majuh, while you peks de goods."

Urquhart rubbed lather into his cheeks. "You stay with the sergeant, Albumen, I'll do the shaving." He'd be sorry to part with these razors. The steel was the finest he'd ever encountered. Well, there was one way he could retain possession: by taking Jennifer Keating to Texas . . . He swore suddenly and hastened the shaving. Corbillat asked if Urquhart had cut himself. "No," Urquhart mumbled, and added, "not the way you mean." Corbillat eyed him sharply, then continued packing. Urquhart dried his face on a towel of flour sacking, placed the razors back in their velvet beds, and closed the leather case. Re-entering the cabin, he saw the girl standing near the table. "And again, a thousand thanks, Miss Jennifer. Your father had an appreciation for good steel."

"I'm thinking it is equaled by your own," the girl replied. "As for the razors, I'd like you to take them, along with this." She placed on top of the leather case, the small volume of Prescott Deveraux's verse.

Urquhart stared at her. "Uh—er—thank you—but why give the book and the razors to me?"

"There is no one here to use the razors." The girl's

red lips curved. "As for the book, you like it; at least you liked one poem. When a man likes a thing well enough, it should belong to him, but only when he is certain he likes it well enough. I think you are certain, about the poem and the razors, anyway."

Urquhart eyed her quizzically. "Meaning, Miss Jennifer, I'm not sufficiently certain on other matters?"

"That is a thing it is not for me to say." Her voice sounded faintly accusing. Urquhart dropped the subject. He went on trying to make it clear her gifts were greatly appreciated, though the reason for them, he insisted, was beyond his comprehension. She said quietly at last, "Perhaps it is just that I want you to have something of mine, of this place, to help you remember. . . ."

The sweet huskiness of her voice brought a quick sharp breath to the man's throat. "It's not likely I'll need anything to remind me of you, of this room," he said. He cast a quick glance about the place, his gaze picking out the fireplace with its kettle suspended on an iron crane, the books, the blanketed bunks, the table with its twin benches, and the rocking chair. His eyes returned to the table. It was there he had been stretched, raving, while the girl probed and extracted the bullet that had threatened his life. "On my side, there is a great obligation. There are things money cannot buy, even if I had money to pay. I can't even thank you properly." He'd been twisting, absentmindedly, the carnelian ring on his finger, while he talked. Now, impulsively, he removed the ring and offered it to the girl. "It occurs to me,"—he tried to make his tones light and easy—"that going-away gifts may be exchanged."

She glanced quickly at the ring; her eyes searched his face. "You are certain you want me to have this?" she asked gravely. "You are sure?"

"I'm sure," he replied, and there was no mistaking the assurance in his voice. He saw the flush in her cheeks and knew that she was pleased.

Unconsciously Urquhart had drawn closer to the girl. From her thick blue-black hair came the perfume of powdered orris-root, and his heartbeat quickened at the sweet fragrance of her young body. His right arm settled lightly across her shoulders. She glanced quickly up at him, and there was no sign of withdrawal in the long-lashed eyes, though he could scarcely hear her when she spoke, "I want you to be very sure, Darius Urquhart. You must not forget I am one-half a Cherokee." A choking sensation rose in Urquhart's throat, and his arm tightened.

A sudden wave of confusion engulfed him. Abruptly, a sound reached Urquhart's ears: turning his head he saw Jennifer's grandparents dismounting from their mule, before the doorway. Urquhart reluctantly withdrew his arm and stepped back. For a moment longer his eyes lingered on Jennifer's slim loveliness, but the spell had been broken. He realized only that for a brief moment he had been very close to understanding something Jennifer had been endeavoring to make clear. When next he turned, the two old Indians were entering the cabin. Each voiced a greeting in Cherokee to Jennifer who responded tersely, the usual guttural syllables taking on a liquid quality as they flowed swiftly from her red lips.

Urquhart waited a moment longer, saying to the girl, in a voice that wasn't quite steady, "I'm glad you have the ring." Picking up the razors and volume, he turned to leave. His lips felt stiff when he tried to answer the friendly, toothless smiles of the old Indians as he brushed past.

Corbillat already had the horses saddled, while the Negro was lashing a canvas-covered pack on one mule. Urquhart handed the case to Albumen. "Take care of these blades." The small book, he thrust within his shirt.

"We're 'bout ready to stir up the dust, Rius," Corbillat said, then frowned, "Somehow, I can't find your saber and scabbard. I spoke to Miss Jen yesterday but she ain't seen it. I rec'lect takin' off that scabbard when we undressed you that day. The sword set around the cabin three-four days as I remember—"

"Let's forget it," Urquhart said shortly. "We've got our cap-and-balls, and those two repeating rifles. In God's name what would I want of a saber now?"

Corbillat shoved back his flop-brimmed hat. "Damned if you don't act like somethin' was gripin' you. All right. C'mon, man, stir those stumps! Dicey Nell will've left Texas before we get there."

"Yassuh, sahgent, suh. We's ready foah depahtin', jist de minute Ah gits dis saddle on Gomo'ah."

The next minutes passed all too swiftly. Jennifer and her grandparents had come outside where the horses waited. Albumen was mounted on Gomorrah, holding the lead rein of the droop-eared Sodom. Corbillat

79

shook hands brusquely with Jennifer and the old folks, then mounted and glanced impatiently at Urquhart.

Jennifer's eyes followed Urquhart's every move as he took the withered hand of the grandfather. The old Indian removed his hat and said, *"Higinalu."* Urquhart glanced questioningly at the girl.

Jennifer interpreted, "He says you are his friend. The word,"—speaking slowly and distinctly—"is *'higinalu'.*"

Urquhart attempted the word, *"Higinalu,"* the unaccustomed syllables falling flatly from his lips. He tried it next on the grandmother and did better. The old woman made a ducking bow showing toothless gums in a wide smile, repeating the word and adding, *"Asgaya 'siyu."*

Urquhart looked to Jennifer. Jennifer said, "She says you are a good man."

A wry smile crossed Urquhart's mouth. "I've always found old people very tolerant."

"She's not forgotten, nor has my grandfather, that you arrived here, one day, in time to prevent certain things—"

"Through luck only," Urquhart said. "As I see it, the luck worked mostly for my benefit. I've tried to thank you, but I find it impossible. I can only say—well—*higinalu.*"

"No more than friend?" the girl asked gravely.

"It's the only Cherokee I know," he reminded her.

"I could teach you much more, Darius Urquhart."

"I've already learned a very great deal from you, Jennifer."

She glanced down at the ring, and he saw she had already wound linen thread about the silver band to make it fit the better. Again she raised her eyes to his and held out a slim hand. It felt warm and firm in his grasp, with a hint of steel in the long fingers. She said, "I will be seeing you again." It was a statement; not a question.

"I think so," he nodded. "After I have been home and rebuilt my house, I'll return to Carolina, perhaps. Will I find you here?"

"That is a thing that cannot be answered now," she returned gravely. They stood there in the warm, sunlight. The grandparents were forgotten, as were Corbillat and the Negro and the blue sky and the tall pine trees, green against the blue. The man stood very straight and tall, the sunlight bright on his rust-red hair, still holding the girl's hand. After a moment he reluctantly released it. Jennifer said quietly, "You'd better go now, Darius Urquhart. The sergeant is growing impatient."

"I'm not sure," his words were uncertain, "that I want to leave. I find this leaving very difficult, now the time is come—"

"That is just it," her calm voice interposed, "you are not sure. So it is best that you go, Darius Urquhart."

She held his eyes a moment longer, before he mounted the black gelding. Urquhart was conscious of nothing except that he was leaving Jennifer, and that the leaving brought to his chest a definite pain.

And then the horses were traveling between tall pine trees; only then did Urquhart remember that the word "good-bye" had not left his lips. After a time he turned and looked back. Jennifer Keating stood as he had left her, a slim figure against the surrounding background of pines. As he glanced around, the girl raised her right arm, palm out, high in the air, held it an instant, then allowed it to drop slowly at her side. Urquhart raised his wide-brimmed felt hat, and again settled to the saddle as a wild persimmon tree obscured further view. The animals moved more rapidly through the forest which gradually thinned out, as they came to a road running south across rolling fields.

PART TWO

SABINA

1

GAULT MADISON, OWNER OF THE POT-HOOK RANCH, considered Corbillat's tale—a tale of running contraband cotton from New Orleans and of a near duel in which Urquhart had been involved. He allowed his eyes to wander thoughtfully around the patio of San Antonio's Menger Hotel, and shoved a Stetson to the back of his greying blond head; his right hand tugged abstractedly at sweeping moustaches. He was approaching fifty and was a trifle paunchy about the middle; one leg of his trousers was tucked sloppily into a boot, the other hung at ankle length. Shifting his bulky shoulders against the back of the wide-armed wooden chair, Madison called a Negro to replenish the glasses. "You know somethin'?" Corbillat said. "There's been times in the past years when I'd have given every chance for life I owned, just to get back to San Antonio and a glass of Menger beer. Ain't no man ever brewed lager suds like Charlie Degen. But we got here, finally, and I still almost couldn't believe it until yesterday mornin', before daylight, when we passed through and I saw the moonlight shinin' on old Alamo Mission, and I says, 'San Antonio, welcome your prodigals—' Lord A'mighty, I'm glad you spotted me crossin' the Plaza. Me'n Rius was fixin' to ride over and see you, soon's possible."

"Incidentally," Madison said, "I got married last year."

Corbillat's black eyes bulged. "You? Gault! I never did figure you as the hitchin' type. Wa'n't it you we used to figure would take care of populatin' South Texas?" He stopped in confusion. "Well, congratulations. I was so surprised I reckon I—I—is she from around here?"

"Louisiana girl," Madison explained. "She left last week for a visit home. You'll meet her when she gets back. You know, Dix, there's a time when a man needs a woman to run his house. I've been luckier'n most, durin' the war; you know how it is." Corbillat said he knew how it was, though his expression belied the words.

"The Injuns kicked up hell with Urquhart Oaks, didn't they," he said to change the subject. "Even knowin' like we did that the house had been burned, it was a blow to make a man sick. I never see Rius look so white as he got. He just stumbled through them ashes, pickin' up bits of twisted metal and throwin' 'em down, and never sayin' a word, and then lookin' up toward the chimneys, like he couldn't believe the place wasn't still there. He didn't say much, just 'We're goin' to have some buildin' to do, Dix.' Even when I walked across that flagstoned gallery where the pillars used to stand, I couldn't hardly savvy the old house was gone. Damn them Comanches!"

Madison agreed. "Injuns took to raiding when they learned the whites were fighting each other. There wasn't much we could do. I rounded up some greasers when I heard the Comanches were coming, but we was too late. The house and other buildings were in flames. We fought off the devils, and I managed to rescue the family Bible and property papers before the house was gone complete, but that was all. I'm glad Diomedes Urquhart didn't live to see it."

"San Antonio looks like she'd growed," Corbillat said.

Madison nodded. "Around ten thousand population. More, counting Union troops." He sighed. "You should have seen this town after Kirby Smith first sur-rendered his army. Our men come scrabbling back through here, mad as hornets! Couldn't believe we'd quit." Corbillat reminded Madison belligerently that it was the Yanks who'd wanted to quit first. Madison changed the subject, "What was the idea of bringing that Negro and those mules to town?"

"The mules is to draw the wagon; the Negro to drive." Madison said he hadn't seen any wagon. "That's why we come to town," Corbillat explained. "We got to have a wagon. I'm fixin' to buy one, someplace. And then I got to get timbers—say, is that lumber yard on Commerce Street yet?" All this, Madison pointed out, required elucidation. Corbillat said, "Urquhart Oaks needs rebuildin'. Rius ain't got money for carpenters, so him and me will build it. The foundation is there and the chimney's standin'. But we need lumber and a wagon to haul it."

"You got time for another beer." Madison called a waiter and when he arrived with fresh glasses, paid with an octagonal piece of gold. Noting Corbillat's curious glance, Madison explained, "They come from California. I don't mind telling you, I've got plenty of these yellow slugs."

"We heard around Galveston," Corbillat said, "there wa'n't no Texans with money a-tall, let alone gold."

"That's the general condition. I told you I'd been lucky. Now, regarding this building you and Rius are planning. Where you going to live while you build?"

"When we come back we found some Mexicans livin' along the south bank of Crinolina Creek, and makin' 'dobe bricks, so Rius made a deal with 'em to build a 'dobe shack to live in, until the big house is done. Dam'd if I know how them Mexicans come to settle there."

"I'm to blame. You remember there used to be a settlement of Mexes living on my holdings. When I got married, I told 'em to move someplace else—"

Corbillat snickered. "Didn't want your new missus wonderin' how come so many of them Mexican kids had blue eyes and light hair, eh, Gault?"

Madison looked sheepish. "Well, you know how notional a woman gets. I didn't owe those Mexicans anything. I'd taken care of the whole pack and passel of 'em for years, though I admit they were good company. Those two families over on your place, I told 'em they could settle there. Didn't figure Rius would object. Now about this wagon, there's no sense Rius spending his money, when I got several." Corbillat said he knew Rius wouldn't want to be beholden to any man. Madison looked hurt. "By God!" he swore. "If I can't loan to the son of my oldest friend, I want to know! I got an old linchpin wagon, just right for heavy haulin'. Got a buckboard you can have too. And you'll need horses and mules." Corbillat stated they already had mules, them the Negro had brought. Madison grunted. "You're going to need more'n two mules. And you won't get your timber today. All's you can do is order, and come after it when it's cut. If you're ready, let's leave. I want to see Rius."

They left the patio and passed through the lobby of the Menger to the plank sidewalk. A few cowmen, chairs tilted back against the white wall, spoke to Madison and received a nod. At the sidewalk, Albumen waited with Corbillat's horse and Sodom and Gomorrah. Madison laughed. "You can't expect to haul much with those critters, Dix. Hell! Those mules aren't hardly burro caliber."

Corbillat eyed the mules as though he'd never seen

them before. "That's a fact. They don't look like Texas mules."

Madison placed one foot carefully in a stirrup, the saddle creaking under his bulk as he lifted himself to the back of a big grey gelding.

Corbillat reined his horse close to Madison's and they moved off, the Negro and mules following, across Alamo Plaza, its surface a cracked mosaic of sun-baked mud where, a week previously, frogs had croaked in rain puddles. At Commerce Street, the men turned right to cross a plank bridge over the winding San Antonio River, and threaded their way past a train of mule-drawn freight wagons entering the city. The street was narrow, lined on either side with buildings of rock and adobe. A number of blue uniforms brought scowls to Corbillat's dark features, though he kept silent; a few men still wore the remnants of Confederate clothing. Arriving at Main Plaza, Corbillat purchased supplies, before the riders turned their mounts northwesterly out of the city. Ahead lay rolling hill-lands, green and brown under the bright afternoon sunlight, their hollows lavender with shadow. Toward the south, cumulous clouds banked white against blue sky. Corbillat filled his lungs with air. "Texas," he said lovingly, "Texas! Never did believe I'd actually get back home."

2

THE OLD ROAD, NOW GRASS-GROWN BETWEEN THE RUTS, undulated across a terrain spotted thickly with stands of cedar, mesquite, post-oak and prickly-pear. A neglected cottonfield lay along one side of the road for a distance, before the riders topped a rise to descend a long corridor of ancient Spanish oaks with, at the end, a cleared space where the great house had stood. Beyond lay Crinolina Creek, flowing between cotton-wood- and willow-shaded banks.

"Where the devil's Rius?" Corbillat sputtered, reining near Madison. Almost immediately they sighted Urquhart down near the stream, engaged in building a cottonwood pole corral. A smile lighted his features when he spied Madison, and he came hurrying to greet him. His shirt was soaked with perspiration; his trousers, tucked into boots, dusty. His sombrero showed sweat stains in the band. "Gault! Lord above! It's good to see you again."

Madison climbed down from the saddle, his right hand closing tightly about Urquhart's, his left clutching Urquhart's shoulder. "It's been a long time, son." His eyes were moist. "God! You grow more like Diomedes every day. You've broadened through the chest."

The sun was low now. Albumen started a fire and delved into supplies. Corbillat had gone to the creek with the horses and mules. Urquhart and Madison sat not far from the fire. ". . . yes," Madison was saying, "Dix gave me a complete account of what you've been through." Diomedes Urquhart's death in battle received some comment. Terry's Rangers came in for mention. "There wasn't but few of Terry's Rangers got back," Madison said. "You boys certainly made a record. Why'n't you ever write me? For a time I thought you were dead."

"I kept thinking we'd be getting home soon . . ." He left the sentence unfinished.

Madison said, "You'll find changes when you get time to look around. Even with the war, San Antonio's boomed. There's a factory started there, for making ice. Imagine! And there's people using gas-light."

Corbillat came up and threw down an armful of fire-wood. "Say, Rius, has this old stud-hawss told you he got himself tangled in double harness, while we was away?"

"Married? You, Gault?" Urquhart's grey eyes widened.

Crimson seeped into Madison's features. "That's it," he nodded. "Louisiana girl—Sabina Nielsen that was—from Alexandria. Her folks came from St. Looie to Alexandria twelve years back. Her father went into cotton brokerage. War just about finished him. Sabina's home on a visit, now. Her father's sick. You'll like her, Rius. Nearer your age, than mine . . ." His tones dwindled. He changed the subject: "What you figuring to do, now you're back?"

"Raise beef. Soldiering and raising cotton and beef are all I know. Soldiering's done. There'll be no money in cotton if we pay for nigger labor. Cows seem all that's left."

"There's plenty cows." Gault Madison tugged at his grey-blond moustache. "They've done nothing but breed and run loose through four years of war. There's some I've seen down in river bottoms and back in the *brasada*, with horns spreading six feet and covered with moss. For a fact! Wild as antelopes and nigh as fast." Darius Urquhart remarked he appeared to have a job of branding ahead. "Branding?" Madison snorted. "Hell's fire! I'll say so. There's been practically no branding for five years. Don't waste any time trying to locate your own cows. Just head into the thickets and when you catch a critter slap your iron on him. That's what everybody's doing—especially a heap of hombres who never even owned a horse before the war. Now they're aiming to be cattle-kings. I don't figure they'll get far. Not with cattle prices down and things so unsettled."

Albumen served food. The men sat crosslegged on the earth, eating from tin-plates. Darkness settled over the land, relieved only by leaping lights from burning mesquite roots. Fireflies glowed and diminished against surrounding darkness. Corbillat got a bottle of bourbon from one of the sacks; Madison produced cigars. Albumen, after eating, gathered the dishes and carried them to the stream, where Crinolina Creek was making sounds through the willows like the soft rustlings of women's skirts.

Madison said awkwardly, "Rius, I don't want to turn my horse into any corral where he ain't welcome, but Dix says money is short." Urquhart nodded and Madison continued, "It's going to cost money to

90

rebuild Urquhart Oaks. Where you aiming to get it?" Urquhart supposed that banks were still lending money. "Yes and no," Madison stated. "About all you've got to borrow on is land. There's more land in Texas than any place else. Hell! I can buy all I want at two-bits an acre. You can't borrow on your herds, yet. Try for a bank loan if you like, but you'll be disappointed." Urquhart said somewhat stiffly that an Urquhart's word had always been good. "I'm not denying that," Madison said, "but you'll find it won't bring as much money as before the war. Banks have to protect theirselves. And there's too many of these damned Yankee carpetbaggers ready to grab property that's foreclosed. You want to see some Yank living here?"

Corbillat swore bitterly. Urquhart remarked that Madison seemed pessimistic. "You will too, when you've been back a while," Madison said. "You haven't had a chance to size up Texas. Anybody loyal to the South gets short shrift these days. Things are damned bad! U.S. Treasury agents swarming like a plague of locusts, all over the state, confiscating cotton and everything else that belonged to the Confederate Government. Stand up for your rights and you're li'ble to get kicked down. You want to mind that, when you go into San Antonio. They got us whipped and now they're stompin' us—unless one way or another we arrange matters."

What, exactly, Urquhart asked, did Gault mean by arranging matters? "If you got money," Madison explained, "you can buy a skunk off, now and then. For a time we've got to ride along with the bastards. The main thing to remember is to keep clear of trouble. Rius, I don't like to be spreading gloom, but that's how things are. I want you and Dix to be careful. Learn that now! You'll see how it goes: every time a Union man or a Negro gets arrested, ten to one they get off scot-free, but let you or me get arrested and—"

"Ain't no Negro goin' to get uppity with me." Corbillat spat into the fire. "The day ain't come in Texas when—"

Madison said heavily, "If you're going to take that attitude, Dix, you better stay home, and not go where you'll meet anybody you don't like."

Urquhart said, "You make it sound bad, Gault. If things are that way, it's going to take time to rebuild the house."

"That's something I've been leading up to. Rius, I've got money to do all the building you want. I'd like you to take it—on your terms—" Urquhart interrupted to say he'd not come back to Texas to trade on his father's friendship. "Why damn your hide, Rius," Madison snorted, "it's nothing of the sort."

"I just can't do it, Gault. Going to a bank is one thing: taking your money is another. I appreciate your offer, but rebuilding Urquhart Oaks is something I do my own way. The loan of a wagon is a matter of friendship; taking your money is something different. If I borrow from a bank, risk is part of its trade; in the long run, banks don't often lose. You're a friend, and I won't gamble with a friend's money. That's settled."

"By God, I guess it is." Madison sounded wistful.

Corbillat ejaculated a question as to Madison having money to lend when other Texans were broke. Madison smiled. "I told you I'd been lucky. I'm one of few Southerners who made money out of the war. I wanted to go with Terry's Rangers when Diomedes did, but the fool doctors insisted I had something wrong with my heart. Damn' foolishness! I'm sound as an oak. So I contracted to furnish stock and beef to the Confederacy. I made a lot of money." Corbillat remarked that Confederate money was worthless. "I didn't keep Confederate money," Madison confessed. "I've got connections in San Francisco and Denver. Fast as I got any Confed money, I changed it into British gold. I changed my gold into money of the United States. I bought cotton in Texas and shipped it through Mexico, to England. That paid big too. The Britishers needed cotton to keep their mills running."

Corbillat wondered uneasily if many other Texans had converted their Confed money into American gold. "I wasn't the only one," Madison replied. "There were plenty of Union sympathizers in Texas. Probably the idea don't set well with you, but at least I tried to fight for Texas. The war was over for me, when Terry's Rangers wouldn't let me ride with 'em. And any money looks good to me."

Albumen was busying himself with boiling water, whisky, sugar and tin cups. The air had turned crisp. More wood was placed on the flames; sparks danced upward and were lost in the stars. Urquhart said quietly, "Gault, you speak as though you figured from the start we'd lose the war."

"You've hit the nail on the head. I wasn't the only one. Diomedes and I, neither of us could see a chance for the Confederacy." His tones turned bitter. "He at least had a chance to fight for Texas. I could never see the South winning. You had the hope of winning. I didn't even have that, but I did everything possible for our side while war lasted. All the gold I made didn't go into my pockets; there were times when it bought a hell of a lot more for our forces than Jeff Davis' shinplasters. So don't hold it against me, if I made money out of war. I wasn't doing what I'd wanted. Toward the last, when we commenced to run out of men, I could have got in, even with a heart-decline or whatever the sawbones claimed I had, but by that time it looked like I'd best stay home and make money to help those who came back." His voice was pleading for understanding.

Urquhart said, "Nobody's holding it against you, Gault. We play our cards the way they're dealt to us."

"And you won't reconsider about building your place with my money?"

Urquhart said evasively, "I'll think it over." He accepted from Albumen a cup of hot toddy.

The Negro gave Madison and Corbillat their toddies. "Mistuh Madison, suh, could I asks you a query? . . . Did y'all in youah sashigatin' round dese pahts, eveh see hide or hair of a Negro gal name of Dicey Nell White. Sawta on de yaller-complexion side, her, wid a blandishin' look in she eye, and a sawta hip-swivelin' gait."

"No. Why you asking me?"

"Ah done asks most ev'body. Ontil one day de sah-gent allows as how Ah'm jist wastin' of mah time, and he tells me Ah should procrast'nate ontil we gets t'see you, y'all havin' de 'quaintance wid nigh all de gals in Taixus—white, raid, yaller and black—"

Corbillat emitted an abrupt strangling sound and commenced coughing, his face crimson. "Ain't no word of sense in what the man says, Gault," he protested feebly. "You, Albumen, you tell Mr. Madison, *pronto*, you've made a mistake."

The Negro backed hastily away, firelight shining on his ebony features. "Yassuh, no suh. Ah figgehs Ah teks in too much terr'tory. Comes to rec'lect. Ah cain't seems to remembah no mention of black—jist raid and yaller and white—"

"Albumen!" Urquhart's lips were twitching. "You'd best hustle down and see if those mules are hobbled safe." He turned to Madison. "The man's come all this way, looking for his daughter, Dicey Nell. Back in Carolina, he heard she'd come to Texas."

Albumen vanished in the surrounding darkness. "You know how a Negro is, Gault," Dix said sheepishly. "Never can get a fact straight. Knowin' me like you do, you couldn't believe I'd make a remark—"

Madison chuckled. "I know your tendency to brag on your friends, Dix, but I reckon you over-compli-mented me. Nope,"—reminiscently—"I can't say I ever do remember any black. You must have some-body else in mind." Corbillat mumbled a reply to the effect he must've had, and besides he hadn't said any-thin' like that in the first place, and even if he had any damn fool should know there's a limit to any one man's endeavors.

Beyond the circle of firelight a cricket chirped an accented beat to the music of Crinolina Creek. Urquhart talked quietly of the journey from Carolina and of adventures that had delayed them; of cotton-running in New Orleans and a gamblers' quarrel which had almost led to a duel; of a fire which had robbed them of profits from the contraband—profits which would have financed the rebuilding of Urquhart Oaks.

"I was thinking, Rius," Madison said, "about that feller you nearly fought a duel with. Did you say his name was Harnish?" Urquhart nodded: "Captain Drake Harnish." Madison went on, "There's a man in San Antonio, named Harnish. Big jasper—tall as you, heftier—a heavy black moustache, curled at the ends. Handsome cuss, but I can't cater to him. If his name's Drake, I don't know." They considered Harnish's appearance; the descriptions appeared to tally. Urquhart shrugged. He didn't think it could be the same man. What was he doing in San Antonio? "He's an agent for the Freedman's Bureau," Madison replied.

Corbillat asked, "What in hell is the Freedman's Bureau?"

"An organization Washington set up to see the Negro gets equal rights with whites. It's planned to give every freed Negro a mule and forty acres."

"My Gawd!" Corbillat snorted. "What's runnin' the South now, idiots? Forty acres and a mule! Can you tell me where in Gawd's name they expect to find all them forty acres's. You'd be bound to take in all Texas to

96

locate that much land, and there ain't no Negro goin' to own Texas soil! Mules! Acres! Votes! What in the name of seven bald steers is the country comin' to? Does Washington cal'clate it's runnin' us?"

Madison said, "I reckon it does."

"This Harnish you mentioned," Urquhart said thoughtfully, "is the agent for the Freedman's Bureau?" "Only one of many, many agents," Madison growled. "That being the case," Urquhart continued, "he's probably not in sympathy with the South. If he does prove to be the same Harnish, I might be in for trouble with him. That Harnish in New Orleans, I had a feeling I'd seen him before some place, though I can't think where. The Harnish in town isn't a Southerner, is he?"

Madison said, "Christ, no! I don't think he's a North or South sympathizer, either one. He's just a Harnish sympathizer, out to line his pockets. He ain't fanatic on the Negro subject like some agents. He was in the Union Army, though. He had a brother killed serving with the Yanks. But I don't think Harnish has any grievances that can't be cured with money. He's figuring to quit the Freedman's Bureau, and start himself a business in San 'Tonio—bar, gambling, girls."

Urquhart stated, "If this Harnish proves to be the same man, I won't run away from trouble, but I'd just as soon not have anything to do with him."

"Let's forget him for the time being," Madison suggested. "I'll mosey around town and talk to him, next two-three days. Sort of feel him out. Meanwhile, you'd best stay away from San Antonio, until you've heard from me. Don't forget what I've told you about conditions hereabouts. Any man who's been in the Confederate Army has got to figure on playing with loaded dice whenever he goes against Union men." He rose. "Well, I'd best be getting along to the Pot-Hook."

"Dix bought new blankets today," Urquhart invited. "We'd be glad to have you stay and try 'em, Gault."

"Thanks, Rius, but I can be home within the hour. I'm figuring to set fresh mash tomorrow mornin'—got my peaches and apples ready—"

"That reminds me," Urquhart said, "did you set out that young orchard of peach and apples down near the Mexican shacks? I noticed 'em first thing when we arrived."

Madison nodded. "I was setting out more trees for myself, and I happened to have some left over. Figured you might like 'em. Jerk 'em out, if you don't. Otherwise they'll be bearin' good come three-four years."

"I do want them. Father always intended to set out an orchard. I'm thanking you, Gault."

"Don't mention it . . . Yes, I'm still making peach-and-apple brandy. I'll bring you a couple jugs next time I come. Or you get 'em yourself, tomorrow when you come for those wagons. You'll be needing horses and mules, too. I can let you have—Now, wait a minute! Don't be so damn' independent. If you don't take that extra stock off my hands some God damned Treasury agent from Washington will come along and confiscate them. You want the Yanks to get that stock?" Urquhart admitted that he didn't want anyone in Washington to get anything that belonged in Texas.

"All right, it's settled," Madison concluded. "Here comes your man with my horse. I'll see you tomorrow."

3

BY THE END OF THE WEEK THE MEXICANS HAD FOUR walls of the adobe house up, and were testing for proper draught the fireplace built against one end. The corral near Crinolina Creek was finished and now held a dozen horses.

Urquhart and Corbillat had finished breakfast, and Albumen was clearing up when Madison rode in. He lifted his big frame down from the grey, dropped reins over its head and came in to the remnants of the campfire. "Appears like you're getting settled."

"We should be in the house, soon," Urquhart nodded, "then Dix and I are going to see about rounding up some cows."

Madison seated himself on the earth. "I dropped by the lumber yard, yesterday. Your timbers are ready, when you want to fetch 'em. I'll ride with you when you go. I suppose Dix will stay here." He appeared concerned about Corbillat's going into San Antonio.

"What about this Harnish fellow?" Urquhart asked.

"I don't figure there's going to be any trouble in that direction. Yes, he's the same one you ruckused with in N'Orleans. He certain acted funny about the business. I ran across him yesterday in Weintraub's Saloon, and asked was he ever in N'Orleans. First, he said no, that he'd got out of the army as soon as the war ended. I

99

mentioned careless like, that a friend of mine, Major Urquhart, had had a mite of trouble with a Union captain over there. Harnish got red and wants to know where said friend is now. I stalled that off for a spell. Finally he admits having been in N'Orleans a short time; and said he did have words with a fellow one night. Finally he admits he got challenged to a duel one night when he was drunk, but that he was ordered back north before he could keep the appointment."

Urquhart smiled. "That's pretty much the story, except it was Harnish who did the challenging."

Madison frowned. "I can't figure why, but fact is, Rius, I figure he's scared of you. He acted like he didn't want that old trouble reopened."

Corbillat said, "Texas ain't big enough to hold him and you both, Rius—"

"Just a minute, Dix, Texas is a big state. Perhaps it is big enough for both of us." Corbillat muttered something about upholding the Urquhart honor. "Nothing's happening to the Urquhart honor," Urquhart smiled. "I'll fight if Harnish wants it that way. According to Gault, he doesn't, apparently. Any friction at all between Northerners and Southerners only prolongs a war that's supposed to be ended. I have enough troubles without going out of my way to find more."

"I won't say you're wrong. I just don't like it. If he's evadin' trouble, there's no good reason behind it. Maybe,"—Corbillat brightened—"if he's aiming to quit the Freedman's Bureau, he won't swing so much weight. If he's plannin' to open a business, he wouldn't want to offend anybody that's as popular as an

Urquhart. He'll want trade."

"Maybe you're right," Urquhart agreed. "Gault, I'll hitch that wagon, and we'll start."

Corbillat stood watching the wagon as it rolled toward the first rise, Gault Madison on the big grey, jogging at its side. Corbillat shook his head. "You, Albumen," he shouted suddenly, "c'mere!"

"Yassuh, sahgent, suh."

Corbillat leveled a forefinger toward the departing wagon. "There's somethin' to see! An Urquhart—an Urquhart, mind you—toolin' a span of mules just like some poor white trash, or a Negro."

"Yassuh, Ah sees he. Lookin' rat pert an' handsome, don't he?" Albumen said innocently.

Corbillat heaved a sigh. "Reckon like Gault says, things have changed. I'll be learnin' a passel of new ways, before I get through I reckon." The wagon passed out of sight. "I'm goin' over and see can I lend them greasers a hand with their buildin'. Soon's you've finished reddin' up the camp, you come along down to them walls. Beginnin' to look like everybody's got to work around here."

Urquhart and Madison reached San Antonio before noon, and went in search of Drake Harnish. Except for growth, San Antonio looked much as it had before the war. An inspection of saloons in the vicinity of both Main and Military Plazas failed to reveal any sign of Harnish. At an office of the Freedman's Bureau, a large room filled with desks, Negroes and lethargic white government clerks, Madison elicited the information that Harnish hadn't been in for two days; he might be found at Weintraub's bar on Commerce Street, or at his new building being erected on Laredo.

Urquhart and Madison walked west on Commerce Street to Weintraub's Saloon. A mahogany bar stretched along the right wall, behind which was a mirrored backbar, glasses and bottles. Weintraub, a middle-aged German with red cheeks and brownish hair, presided over the counter where a knot of men were clustered at one end. He came forward, beaming, "Mister Urquhart! Haf you from the war been long back? Is goot to see you again. Und Mister Madison. So many time you haf come to my place and you do not tell me home is Mister Urquhart." They shook hands. "The beer I can recommend. With ice now is better."

Foaming glasses were placed on the bar. "Louie," Madison said, "has a man named Harnish been in today?"

A shadow passed over Weintraub's features. "Iss here now." He jerked a disdainful thumb toward the group at the opposite end of the bar. Harnish hearing his name spoken, had already spied Madison and Urquhart. He detached himself from the knot of men and came toward the front of the saloon, a rather forced smile on his face, the curling ends of his moustache seeming to wilt visibly, as his pale blue eyes, beneath thick brows, fell on Urquhart. "I—I hadn't realized, Mr. Madison," he said, "that your friend was already in this section of the country."

Weintraub waddled away and the three men faced each other, Urquhart's eyes cold. Again, almost instantly, the feeling of having seen Harnish some-where previous to their meeting in New Orleans, swept over Urquhart, but the exact locality of the meeting baffled him. Harnish wore a black coat of the Prince Albert type, grey trousers, boots. A gold watch-chain stretched across his fancy waistcoat; there was a flat-topped wide-brimmed hat at the back of his heavy black hair. He looked uncertainly at Urquhart.

"I suppose you want to appoint another place for our meeting, Mr. Urquhart."

"That," Urquhart replied coldly, "I leave entirely to you. I kept one appointment for which you failed to appear. Nothing assures me I'd be doing anything but wasting my time in a second appointment."

Harnish flushed. "For my failure to appear you have my apology. It was unavoidable. Mr. Urquhart, I assume you fought on the side of the Confederacy. At any rate, you realize that Army orders can't be ignored." Urquhart nodded, pointing out, however, that now they were no longer under military supervi-sion . . .

Perspiration appeared on Harnish's forehead. Madison, looking uneasy, broke in: "I can't see any reason for you two renewing that old quarrel. The war's over. There's no use for further fighting. All this country wants is peace."

Harnish looked gratefully at Madison. "My senti-ments exactly"—in assumed heartiness. "I've seen enough of bloodshed. I lost a brother in the war. Lieu-tenant Brett Harnish. Perhaps, Mr. Urquhart, you, too, lost someone dear to you." Urquhart ignored this and asked where Harnish's brother had been killed. "In North Carolina. just before the war ended," Harnish told him. "He was with the 16th Ohio Cavalry—" Urquhart broke in to say that he, himself, had seen action in North Carolina. Harnish's pale blue eyes opened wider. "Perhaps you met my brother on the field of battle. Perhaps . . ." He allowed the assumption to go unfinished.

"I doubt I killed your brother," Urquhart said. "I was put out of action pretty early in the engagement." His dislike for Harnish was turning to an active loathing. Neither could he remember having faced the 16th Ohio Cavalry. in North Carolina. At any rate, the man had been a soldier, as had his brother, Urquhart mused. Any man, even an enemy, who has faced your gunpowder, is entitled to some respect.

Harnish said, "You're as sick of war as I am. I'm all for offering you the hand of friendship." Urquhart puzzled over the man's attitude. One fact stood clear: Harnish wished to avoid trouble. "This may sound strange," Harnish was saying, "coming from a former enemy, Urquhart. True enough. I fought for the Union, feeling our country should be held together, at any cost. but you realize there are times when a man is not free to follow his inclinations. The Confederacy always had my sympathy. Between you and me, this talk of making Negroes equal with whites is damned foolishness. Nor do I feel that the better side won the war. But let's not talk of wars."

For God's sake, Urquhart was thinking, let's not talk of anything. I'd like to get out of here, as far away from this fellow as possible. Urquhart looked appealingly at Madison who got the idea. Madison cleared his throat and said, "You two had better bury the hatchet and shake hands. What do you say, Rius? Harnish appears willing."

Urquhart swallowed hard and reluctantly accepted the hand Harnish extended. It felt cold and clammy to his grasp. He dropped it abruptly as a feeling of revulsion swept him. Harnish looked relieved. "Now will you gentlemen afford me the honor of drinking at my expense?"

Urquhart was about to excuse himself when Weintraub came bustling down the bar with word that drinks were on the house. Harnish took whisky, Madison and Urquhart glasses of beer. "What is it your new establishment you are calling, Mr. Harnish?" Weintraub asked.

"The Dromedary," Harnish replied. Madison asked if that frame structure going up on Laredo Street, north of Dolorosa, was Harnish's. "That's the place," Harnish nodded. "We intended to have a one-story building; you know, a bar, quiet games, a few pretty girls to dance. Then I thought, why not a second story, with rooms? Gentlemen only, you understand." He winked.

Urquhart had some lumber to pick up, he stated. He found himself, against his will, shaking hands a second time with Harnish. Ten minutes later, he and Madison were heading to get the wagon. "Look here, Gault," Urquhart demanded, "did you give Harnish some money—pay him off—to avoid trouble with me?"

"Swear to God, I didn't, Rius," Madison insisted.

Urquhart shook his head disgustedly. "It's going to be difficult living with myself when I think I shook hands with him. But what else could I do? It was clear he didn't want that quarrel renewed. I don't understand. He's got the influence to make things very bad, if he were so inclined."

"I know," Madison agreed. "Don't quite understand it myself, Rius. Unless he doesn't want it known he ran out of a ruckus—military orders or no. From what I've seen of Harnish, I don't figure he had any military orders—not any that called him away that quick. But he wants peace, it's to your advantage. Shaking hands with him was a compromise you had to make. You're going to learn that we've got to compromise until we can get all Yanks out of Texas."

"All right," Urquhart said, "I'll compromise when necessary, but I still don't like it." He smiled suddenly. "I'm commencing to sound like Dix. Come on, let's pick up that lumber."

4

IT WAS THE BEGINNING OF MANY COMPROMISES FOR Urquhart. As the months passed there seemed no end to the indignities which could be heaped on Southerners by a victorious North. Texas was being governed, not as an independent state with states' rights, but as a military province of the United States. Fights, disorders of various types, were frequent; in any dispute involving a Southerner and a Negro, or white

Union sympathizer, the Southerner generally came off second-best in the courts. Texans were arrested on trumped-up charges whenever they found themselves in conflict with carpetbagger ambitions. If the carpetbaggers gained their objectives, Urquhart and his kind would, apparently, have no rights.

It was said, and perhaps with some justice, that Texas was more hostile to the United States than any other former stronghold of the Confederacy, but those who made this accusation failed to remember that the Texans had, only thirty years before, waged a bloody war to gain independence from Mexico, and that such men do not accept readily the arrogant rule of a second despotic dictatorship.

With Corbillat's belligerent spirit in mind, Urquhart strove to keep Dix occupied with ranch affairs to prevent his going to San Antonio. However, Corbillat did spend a few nights drifting about town, frequenting places where Harnish might be encountered. After three meetings with the man, Dix was forced to admit that he had no recollection of ever having seen him before. "If you've met him before," Dix said, "it must have been sometime when I wasn't with you. I wouldn't trust him no farther than I would a rattlesnake. But he's sure a fancy Dan with ladies."

"Probably I just imagine I've seen him before. We'll shy clear of him and attend our own business."

Urquhart had but one object in view: the rebuilding of Urquhart Oaks. The hot-headed Corbillat had learned to hold his tongue and avoid arguments. Neither of them visited San Antonio often; it was generally

Albumen who drove in for supplies, and Albumen's conversation in town had largely to do with inquiries relative to Dicey Nell, such inquiries to date having brought no satisfaction. Word of the Negro's whereabouts resulted in a visit by an agent of the Freedman's Bureau, who insisted a contract be drawn to cover Albumen's job at Urquhart Oaks. This was done, signed by Albumen and Urquhart and the agent; Darius found himself contracted to pay the Negro twenty dollars a month, and the agent departed smugly. Thereupon Albumen, muttering something about fool ideas of Northern white trash, had employed his contract to start the evening's fire.

"Though I'm damned if I know," Urquhart frowned later, "where I'd get twenty dollars to pay the man each month. We're busted flat, Dix."

"Not while you got land and cows," Dix asserted stubbornly. "Quit worryin'. Ain't missed any meals yet. Beef prices will come back."

"Will they come back in time?" Urquhart said glumly.

They were, at the moment, deep in the *brasada,* near a point where Crinolina Creek forked south. At their feet lay a prone brindle calf, its front hoofs lashed with "piggin' string." Around the small clearing in which they'd roped the calf, grew a tangled jungle of mesquite, catclaw and prickly-pear. A running iron was heating among the coals of a small fire. Corbillat drew it out, examined it, said, "Here goes!"

Urquhart took up a position at the rear of the calf, seizing one of its hind legs and pulling it back as far as it would go, the under leg being held in position by his booted foot. Corbillat settled his weight on the animal's forequarters and deftly drew, with the running iron, on the calf's left ribs, the U within a circle which represented the brand of Urquhart Oaks. A thin spiral of smoke redolent of burning hair and scorched flesh stung the nostrils of the men and mingled with the odor of perspiration and smoldering wood. The calf struggled frantically. Corbillat dropped the iron on the fire and seized his knife. The flies increased at the scent of blood. The calf's struggles and bawling were intensified. "Damn! If we only had a third man to do this while you and I held—" Corbillat panted, then "Look out! He'll dung on you!" Urquhart scrambled quickly to one side, and Corbillat moved to the animal's head with his knife, muttering, "Underslope, right and left," as he never failed to do while earmarking Circle-U stock. Urquhart slipped off the piggin' strings, the calf got somewhat dazedly to his feet, then suddenly departed, bawling loudly, to go crashing off through the brush.

Corbillat wiped his hands and knife on his stained leather shotgun *chaparejos,* and mopped perspiration from his face with a blue bandanna. "That's the first calf we've seen not followin' a cow, in several days, Rius."

"It's all right with me when they're not full-grown," Urquhart said. "Most of those mossy-horns we've been turning up are too wild to work easy. But I think we're making progress. Of course, Gault's turning his crew over to help out last month, made a whale of a difference. Otherwise, I doubt we would ever have got caught up with the branding."

"You're not runnin' off at the head when you say Gault helped. Biggest-hearted hombre I ever knew." Corbillat rolled and lighted a cigarette. "I don't know why you won't let him loan you the money to finish up the house."

Urquhart's lips tightened. "We've been through all that before, Dix. I won't gamble with his money. The way things are going, I don't know if I could ever pay him back—"

"You aimin' to just let that house ride until you get rich? How you think it looks with those joists and bare studs, juttin' up on that foundation like a skeleton? We ain't done no work on that house since the first couple months we were back—"

"It looks better to me that way than it would finished if it wasn't paid for. Take a look at that grey sky. There's a chill to that breeze. Could be a norther coming. We'd better get home."

It was dark when they got in. The wind had turned cold. Within the small adobe house Albumen was placing slabs of beef in a pan, by the light of an oil lamp. A few straight-backed chairs stood about; a bunk had been built on either side of the room. The table was of bare pine; the floor of beaten earth. Flames danced in a fireplace; a coffee-pot stood on the hearth. Outside, a small adobe wing had been built against the chimney for warmth; it was here that Albumen had his bed.

Albumen lifted his head when the men pushed open

the door. "Suppeh raidy to lay on, jist 'bout. Y'all had visitehs, today. Mistuh Madison and dat Hawnish man." Urquhart asked sharply what Harnish had wanted. "Jist say he mekkin' sociable call. Befoah he left, Mistuh Madison arrive. Say he ve'y anxious see you on impawtant business. Y'all siddown now. De beef meat fruzzlin' in de skillet."

Supper finished. Urquhart donned a heavy coat and went out to saddle up. It was near eight-thirty when he spied the lights of Madison's place, shining through the branches of cottonwood. A windmill creaked in the night wind. Through the closed door of the bunkhouse came a murmuring of voices from the Pot-Hook crew. Buildings were scattered about: barns, a blacksmith shop, cook shanty, corrals. Smoke drifted from the chimney of the main house. An oil lamp in a window cast a rectangle of light across a broad gallery. There was a blue haze of burning cedarwood smoke in the air. The wide front door of the house opened, as Urquhart was dismounting and Madison said, "Thought I heard you ride up. You want to put your horse in the corral?" Urquhart said no; he intended to return early; it looked as though a norther was making up. He crossed the gallery and entered the comfort-ably-furnished front room. Animal skins were strewn about the floor; there were easy chairs at either side of a table covered with old newspapers, magazines, bits of harness, a pair of rusty spurs, cigars, a battered pipe and a lamp. A huge fireplace held blazing cedar logs. An iron kettle was suspended on a crane. Madison tilted a jug above a pair of glasses and poured hot water from the kettle. "This fruit-brandy toddy will take off the chill, Rius."

Urquhart tossed his hat on the table and settled to a chair; tasting the toddy, he announced it good. Madison sat down. Urquhart mentioned Harnish. Madison said, "Nothing to worry about. He's just trying to be friendly. He visits around often. Been here more than once. Maybe he figures to drum up business for his Dromedary." Urquhart said that he'd heard the Dromedary was thriving. Madison nodded. "Half thought I might find you home today. What you been doing?" Urquhart explained he and Dix had been cleaning cows out of the brush. Madison asked, "Does it ever occur there's plenty of time ahead for that? You can't do that job in nothing flat, son. You're wearin' yourselves ragged. Yes, I know, Dix insists on doing what you do, but—hell's-bells! why'n't you wait until beef prices start coming back?" Urquhart wanted to know when that would be?

Madison drank deeply from his glass. "I'm damned if I know. Texas is overrun with cows, but at two-three dollars a head it don't pay to drive 'em to market. Mostly, I'm paying my crew just to stay on. Any time you want a few hands, say the word; I have to pay 'em anyway." Urquhart mentioned he'd already accepted much help from Madison. "Bosh! But this price situation is insane. The country needs meat. All that remains is to drive to market—when prices rise."

"Some are trying it."

Madison nodded scornfully. "Sure; small bunches. But no Texan is making money. I was talking to a feller in town yesterday. He tells me there's been traders through his country, giving harmonicas and alarm clocks and oil lamps for cows. When you can get a beef animal for a clock, the cattle business is knocked to hell. You spoke about driving to market. Consider herds that were driven north last summer. They reached the Five Nations country and ran into Indian trouble. Herds that swung east toward the railhead at Sedalia, Missouri, had difficulties with farmers who claimed our herds brought Texas fever to their milch cows. They refused to let the Texans pass. That meant fight or look for another route. Selling cows is one thing; shooting at farmers and getting shot at is another. Gangs up that way, calling themselves farmers, refused to let Texas cattle pass, unless the drovers paid two-three dollars a head. Right off, there went the profits—or more shooting and killing. Texas fever! Bah! Those farmers in Arkansas and Missouri are just trying to fix the blame on us, for some sickness that hits their herds. If it's Texas fever, why doesn't it affect our stock? Answer that?"

"There might be something in what they say, Gault. Perhaps Texas cows have built up an immunity. We know it kills northern cows. Could it be something carried on our cows from Texas—say, a weed-pollen, or an insect of some sort? I've heard it's something dropped in the slobber of herds on trail, but I don't know."

"I don't know either and I don't give a damn," Madison growled. "I figure it's all talk to keep Texas from getting back on its feet, and that talk has a lot of

Northern folks scared to buy our beef, even if we could get it there, which we can't." Urquhart remarked that building a railroad into San Antonio might be one solution to the problem. Madison agreed. "But you know damn' well, those skunks in Washington ain't goin' to allow anybody to build a railroad in here, if it would help Texas." He rose, violently angry, from his chair and replenished the glasses. "But this isn't what I wanted to talk about. I've got a contract to deliver six hundred cows to Indianola. You want to take that contract off my hands? . . . I don't want it; I've got enough money." Urquhart asked the price. Madison said, "One dollar a head."

Startled, Urquhart said, "My God! A dollar a head!"

"This company that wants the cows don't care anything about beef. All's they want is hides. Maybe they'll render some tallow. They're building a factory on the Gulf. It wouldn't be necessary for you to deliver prime beeves. There's old stuff to be snaked out of the thickets. It's not like you had to do the skinning yourself. Just drive the critters down and deliver. Hire a couple of Mexican *vaqueros* for the drive; if you're not too damn' independent, take a pair of my hands. And six hundred dollars is solid money."

Urquhart nodded. "I'll do it, Gault. And thanks."

"No thanks needful." Urquhart refused another drink. Madison poured himself a glass. He said, "Sabina'll be home some time after the first of the year. You know, my wife." Urquhart had almost forgotten Madison's marriage; the man so rarely mentioned it. "I've got to do a heap of reddin' up around here, or she'll be sorry she come back. Fact is,"—growing confidential—"I wasn't sure she was coming back. We had words before she left, and she's stayed so long that—"

"Look here, Gault," Urquhart interposed, "it's none of my business, but you do appear to have a powerful liking for that brandy. It's pretty heady stuff. Don't tell me anything you'll regret."

"Damn it, who can I tell? A man just has to talk now and then." His eyes roved about the room. "This was all new furniture when we got married. I reckon I haven't cared for it the way I should. Minute I read she was coming, I headed right for Tannbauer Brothers', and ordered a piano. It's due here before Sabina arrives." He added a bit wistfully, "Maybe it will please her." Urquhart asked if Mrs. Madison was interested in music.

"Hell, yes. Played since she was a youngster. First time I ever saw her in Alexandria she was at a piano. I'd gone there to see her pa, about getting cotton I planned to ship through Mexico, to England. His business had gone to pot, during the war, and he didn't have the gumption to make things go. I took off his hands such bales as he had in his warehouse. That gave Nielsen a breathing spell, but he was headed hell-bent for bankruptcy. All I did was stave it off a mite." Urquhart suspected that Madison had been helping ever since. "Well, one thing led to another and finally I asked Sabina to marry me. Maybe it was a mistake. She told me before she left, that Nielsen had talked her into marrying me. Later, she said she was sorry and that it wasn't true; it was just said because she was mad at the time." Madison shifted his big frame uneasily. "I never could get those words out of mind, though. I don't figure she was ever happy here. She's been educated. My friends generally don't seem to fit in with her. One time in San 'Tonio, we got acquainted with a couple of Union officers. They weren't bad fellers, but when they fell into the habit of visiting here, I knew it wasn't me they came to see. I told Sabina I didn't like it. And then we had words. When the letter came that her pa was ailing, she hightailed for home. Jared Nielsen died a month after she got to Alexandria. The letter that come yesterday said Sabina's ma had passed on too. Sabina wants to stay in Alexandria until the estate's cleared up, she wrote, though what in God's name estate there is, I can't think. I'm hoping, Rius, you'll help make things pleasant for her, when she gets back. You having an education and all . . ." His words drifted to silence and he reached for the jug to fill his glass.

That night, riding home, the picture was clear in Urquhart's mind: Madison and Sabina had been sacrificed in an attempt to forestall an inevitable bankruptcy. The girl had been persuaded to marry Madison for his money; perhaps, she had been willing to accept such a situation. Urquhart, while attempting to appreciate her position, was quite sure it would never be possible to like Sabina Madison.

5

IT HADN'T, URQUHART REFLECTED, SEATED IN THE MAIN room of Madison's house, been a bad spring. The harmonies issuing from Sabina Madison's piano scarcely infringed on his abstractions. The year was into June now. Not that the pleasant weather was solely responsible for Urquhart's lightened frame of mind; Sabina Madison had had more than a little to do with it. Prosaic as it might seem, he had in pocket a few dollars he could call his own; the drive to the hide factory at Indianola had netted him nearly six hundred dollars. Urquhart wondered where that money had gone? He never had got around to buying more lumber for the house; the bare studs and rafters stood as before. But there'd been many things to buy: a new saddle, a buckskin horse of Madison's which he'd refused to accept as a gift; clothes cost money, especially one outfit with a long blue coat and fawn-colored trousers, strapped at the bottom. But a man couldn't accompany a woman like Sabina Madison into town, looking like a yokel. The Casino, in San Antonio, had staged entertainments throughout the winter and early spring. The first two times, Gault had accompanied them; the third time, when they reached town Madison had explained there was a man to see on business, and Sabina and Darius had gone alone to the Casino. . . .

The music from the rosewood piano drifted to silence. Turning, Sabina Madison's velvety sloe-brown eyes sought out Urquhart. "Now, tell me, Darius," she asked in a mellifluous tone, "which was it—Chopin or Mozart?" Sheepishly, Urquhart admitted he didn't know. Sabina said scornfully, "Not tell the difference between Mozart and Chopin? Darius, you're mortal stupid." Her laughter carried an edge. "Perhaps," she conceded, "it's all due to my faulty technique. My teacher once advised that I attempt nothing but the lighter things." Urquhart assured her he found nothing wrong with her technique. He had no ear for the classics.

"Trouble is," Gault Madison offered, "no man's going to care for those little tinkling tunes, Sabina. Now, if you'd play *Dixie*—"

Sabina said "Fiddlesticks," adding that she'd not put in a good many years of study, just to play trash. Her white hands crashed angrily on the keys. Madison eyed her quietly, then asked if Urquhart were ready for another drink. Urquhart refused. Filling his own glass, Madison relaxed in his chair. Urquhart had to admit, secretly, that he himself preferred *Dixie*. Sabina had drifted into something with a great many runs in it. The light from the oil lamp with its round, frosted globe, formed highlights on Sabina's pale gold hair, gathered at the back in a silken snood. In a way Sabina resembled the notes of her music, light and airy, with a tune that never seemed to get anywhere.

At any rate, Urquhart consoled himself, he could keep abreast of Sabina where books were concerned. That new bookstore on Commerce Street was a Godsend: you could order a book from New York or Boston, and it would arrive within a month. Sabina often asked him to ride in with her to look over the catalogues, or help her choose new stationery. It seemed he was always accompanying her somewhere. Gault had suggested he wanted her to learn the country. She rode side-saddle, of course, as a lady should. Urquhart glanced at Madison, nearly asleep in his chair, and envied him, doubting that Sabina lived in the right house. Her slim poise—or something very like hers, Urquhart hastily corrected his thoughts—belonged at Urquhart Oaks. Lord, the next money he got, he must remember to order lumber.

The piano fell silent, and, Sabina, in a brown dress of light wool, with full skirt and bodice trimmed with a great many buttons, rose. Urquhart placed a chair for her. Madison opened his eyes. "That piece was sure pretty, Sabina."

"A lot you know about it, Gault." she laughed coolly, "you were asleep. You should get to bed earlier." Madison started to protest that that didn't seem to be much use, when she interrupted him, addressing Urquhart: "He didn't come home at all, last night."

"I explained why." Madison said. His eyes went quickly to Urquhart. "I had to ride into San 'Tonio to see Hugo Shepard on business. We talked late, so I figured I'd best spend the night at the Menger." Sabina asked in a light voice if he were sure it was the Menger Hotel at which he'd stayed. "Of course it was," Madison insisted. "Where else should I stay?" A cool smile played about Sabina's lips. Urquhart stirred uncomfortably.

"Stay where you wish, by all means, Gault," Sabina

119

said quietly, adding she'd probably have swooned from ennui, if Mr. Harnish hadn't dropped in.

Urquhart stiffened. "Harnish? Did *he* call on you?"

Madison explained that Harnish dropped by now and then. Urquhart remarked testily he should think Harnish's business would occupy his evenings. "Drake's got a manager for the Dromedary, now," Madison said. "He's certainly coining money in that place. Between his games and his bar—"

"Darius," Sabina interrupted, "you don't like Drake Harnish, do you?" Urquhart replied that men like Harnish never appealed to him. "You Texas men," Sabina sighed. "Why do you keep alive the hostility for Northerners? I've always found Mr. Harnish a perfect gentleman." Urquhart smiled and wanted to know if Harnish could detect the difference between Chopin and Mozart. Sabina colored and stated she'd never asked.

Madison cleared his throat and mentioned that Harnish had it in mind to go in for stock raising. He'd been to the Pot-Hook the previous evening to learn if Madison knew of properties for sale. Urquhart said he hoped Gault didn't. "That's what I'd have told him if I'd been home," Madison nodded. "With beef prices like they are, I wouldn't advise anyone to go into cattle now."

"Speaking of beef prices," Urquhart cut in, "Cyrus Harper rode over to see me yesterday. The way Harper sees it, Texas has got the cattle; the country east of the Mississippi needs meat. We've got to find a way to get the cows out." Madison replied any fool knew that much, but what did Harper have to offer? Urquhart explained, "He wants me to join him and drive a herd north—five hundred of my cows and five hundred of his Rocking-H animals—and see if we can't find some good route to Missouri. He tentatively plans to head toward Kansas City—"

"Bosh!" Madison said. "You'd run into the same troubles every other drover has. Indian trouble, or the gang that's either bawlin' about Texas fever or charging so much to let you through, you'll lose all profit. No, the thing to do is keep things in order here, until Washington realizes that it's got to give us a chance. What'd you tell Harper?"

"About the same. I said we'd best hold off until conditions improved. He finally agreed with me, but I could see the idea wasn't entirely out of his mind."

"You took the only sensible view." Madison lifted the jug toward his glass.

"Do you really need that, Gault?" The strained quality of Sabina's tones caught the attention of both men. Her face was white. Madison replied lightly that maybe he didn't exactly need it, but he felt in the mood for another drink. Anger flared in Sabina's cheeks. "If it's not fruit brandy, it's politics; when it's not politics, it's beef-raising and horseflesh. Do you imagine Darius cares for nothing else—?" Hastily, Urquhart interposed the information that he liked to discuss beef-raising. Madison carefully replaced the jug at the side of his chair, saying with a short laugh that maybe Rius could understand why he didn't always remain at home in the evening. And if it still wasn't clear, he could add a few details concerning other matters. "I don't think, Gault," Sabina said icily, "Darius cares to hear us quarreling."

"Probably you're right," Madison returned, and reminded his wife it wasn't he who had brought up the matter to which she objected. But it was, she insisted. Urquhart got to his feet: it was time for him to be starting home. Madison said, "No, you stay here and talk to Sabina." He struggled to his feet, face red. "I want to go to the bunkhouse and talk to Jeff Strunk." Jeff Strunk was the Pot-Hook foreman.

Urquhart sank back in his chair as Madison left. "I still think I'd better be on my way."

"No, wait," Sabina urged. "I want to talk to you about that book by Sir Walter Scott I've been reading . . ." She paused, listening while Madison's steps reached the back of the house. They heard a door slam. Sabina said, "You see how it is, here? How long do you think I can stand it?" Urquhart said, lamely, he didn't have an opinion. "You know better than to say that, Darius." Tears welled into her eyes, and she brushed futilely with a wisp of cambric. "Him and his business with Hugo Shepard. I knew he was at the Dromedary last night."

Urquhart asked harshly, "Did Harnish tell you?"

"It wasn't necessary for him to tell me. Mr. Harnish has never been here before in the evening. He must have known where Gault was."

"That doesn't signify that Gault was at the Dromedary. Don't rush to conclusions, Sabina. Gault does have many business interests; he has to attend them properly."

She said, angrily, "You're as cruel as he is, taking his part. Don't you think I know why he stays away all night? I'm no child, Darius. Not that I care what he does. If he doesn't want my criticism, I don't think he should criticize me. If he doesn't want men like Harnish coming here at night, he should stay home—"

"I think," Urquhart said quietly, "I'm in accord with any view Gault takes, where Harnish is concerned. And if Gault doesn't stay at home, there must be a reason, Sabina. Have you done all you should?"

Sabina said hotly. "You've no right to ask." Urquhart replied, his face flushing, he was perfectly aware of that. He begged her pardon. Mollified, Sabina continued, "What has Gault told you about us?" Very little, Urquhart assured her, though he'd suspected that Gault wasn't happy; perhaps she wasn't either. "Happy?" A scornful laugh broke through Sabina's tears. "It's just bearable, that's all. I'm going to leave this house." Her voice rose wildly. "I'd not have remained this long, if it weren't for you. Things have been mortal pleasant with you, Darius."

Urquhart broke in uncomfortably, "Don't talk foolishly, Sabina. You don't realize what you're saying. Why not run along to bed? You'll feel better in the morning. I've got to be getting home." He gained his feet.

Instantly, Sabina was clutching desperately at his arms, begging him to stay. "You mustn't go, Darius. If you leave me, there'll be nobody. Dear Darius, can't you take me someplace—away—?" For just a moment she was warm and close against him, sobbing hysterically against his breast, her lovely eyes brimming, her rounded arms meeting at the back of his neck. Urquhart's arms tightened about her shoulders. Sabina's tear-stained face lifted to his, her soft lips seeking his mouth. With an effort he stepped back, disengaging her arms.

"It won't do, Sabina," he said, exhaling a long breath. "You and I aren't cut out for anything like this." He maneuvered her back to the chair and she half-collapsed, still protesting through a renewed flood of tears. What else he said, he wasn't sure, by the time he'd found his hat and had closed the front door behind him. Pausing a moment on the gallery, he could hear slow footsteps as Sabina made her way to a bedroom. Dimly there came from within the house the sound of a closing door, the deep silence broken only by the sounds of night insects at the edge of the gallery.

Urquhart sighed and with his handkerchief dabbed at his moist forehead, then started toward the bunkhouse. The moon was lifting above the hills to the east now, and a breeze agitated the cottonwood leaves.

Urquhart entered the bunkhouse. His eyes ran swiftly about the long room, lined at one side with a double tier of bunks. He nodded to Jeff Strunk, a tall taciturn ex-Confederate cavalryman, and to several others, before his eyes finally fell on Madison at the far end of a long bare table, filling tin cups from a jug. Madison said, "You leaving, Rius? I'll walk to the corral with you."

Only when the corral gate had been once more shut and Urquhart was mounted, did Madison open his lips.

124

"Look here, I'm right regretful that unpleasantness arose while you were visiting. No, son, you can't brush it off with polite words. You take my advice and don't you never get married. I've done my best, and I intend to keep on doing my best until . . . Maybe I'm not the right man for Sabina. She's like sunshine on ice, shiny and bright—and cold. I think that Harnish bastard told her I was at the Dromedary, last night. All right, I was for a little spell. But dammit to hell—!" He paused. "Those fool army medics said my heart wasn't too strong. Sometimes I wish it would stop, altogether—" Urquhart interrupted to say Madison was making foolish talk. "That could be," Madison conceded, "but when you reach my age, you sometimes figure you don't give a damn, and you might as well get what's possible out of the time remaining. Those friends Sabina has out from town, aren't my kind. Either we listen to that tinkling piano, or if politics comes up I have to listen to what a good job is being done in the Reconstruction of Texas. You think that ain't enough to make a man mad? More'n once I been on the point of tellin' Sabina I don't aim to stand it no more, but somehow I keep quiet, until we have a blow-off, like tonight. Then things run along peaceful for a spell." Madison paused. "Try to forget it, Rius. And don't let this keep you from visiting. You seem to be all Sabina and I have in common."

The moon shed a soft light across the hills, while Urquhart rode toward home. What was a man to do? He couldn't in honor, continue to see Sabina. Sometimes things get out of hand and a man—yes, and a woman too—get beyond their depth. Nothing at all must happen to hurt Gault. But if he suddenly discontinued his visits, Gault would wonder why. There was the bad heart, too. If Gault should die suddenly. . . . ? A vision of a rebuilt Urquhart Oaks rose in Urquhart's mind, and he saw the slim loveliness of Sabina standing between the tall white columns of the gallery . . . Urquhart swore suddenly and jabbed spurs to his horse. The horse moved swiftly down a long gradual slope, splashed across the upper reaches of Crinolina Creek, and, abruptly, Urquhart realized he was on his own property. "I wonder," Urquhart speculated, "how long a man can think thoughts like I've been having, without hating himself?"

Corbillat came from the house to meet him, as he was unsaddling at the corral. Dix said, "Did you enjoy yourself at Gault's, or was Sabina ticklin' her piano keys all evenin'? If you was to ask me . . ."

"Nobody has asked you," Urquhart said irritably. Dix fell silent. Urquhart went on, "I've been thinking things over, Dix. Do you remember what Harper mentioned the other day?"

"About makin' up a small herd and seein' could you find a route through to Kansas City. Yeah! I figured you was against the idea."

"I'm commencing to think it might be worth trying. First thing in the morning I plan to ride to see Harper and tell him I've changed my mind. It shouldn't take you and me long to round up five hundred cows."

"C'rect. But what'll we do about a crew? We'll need more'n just Albumen for cookin'."

"Harper said he'd furnish the crew," Urquhart reminded. "We'll leave Albumen home. You and I will be working hands. Unless I'm wrong, Harper wants us for moral support, more than anything."

Dix chuckled. "I ain't sure morals like mine will be much help. Hell, yes! I'd just as soon stir up some dust up Kansas City way." Urquhart looked relieved. Dix frowned. "Look here, Rius, you act like you was runnin' away from somethin'. Anything happen at Gault's—?"

"I didn't say that, either," Urquhart said shortly. "Maybe I want to stir some dust, too. Let's start looking ahead a bit. We'll be starting north in two weeks."

6

THE YEAR WAS INTO NOVEMBER WHEN THEY RETURNED to Urquhart Oaks and an overjoyed Albumen White, early one morning. Sunlight, slanting through the branches of oak, glistened brightly on the fallen leaves below, wet from the previous night's frost. The Negro's eyes grew moist as he ran to take the horses' reins. "Sweah t'Jehovah, Ah ain't neveh seen time so pr'cawstinatin', sense y'all left foah up No'th. 'Peahs lak de days jist dribble. Howcome you'ns look so whupped down? Dis Negro suah got t'begin feedin' y'all up hawty, so's t'put some talleh back, on de bones."

Corbillat and Urquhart about noontime rode to the Pot-Hook, Corbillat reminding Urquhart all the way that there wa'n't no air like in Texas. The heat increased and there was a definite welcome in the shade of the Pot-Hook gallery where they found Madison sitting, gazing out with listless eyes. The jug stood at Madison's side and he was in the act of filling his glass, when his gaze fell on the approaching riders. Heaving his bulk up, he unleashed a wild yell of greeting, then bawled to the Mexican girl-of-all-work to "come a-runnin'" with extra glasses. Hearing the sounds, Jeff Strunk came hurrying up from the bunkhouse. Corbillat and Urquhart left their horses standing at the edge of the gallery and shook hands with Madison and Strunk.

"Damned if it don't do me good to see you back," Madison exclaimed. Looking at him, Urquhart decided Madison needed something to do him good. He had lost weight; flesh sagged loosely about his jowls; there was more grey in the blond hair and his blue eyes had lost their keenness. Urquhart noted his hand shook a little. "Shame Sabina isn't home to welcome you," Madison went on, when they'd found seats along the gallery. "She's been staying in town with friends. What about the drive? I've been hearing talk about a market up in Kansas. Was your trip profitable?"

"In experience, yes," Urquhart replied. "I can't say so much as concerns cash. It was Kansas we drove to, Gault. Who else you hear of who went up that way?"

"Just heard indirectly," Madison said. "There was a piece in the *Alamo Star*, about cattle being shipped east from a town named Abilene."

"That's the place," Urquhart nodded. "Abilene. Not

much of a town. Just a few shacks and log cabins. When we left here, Harper and I figured to get through to Missouri. Then one day—we'd just crossed the Red River, and that wasn't any picnic, either—a rider cut our trail who'd been sent out from Abilene to contact herds. He told us railroad shipping and stock buyers would be available in Abilene by the time we got there, so we swung due north again, figuring no matter what direction we took, it was a gamble."

"A losing gamble, I take it," Madison put in.

"It may not always prove so," Urquhart said. "There's a man up in Abilene—Joseph McCoy, by name—who got an idea if he could furnish shipping for Texas cattle, we'd all benefit. He's persuaded the Kansas Pacific Railroad to lay tracks to Abilene. McCoy's contract with the railroad gives him a percentage on all freight shipped from the point. In return, McCoy has bought up land, erected cattle pens and yards—even had a hotel under construction when we left. If business holds up, Abilene is bound to boom. The country needs the beef; the railroad wants the business. Texas needs a way to dispose of her cattle. Theoretically, all we have to do is drive our cows straight north to Abilene."

"Theoretically? There's a catch to it then?"

Urquhart sighed. "There was this year. Lord! The difficulties we encountered between here and Abilene. Day after day, the rain poured. You know what that does to grass. It grows, but so much rain made it rank and washy; no nutrition in it. The few days it didn't rain, the air was so sultry you could scarcely breathe.

We figured to drive fifteen miles a day on an average." Madison interjected a remark to the effect that shouldn't be difficult. "Under ordinary circumstances, no," Urquhart agreed. "But circumstances can't be called ordinary when every river is so swollen from rain it's a job to get the cows across. We waited several days at both the Colorado River and the Red, until the water went down, and we should have waited longer. A lot of cows got drowned. Then, about the time we got through the Nations country, cholera hit the herd. Between that and stampedes every few nights, you can guess how things went."

"Any Indian trouble?" Madison wanted to know.

"Nothing to speak of. Maybe we were lucky. Shortly after we crossed the Red, a bunch of Kiowas tagged us for a week, begging food and trying to steal our horses at night. We bought 'em off with a couple of beeves. Farther north, some Arapahoes swooped down, but as soon as we unlimbered our guns they scattered."

"What caused the stampedes?" Strunk wanted to know.

"Nigh everything you can think of," Corbillat said. "The critters got so spooky they'd run at the drop of a hat. Lightning storms, the scent of a coyote, a sudden movement from a rider, would start 'em off."

"That's the way it went," Urquhart nodded. "What with the lack of good grass, and the animals running off flesh, you can imagine what condition the stock was in when we reached Abilene. So the price per head wasn't anything to rejoice over. By the time I'd paid Harper my share of expenses, I didn't make much."

130

"And another year," Madison grunted, "you might even make less."

Urquhart said, "The cows were here. It wasn't as if we'd had to buy them, so I suppose anything I made was pure velvet." Madison asked why they hadn't sold their "ganted-up" cattle to some buyer to fatten. "We considered that," Urquhart nodded, "but there's a shortage of corn up north this year, and it wouldn't have been profitable at the price a buyer would have to pay for feed. So we figured we'd best sell while we had a taker. I was talking to a buyer up there, and he told me the east would have to be educated to eating Texas beef. Some people claim it's so stringy, it's not palatable."

Corbillat stated indignantly, "There ain't no juicier eatin' than a prime Texas steak." Madison agreed and put another question to Urquhart.

"Yes, we returned by the same route," Urquhart answered. "Harper and I wanted to see what those rivers looked like when they were down. Two or three were still pretty full. Yes, all but three of the crew came back with us. Rafe Scanlan—I don't think you knew him—was drowned when we were crossing Red River. Pedro Sequado's pony spilled him in a stampede one night and broke his neck. Brock Porter was anxious to see his girl in El Paso, so he left us at Abilene." Strunk wanted to know if Urquhart considered driving to Abilene another year. "Jeff, I might and I might not. Driving north has a lot of men interested now; but I'd prefer to wait and learn how things pan out for other stockmen. You see, there were about thirty or forty thousand cattle reached Abilene this year. News of that will spread and—"

"You mean to say," Madison interrupted, "that thirty or forty thousand cows were actually bought and shipped east?"

"Without a doubt," Urquhart answered. "There'll be considerable more driven north next season. Joseph McCoy's planning to advertise through Texas this winter, so stockmen can know what to expect. He's sending out men to establish a trail through Kansas, to show the way. McCoy's doing his part; it's up to Texans to get the cattle there. But I'd wait before I tried it again. Next time, I'd know better how to go about things. In the first place, I'd not drive a mixed herd— just prime steers, say threes and fours. Another thing, I'd start north earlier, so as to get advantage of the best grass, without throwing too far off trail for my grazing. If it ever reached a point where there was a steady flow of stock headed for Abilene, the first ones on the trail would get the best grass. Something else: instead of an ox-drawn wagon for carrying supplies, I'd use four mules. Oxen are too slow. With the crew we had, we could have driven more cattle at the same expense. I figure a herd of three thousand would be right. If shipping from Abilene proves successful, it will be the salvation of Texas."

"Speaking of wagons," Gault Madison said, "about a month back I was talking to a hand that made a drive into New Mexico, last year, for a couple of stock owners named Charles Goodnight and Oliver Loving, and they'd rigged up what they called a cupboard wagon, fixed with a regular pantry built on one end. All's the cook had to do was let down the door of the pantry, which was suspended on rawhides, and he had a table to work on. That way, the wagon-bed was left clear for bedrolls and rations not needed immediate, also water-barrels."

"You have any trouble with Yanks up in that Kansas country?" Strunk asked.

Corbillat suddenly slapped his knee. "Damn' if I believe it, yet," he stated, "but we didn't. Me, I was expectin' trouble soon's we hit that range. But every-thin' was peaceful as a dead pig in the sunshine. Right after the first trainload of cows pulled out of Abilene, they had a big blow-out to celebrate what McCoy said was an historical event. He's struck up a big tent and invited everybody to attend a banquet, with wine and elegant rations and speeches. I never see the beat! I sure expected somebody to go on the prod, but all us Texans heard was talk from Yanks about their friends from the South. Fr'fact! I just settled down and lis-tened to the music and speech-makin', and how this meetin' would be the joinin' of two enemy factions, and the war should be forgot, and the North couldn't get along without the South, and if new difficulties rose, they could be ironed out with talk and not guns. Never did think I'd live t'see the day I'd sit down with a Yank, but I done it."

Strunk stated he'd be damned! "You runnin' a whizzer on us, Dix?"

"Dix is telling it correctly," Urquhart nodded. "Well, the spark that started off the war was blown to life in

Kansas. What's more fitting than that it should be extinguished there. All the Yanks we met, acted as though they were anxious to co-operate."

"That's the spirit we need here," Madison growled, "but things in Texas just go from bad to worse."

Urquhart smiled ruefully. "If that's the situation, I guess the best way for Dix and me to keep out of trouble, is to spend time trailing herds to Kansas."

"You just hold off, Rius, until we see how that Abilene business works out. If it appears promising in a couple of years, I might send a herd up. You wait. I'll see that you get money. There's establishments have sprung up along the Gulf coast, figuring to ship hides, tallow and canned beef east, by steamer, to N'Orleans. I got contracts and you can help fill 'em. It's not big money, but you won't go broke. And you can get rid of your oldest stock—a lot of those old mossy-horns aren't good for anything except canning and grinding into boloney meat. That will leave your best critters for driving north later."

"I wouldn't want to take money out of your pocket."

"Hell's-bells! I don't need money. I only took the contracts to keep some scalawag or carpetbagger from gettin' 'em. There's plenty Radical-Republican sons-a-bitches trying to make money out of our cattle these days. Harnish was saying last week, he's thinking of making up a herd to drive north next year. He heard about Abilene too. Didn't mention where he aimed to get his cows, so I'd keep an eye open. Harnish isn't the man to buy what he can steal. He's coining money in the Dromedary, too. Four men been killed in gun-fights

134

in that place, since it opened. It's the old story—arguments over girls, or some sucker claiming he was cheated at gambling. I put up with Harnish and other Yank bastards, but it's only because that's a wise policy, conditions being what they are."

"Albumen," Urquhart commented, "tells me you've kept two Pot-Hook men riding my holdings, while we were away, Gault. I'm obliged to you."

Madison nodded. "I figured it was best somebody keep an eye on things, with the fellow there alone." Urquhart commented he was getting deeper in Gault's debt all the time. "What the hell!" Madison boomed. "Can't one Texan help another without fooforaw? You'd do the same for me." He reached to the jug beside his chair.

The sun dropped lower, spreading a crimson glow over high-banked clouds. Purple shadows deepened and the yellow on the cottonwoods whispered sibilantly. Urquhart and Corbillat prepared to leave, Urquhart explaining, "We told Albumen we'd be home. He's fixing a special feast for tonight." That being the case, Madison allowed he'd ride back with them: "Not only for the food, but I want to hear more about your drive. Mebbe Abilene might be good for Texas."

7

THE WINTER PASSED SO SWIFTLY THAT URQUHART scarcely knew where it had gone. He and Dix had thrown up brush corrals on the range and worked tirelessly at getting cows branded. Occasionally he made rides to visit Madison. Sometimes, Sabina was there; more often not. Sabina spent much time with friends in town. He suspected Madison was now indifferent to his wife's activities, so long as peace reigned. Sabina never referred to the scene that had taken place that night between her and Urquhart, though there were times when her eyes met his and he realized it wasn't forgotten. Their attendance at the Casino and their rides had never been resumed.

When Madison commented on this one day, Urquhart had pleaded the requirements of his own affairs. It was amazing, he continued awkwardly, how cows multiplied when left to shift for themselves; he and Dix were forever routing out of the brush four- and five-year-olds. He had also been trying to get something accomplished on the big house, but hadn't yet found time. Urquhart supposed it would be necessary, eventually, to engage an architect. Also, he had been teaching Albumen to handle four mules, instead of the single span Albumen was accustomed to. He and Dix had been busy for a time constructing one of those cupboard affairs on a wagon, which they intended to try out when they drove a herd to the Gulf. Several stockmen were building similar equipment for their wagons; someone had named them chuck-wagons. Numerous herds would be starting for Abilene this year.

The weather softened, bringing rains and hot sun. Redbud bushes began to flame into being. Mesquite put out delicate traceries of bright green and the flowers were golden-yellow on the prickly-pear. Calf round-up arrived and Urquhart hired a temporary crew to take care of the Circle-U's end of branding. Afterward a herd was gathered for the drive to the Gulf; the new chuck-wagon was put to the test and pronounced a success. Albumen proved himself as good a driver as he was a trail cook, his only disappointment lying in the fact that numerous inquiries elicited no information regarding Dicey Nell.

Urquhart made six drives to the various beef-canning establishments that year, paying off his crew at the end of each drive, and thus cutting expenses.

By September of 1868, Urquhart could view with pride the money now credited to him in the San Antonio National Bank. It wasn't a large sum, but it encouraged him to consult an architect with a view to rebuilding the big house according to descriptions. It was intended for completion by the summer of '69, at which time Urquhart hoped to have the means to pay for it.

He had by this time, as had Madison, resolved to drive a herd north the following spring. This year more than twice the number of cattle of the previous year had been driven to Kansas, and many stock-owners had already returned to Texas with glowing reports of the prices received at Abilene. Harnish had sent a herd up the trail, though he'd not gone himself, and was well satisfied with his profits. No one seemed quite sure where Harnish had secured his cows; and some nasty rumors were circulated regarding Harnish and the riders who had worked for him.

The word, KANSAS, spread like wildfire through Texas, and numerous stockmen made plans for trailing north in 1869. Such talk removed from their thoughts the painful Reconstruction. In Kansas lay the salvation of Texas. The Lone Star was again in the ascendancy!

Madison secured a contract to ship a number of horses from Galveston, early in the coming year. "My hands are out on the range, now, gatherin' 'em, Rius. You're going to require horses for that drive to Kansas." Urquhart nodded and remarked that four to six horses would be required for each rider. "That being the case," Madison continued, "you'd best get your hawsses from me and break 'em yourself. If you wait until spring, you'll have to take whatever the market offers in horse flesh. Ride over in a week and take your pick."

Something over a week later, seventy-two half-wild ponies were churning restlessly in newly-constructed corrals built along Crinolina Creek. Ensued then the period of breaking the animals to saddle, a fatiguing process, then the more intensive business of teaching the horses their functions when cattle were worked. Each evening Dix and Urquhart were too worn out to do little more than eat and drop into bunks.

One day in October Urquhart rode into San Antonio

to inspect some newly-arrived harness which Vohrmann's General Store was advertising. The harness proving to be not exactly what he wanted, he was headed toward the doorway, when he spied Sabina fingering a bolt of dress-material at the dry-goods counter. At her side, stood Drake Harnish. Conscious of his own work-soiled appearance, Urquhart's disposition wasn't improved at seeing the two standing closely together. As he approached, Harnish was saying something in a low voice that brought a flow of color to Sabina's cheeks. A wave of anger swept through Urquhart; his fists clenched. Sabina and Harnish glanced around as he passed, Harnish speaking pleasantly enough. Sabina put out one hand to detain Urquhart, but with a short nod and a doffing of his hat, Urquhart strode on. An instant later, he stepped into Main Plaza's brilliant sunshine.

"By God," Urquhart told himself, "if Sabina's going to waste herself on a skunk like Harnish, I might's well—" He halted suddenly the speculation that had entered his mind, detesting himself for the thought. He crossed the Plaza and, entering a barber-shop, settled into a chair for a haircut and shave. Under the ministering of hot towels, Urquhart calmed. How long was it since Albumen had shaved him? He must resume that daily routine of the razors. Razors like those deserved better than the neglect he'd been giving them. That much, at least, he owed to Jennifer. He wondered what she was doing these days. It was more than three years since he'd left Carolina. The two old grandparents were likely dead by this time, and Jennifer—well, what else could she do? —probably married to some Cherokee buck. Papooses, no doubt; and the straight back prematurely bent under the bearing of Indian burdens. At his involuntary groan, the barber asked solicitously if the razor pulled.

Minutes later, Urquhart had left the barber-shop and was threading his way between the loitering Mexicans before San Fernando Church, when he saw Sabina approaching alone, carrying a white sun-parasol. She was wearing a dress of dark green taffeta and a saucy bonnet, trimmed with velvet ribbons, her pale yellow hair, gathered in thick waves over her ears. Urquhart lifted his hat, meaning to pass on, but Sabina stepped in front of him, then turning, took his arm, forcing him to adapt his step to her own.

"I thought you might be someplace on the Plaza," she said, as they walked along. "Darius, what were you so angry about, in Vohrmann's? Did you think we'd been talking about you? We looked around and there you were, looking fit to kill somebody." That, Urquhart evaded, must be her imagination; he didn't remember being angry at anything. Sabina clutched his arm tighter and said, "Fiddlesticks! Were you angry I was with Mr. Harnish?" Urquhart denied that, adding, however, that he didn't think much of Harnish as a companion. "I can't see," Sabina pouted, "why you and Gault don't like him. I think he's most amusing, and a perfect gentleman. We'd just met by accident and he'd accompanied me—" She halted angrily and stamped one foot. "I don't have to explain my actions to you." Urquhart agreed that she certainly didn't. He

140

added pointedly his sole interest lay in the fact that she was Gault's wife.

They walked on, Sabina silent, as they turned at the corner of the Plaza. What, exactly, Sabina asked, did Darius mean? "Look here, Sabina," Urquhart said quietly, "I think a lot of Gault. I don't want him hurt. Not in any way. Understand?"

Sabina replied frostily that she'd no idea. "Gault knows I have friends in town. He doesn't object; why should you?"

Urquhart repeated, "I don't want to see Gault hurt."

"You've already said that," Sabina reminded him, hard lights in her eyes. "No one, apparently, ever considers that I could be hurt. I'm not ignorant of the fact, Darius, that Gault also has friends in town, though they may not be so permanent as mine." Urquhart flushed. She went on, "You can't expect me to stay at the ranch, when he comes and goes as he pleases. Either I stay alone, or I sit and watch him and his jug the whole evening through. It was different when you came often; I didn't mind then. This past year you've been avoiding me." Sabina brushed aside his denial. "If you won't call on me, I have to find other friends."

Driven into a corner, Urquhart conceded, there were two sides to every question; perhaps, they'd better drop the subject. They turned, neither speaking now, and retraced their steps to Main Plaza where Sabina said she'd promised to meet friends. "There's Nettie now," Sabina said, pointing across the Plaza to a dark-haired girl seated in a carriage with a Negro driver. Nearby stood two young Union officers, resplendent in blue uniforms. Sabina smiled at Urquhart's rigid features. "I can see you'd not care to cross over and meet the enemy." Urquhart admitted that he wouldn't, though he thought he preferred Yank soldiers to Harnish. Sabina petulantly tossed her head, and with a cool nod left him.

Urquhart gazed resentfully after her, then started in the direction he'd left his horse. Mounting, he walked the animal slowly across the square, his face a scowling mask. What in the devil was a man to do? Gault must be shielded from hurt arising from Sabina's actions. She had, Urquhart considered, made it plain enough: if he would resume their old friendship where it had been dropped, there'd be a cessation of her activities in San Antonio. So far as he knew, those activities were harmless, but a man never knew where they might lead. Not with Harnish nearby. Suppose he did resume with Sabina, Urquhart asked himself miserably; exactly where might it end? Sabina was a beautiful woman with a beautiful woman's provocativeness. After all, there was a limit to any man's strength and a single mad moment of weakness could . . . An unreasoning anger against Madison rose in Urquhart; how in the name of God could Gault be so infernally indulgent? By God, does he—does she, for that matter—look on me as a monk? Do they consider I have no feelings?

He sagged wearily, in the saddle. The burning sun scorched his nape; his lips felt dry and parched. Raising his head he saw he was passing Weintraub's Saloon. Abruptly, he swerved his horse, dismounted and, entering the cool interior, demanded of Weintraub the coldest, largest glass of beer the place boasted. It was forthcoming at once, a veritable giant of a schooner brimming with chilled amber, the creamy foam swelling at the surface and overflowing the sides. "Iss on der streed hot, today?" Weintraub asked.

Urquhart quaffed deeply, wiped his lips and drew a long breath. He took another long drink. "Uncomfortable," he smiled, "but this brew provides a partial palliative, at least, Louie." Urquhart and two men drinking at the far end of the bar, were the only customers, until a man in town's-clothing entered the barroom, laughing hugely, and stopped near Urquhart, where he ordered whisky. Weintraub served him and observed, "A good joke it must be, Mister Wilding. Maybe you tell us, then we all laugh."

Urquhart listened idly while the man explained, "That Lem Carter is sure a card. Always playing jokes on innocent people. Wait'll I tell you—"

Weintraub frowned. "That bummer, Carter. Iss no goot, dat feller! What now does he do?"

Wilding chuckled. "Some girl hit town a spell back, looking for a hotel, and Carter directs her to Harnish's Dromedary, where he tells her they got rooms for girls—"

"Dat is nod funny, if a nice girl she is,"—indignantly. "Surprised I am you should laugh, Mister Wilding."

"Aw, there ain't no harm done," Wilding grinned. "If she's a nice girl, I wouldn't know. Part Injun, I'd say. But a looker! By Jeez, yes! She's in front of the Dromedary now, and Harnish was sure sweet-talkin' her to beat the band. But she's just giving him a cold smile and the levelest look from a pair of eyes I ever see. She knows what Drake's up to. There's a couple of old Injuns with her—a man and a squaw. The old coot's wearing a cavalry saber strapped at his side, and him driving a moth-eaten mule and a crowbait of a horse, hitched to a little of spring wagon with rolled leather curtains." Further laughter. "Funniest damn' thing I ever saw. I heard the girl—she was sitting astride her horse like a man—telling Harnish they'd come clear from North Car'lina—" The speaker paused as Urquhart plunged through the doorway. "Now what in hell come over that jasper, Louie?"

Weintraub eyed the still-violently-swinging doors with bewilderment. "His beer to finish he didn't wait even. Mister Urquhart something must have remembered all of a sudden, maybe."

8

IT SIMPLY COULDN'T BE, URQUHART TOLD HIMSELF! He dashed wildly across Commerce Square, dodged in front of an ox-drawn freight wagon. North of Dolorosa Street, rose the façade of the Dromedary. His gaze moved swiftly along the thoroughfare, until it rested on Harnish at the edge of the walk, conversing with a slim figure on a trim chestnut mare. Disappointment rose sharply in Urquhart's breast: no, that couldn't be Jennifer. Then he saw the spring wagon with the old grandparents on the driver's seat, and there was a quick catching of his breath. His eyes darted back to the figure on the mare, taking in the thick braids of hair, glossy as a crow's wing, hanging at either side of her breast from beneath a sun-faded cavalryman's slouch hat. Drawing nearer, he spied the mannish flannel shirt, open at the throat and the divided riding skirt of tanned deerskin, the scuffed riding boots.

It was her skin that had, at first, made Urquhart uncertain. White, like a cape-jasmine is white, he had said. Now she was deeply tanned, the alteration emphasizing certain physical traits of Indian forebears when combined with the high cheekbones, slightly-hollow cheeks, generous mouth and faintly-oblique eye-brows. Involuntarily, Urquhart stepped between Harnish and the chestnut mare. Harnish had been chuckling over some remark she had made and Jennifer was surveying him with amused tolerance.

Urquhart strove to hold his voice steady, "It's taken you a time to get here, Jennifer." And then he was seeing again the placid gaze of smoky-gentian eyes and hearing her quiet tones. "You'd not be asking us to cross your great Texas in a skip and a hop, would you now, Major Urquhart?" and he saw the gladness come into her face and felt her brown hand firm and warm in his palm. Something hard brushed his fingers and he saw the silver ring with the red carnelian stone on her middle finger, and a lump came into his throat, making breathing difficult.

Harnish said, "You two are acquainted, I see." Without turning, Urquhart replied he'd been expecting Miss Keating's visit for some time. "I see," Harnish said lamely. "I was just endeavoring to make it clear to the young lady the Dromedary doesn't accept female lodgers."

Jennifer laughed and the sound was music to Urquhart. He heard her say, "Was it that now, Mr. Harnish, you were trying to explain? It must be my stupidity was persuading me otherwise." There ensued considerable stammering on Harnish's part, and Urquhart moved to the wagon to greet the grandparents. His jaw sagged at their toothless grins! Urquhart thought, they've changed not a particle—the same faces like wrinkled prunes, the same shapeless cotton clothing. Surely that wasn't their same old mule hitched to this wagon? And the crowbait grey horse at its side—Urquhart felt suddenly weak—was the identical animal he had mounted for his final battle and which had carried him to Jennifer's cabin in the Carolina pines. Behind the grandparents he caught a glimpse of the leather trunk Albumen had brought to the cabin so long ago. Dimly to Urquhart's ears came the old man's voice and the quavering tones of the grandmother: *"Higinalu."* And from some deep recess of memory, Urquhart brought up a choked, *"Higinalu*—friend," in reply, and took the old man's hand in his own, while the grandmother made a ducking bow from the driver's seat.

"They do everything for me except the learning of English," Jennifer said, spurring the chestnut mare to the opposite side of the wagon. He heard Jennifer nodding a light good-bye to Harnish and the circle of onlookers, as the mule-and-horse-drawn wagon got into movement. He walked at Jennifer's side until

146

they'd reached his horse. Jennifer said, "Where are we going?" He told her Urquhart Oaks, naturally. Had he rebuilt the house? Urquhart explained that lack of money had prevented that, but soon . . . Jennifer said next, "Are you sure you want us?" Urquhart said, "Good God, yes," and his voice wasn't quite normal. He added there were two adobe houses (the Mexican builders had moved the previous year) for their convenience; they could have their choice. One had bunks built in. They rode, stirrups almost brushing, with the bright blue of October's sky stretching above; behind them the ancient mule and old grey cavalry horse shuffled through chocolate-hued dust, and the turning wheels of the small wagon protested plaintively, at every revolution, the need for grease.

Urquhart's gaze was continually on Jennifer. The thin leggy girl of the Carolina days had developed amazingly. There was a fullness to the straight trim shoulders, and confidence in the level eyes. He mentioned she rode well. Jennifer smiled, "That was a thing I offered to prove to you when you left Carolina." Urquhart was silent, then said something about her saddle. Those old cavalry saddles couldn't be compared with a Texas rig; she'd have to have one. Jennifer wanted to know about Sergeant Corbillat and Albumen; had the Negro found Dicey Nell? Urquhart gave fragmentary replies in his haste to put his own questions. He mentioned jokingly that often he'd visualized her as having taken a husband. "Instead, you've come to Texas."

"Surely, you'd not be thinking you could rid yourself

of me by leaving North Carolina," she smiled. "I suppose you noticed we found your sword. Grandfather claimed he didn't know we'd been looking for it. He—" the smoky-gentian eyes danced—"he had been using it to prod the pigs on his place." Urquhart chuckled and remarked he, himself, may have put the weapon to similar use during the war. Mention of the war brought a sober expression to Jennifer's face. The Freedman's Bureau was confiscating property on the slightest excuse; Jennifer's cabin had been threatened; she'd lacked money for taxes. For a time she'd done sewing for ladies in Bentonville and managed to make ends meet, but that was difficult. "So when an opportunity came to sell my property," Jennifer said, "I was glad to let it go. When I'd purchased this mare and bought supplies, we had nearly five hundred dollars to be traveling with."

They had crossed the Mississippi at Memphis on a ferry, ranged southwest through Arkansas and entered Texas, stopping first at a small settlement in old Cherokee land grant country, where the grandparents had distant relatives. "They'd be relatives of mine, too, in a way, I suppose." The relatives had moved near another settlement, called Seguin, where they had a farm. Jennifer and her grandparents had remained there two days, and then, she finished a bit breathlessly, "I saw on a map how near was San Antonio, and I thought, perhaps, we could be finding you." And was that, Urquhart asked, the first thought she'd given him? "Of course not," Jennifer replied directly.

Jennifer continued: she had contemplated staying at

a hotel in San Antonio until Urquhart could be located, but the first hotel at which she'd stopped had appeared reluctant to take in her grandparents. "A man in that hotel made a suggestion that I try a rooming house named the Dromedary." Urquhart scowled and explained that some men possessed a perverted sense of humor, and that just as soon as he could locate a polecat named Carter, he'd—"Don't be angry, Darius," Jennifer laughed. "It was nothing. Mr. Harnish was very pleasant. He offered me a room and said he'd find a place for my grandparents. I—I realized at once I wouldn't want his room—" Perhaps, Urquhart interrupted angrily, he'd take care of Harnish before he disposed of Carter. Jennifer reminded him, somewhat tartly, she'd not come to pay a visit only to make trouble. She asked, "Why did you never write me?"

The horses kicked up small clouds of dust beneath their walking hoofs. Urquhart said, "I wasn't certain if a letter to Bentonville would reach you. I could have tried, of course. I did write, in New Orleans, but the letter wasn't sent off." Jennifer asked why and he stated it had been unnecessary, explaining he had been about to engage in a duel and, being uncertain how it would end, had wanted her to know what happened. The writing of further letters had been postponed until he could tell her Urquhart Oaks was rebuilt and ask her to visit him. Jennifer insisted on details concerning the duel. He told her, mentioning Harnish.

Jennifer's eyes widened. "You mean the same man I talked to in San Antonio? Darius, who is he? I have a feeling I've seen him before."

Urquhart glanced sharply at the girl. "That's very odd. I gained that impression the first time I saw him in New Orleans." He told her what he knew of Harnish. Jennifer remarked that he painted an unflattering picture of the man. "He's rather good-looking. I think some women would like that type." Not any woman with sense, Urquhart protested roughly. Of course, Jennifer admitted, she could realize how Darius felt.

"Darius, could we he hurrying a bit," she asked, after a short silence, "I want to see the sergeant—" She turned in the saddle and spoke rapidly in Cherokee in the direction of the little wagon. They touched spurs to their horses and the animals quickened pace.

9

THE FIRST NIGHT THEY HAD ALL TALKED UNTIL THE small hours, both Albumen and Corbillat overjoyed to see Jennifer again. It was decided Jennifer would take the smaller of the two empty Mexican adobes, while the grandparents settled in the larger. Two bunks were torn out of one house and erected in the other. There was certain furniture necessary for the fitting up of the houses. Madison had happened in the day after Jennifer's arrival and, learning furnishing was necessary, had invited Urquhart to take what was needed at his place. Sabina had come home the previous night: Jennifer had better come over and meet her. Urquhart could see Madison was greatly taken with Jennifer; he promised they'd be over that afternoon.

Madison rode ahead to prepare his wife for the visit.

There was a row. She was not, Sabina stated coldly, prepared to meet some Indian girl with whom Darius had lived in Carolina. Madison strove to point out that Sabina had wrong ideas; there'd been nothing like that at all. After all, the girl had saved Darius' life. Sabina sniffed: that made a good story, anyway. But, dammit, Madison persisted, Jennifer Keating was well-chaperoned: her grandparents were with her. Why shouldn't Urquhart Oaks entertain guests? Sabina asked nastily if Darius was considering establishing a Cherokee Reservation at Urquhart Oaks. She was going back to San Antonio at once. She had no intention of lowering her social prestige by entertaining some squat-legged, stringy-haired, flat-faced Indian squaw. What would her friends think? Meaning, Madison asked angrily, friends like Harnish? Mr. Harnish, Sabina flared, was better than some of the Mexican girls Madison had run with, before his marriage. That, Madison said, with an extremely red face, was before his marriage, and he'd be damned if he'd be accountable to anybody for his actions those days. If that was the way he felt, Sabina snapped, she'd pack her clothing and go where she was appreciated. Madison said hotly he could mention other destinations too.

They were still quarrelling when the wagon rolled into the Pot-Hook yard bearing Jennifer and Urquhart. Glancing out, Sabina's eyes widened in surprise. Why hadn't he told her Jennifer looked like a white girl? That, Gault said dryly, was something she'd given him no opportunity to do. He went to the door to greet the visitors, while Sabina rushed to put on what she termed her best house-wear dress, a pale blue with a great deal of ribbon trimming, made from some soft material. In time she had completed her coiffure, in the "waterfall," fashion of the day, and emerged to meet Jennifer. The two women were left alone, while Madison and Urquhart went to a barn to determine what furniture would be needed from the Madison surplus.

If Sabina had expected to overawe Jennifer, she was mistaken. Sabina directed the conversation to the latest fashions; it was a pity hoops had gone out: Sabina adored them. Jennifer averred she had never worn hoops, Sabina prattled on: Had Miss Keating enjoyed her travels? Very much, Jennifer replied; the journey had been a revelation. Yes, she liked Texas. She contemplated buying a place for herself and grandparents. Sabina maintained a preference for Louisiana; the men there displayed a greater culture. If it had not been for Darius escorting her to affairs in San Antonio, she didn't know what she'd ever done. She had tried to help Darius in an appreciation of music, but feared she'd made small progress. Texas men didn't appear interested in classical music. That could be, Jennifer conceded; the only Texans she knew were Darius and Dix. Sabina offered to accompany Miss Keating to San Antonio whenever she wished to inspect the stores. "They've not a great deal, my dear. They're still pushing the fashions of two years back. I think you'll find Texas mortal backward in many ways."

The men returned from the barn and the conversation became general. Sabina played the piano. Supper was served by the Mexican girl-of-all-work, after which

Jennifer and Urquhart drove the furniture back to Urquhart Oaks. Urquhart asked Jennifer how she liked the Madisons. She admitted to a great liking for Mr. Madison, but wondered if Sabina were the wife for him. "She talked considerable of the soical life," Jennifer said, "and of various entertainments at the Casino." Urquhart nodded and said he'd accompanied Sabina to the Casino on a few occasions; the past year and a half he'd been too busy to indulge in such pleasantries. "Do you enjoy her music?" Jennifer asked next. Music, Urquhart stated absentmindedly, was always enjoyable to those who liked it. Jennifer said dryly she'd always imagined that was the case, and asked what he'd been thinking about.

"To tell the truth," Urquhart said, "there's a minstrel show coming to the Casino a week from now. If you cared, we might drive in to see it." Jennifer said she thought that would be nice; particularly if they could go in the wagon: she'd like to wear a dress, she explained, and didn't imagine a riding-skirt was acceptable in town society. Urquhart laughed, "Sabina has been trying to impress you. Wear whatever you like; it won't make a great deal of difference."

A week later, when he escorted Jennifer to the minstrel show, he could scarcely keep the amazement from his features when she appeared in a fashionable gown of dark maroon—purchased in Memphis—with a bonnet of velvet and corded silk fitted about her coiled black braids. Nor did he miss the admiring male eyes directed toward his companion, though the sudden look of jealousy which appeared in Sabina's gaze, when she passed on the arm of a Union officer, might have puzzled him, had he noticed it.

Jennifer's grandparents had settled into their cabin as though Texas were a natural habitat; apparently they cared little where they lived. Their relatives from Seguin had paid a visit, bringing as presents two pigs and some chickens, which necessitated the building of pens to keep out coyotes. "Darius,"—Jennifer looked embarrassed—"do you mind?" Urquhart laughed, pointing out that eggs, and later pork, might bring a welcome change to the diet. The girl went on, "Now they're wanting a small piece of ground for the planting of corn. They're never so happy as when they're hoeing weeds, or grubbing out stones," Urquhart said that her grandparents were welcome to use what land they needed. The following day they were busy preparing a small plot along Crinolina Creek, weeding and digging out rocks and cactus.

Next to seeing Jennifer, Albumen's greatest joy lay in the arrival of his little spring wagon. Could he have located Dicey Nell, life for the Negro would have been complete. The days passed swiftly at Urquhart Oaks. Jennifer busied herself about her cabin. She went with Urquhart on brief rides, but generally he and Dix were training the new ponies to work with cattle.

One afternoon, two weeks after Jennifer's arrival, Urquhart and Corbillat were returning early from the day's work. Urquhart glanced ahead through the willows lining Crinolina Creek and saw blue smoke rising from the chimney of their house. Farther along were the two adobe cabins, while beyond were corrals. Two scarecrow figures were bent over a patch of turned earth. "I'm damned if I can see," Urquhart said, "what those old Cherokees find to hoe in that plot, day after day."

Corbillat grunted. "Yesterday they were grubbin' out rocks no bigger'n a hen's egg; like's not, they'll start sievin' the earth, only I don't know if they could let go the hoes long enough. Them hoes is like somethin' grew on their arms, and even if they let go, or the hoes got plumb wore down to the handles, them two dried-up folks'd just keep goin' through the motions."

The horses splashed across Crinolina Creek, emerged on the opposite bank, and turned toward the corrals. As they approached Jennifer's cabin, Urquhart swore. Corbillat exploded, "I'll be goddamned!"

Near Jennifer's doorway Harnish was just taking leave. He was already in the saddle, looking down at Jennifer in a bright calico dress, who was smiling gravely at him. His pale eyes shifted as Urquhart dismounted. Corbillat rode toward the corral, leading Urquhart's horse. Urquhart strode over to join Harnish and Jennifer.

"Thought I'd ride out and see if the little lady got located all right," Harnish said. Urquhart replied with cold courtesy that guests at Urquhart Oaks generally were made comfortable. "I don't doubt it," Harnish replied. "Nice place you have. Been looking to buy a place myself. I've had two offers for the Dromedary. The place has paid, but I may sell. That herd I sent to Kansas last spring was so profitable that I consider concentrating on cattle."

"Maybe you were lucky last spring," Urquhart observed shortly. "There's as much trouble connected with stock-raising as any business." Harnish agreed that might be so, though his manner indicated doubt. Presently he lifted his hat and trotted off. Urquhart, hat in hand, hesitated a moment.

Jennifer studied his face. "You don't like him coming here, do you, Darius?" Urquhart stated that guests at Urquhart Oaks had the privilege of entertaining visitors, if they wished. Jennifer's eyes widened. "But I didn't invite him. I've not seen him since that first day in San Antonio. He said he was out riding, and stopped to pay his respects." Urquhart asked how long he'd been there. "An hour or so. He tries to be agreeable." Urquhart scowled and remarked that he didn't like people who wore masks, didn't trust 'em.

"Nor I," Jennifer said, "but sometimes it is interesting to try to learn what's back of the mask. There's something fascinating about Mr. Harnish, that, well—" A frown furrowed her smooth brow beneath the parted midnight hair. Urquhart remarked he'd heard of rattlers having a sort of hypnotic power over helpless birds, too.

Jennifer laughed softly, noting his swift anger, and reminded him she was no helpless bird. Anyway, she said, *fascinating* hadn't been the proper word; it was just that Harnish aroused a certain incomprehensible curiosity. "Let's forget Mr. Harnish, shall we? You can be assured I shan't invite him here."

That, Urquhart assured her stiffly, was entirely up to her; he had no wish to cramp the desires of a guest.

Instantly he relented. "I'm sorry I said that, Jennifer. I'm being foolish. Let's forget Harnish."

November passed, and the days built toward Christmas. There'd been one "norther," but otherwise the weather remained clear. Urquhart had not had the time with Jennifer he'd contemplated. He'd looked forward to evening visits, but there'd been a deal of work; when supper was finished he could scarcely keep his eyes open. There was in him an obsession to put Urquhart Oaks "back on its feet," and he could think of little else.

There'd been but few visits to Madison's place. Sabina and Jennifer possessed little in common. Such times as Jennifer and Urquhart rode to the Pot-Hook, Sabina devoted most of her conversation to Urquhart. Sabina had never appeared more beautiful. Urquhart found himself continually comparing her blond elegance with Jennifer's slim dark loveliness. Once, alone with Urquhart, she had said she was staying home because she didn't want to chance missing one of his visits; she had twitted him about staying away, adding, however, she didn't suppose she could blame him: there weren't many men with a pretty Indian girl at home to keep them company. Urquhart had flushed at the insinuation, advising her not to cherish any absurd ideas. Were they absurd? She couldn't keep anger from her voice. She told him frankly she was jealous. Urquhart reminded her she was still married to Gault, and there the matter ended.

Madison announced one evening that Harnish had sold the Dromedary. Harnish was still around town and spoke of going in for stock raising. Mostly, Urquhart and Madison talked of the contemplated drive to Kansas, and in this newfound interest Madison's fondness for the brandy jug was suffering neglect.

Christmas Day found Urquhart and Corbillat out on the range, building a chute for the road-branding to come later, when the herd was gathered for the drive. In the afternoon Dix and Urquhart came in for a dinner of roast wild turkey and pudding and gifts were exchanged. Corbillat joined with Urquhart in presenting Jennifer with a new, double-rigged Texas saddle. Jennifer had laughingly asked if the saddle were intended to help her herd cows up to Kansas, and Urquhart, aghast, quickly explained that ladies simply did not participate in cattle drives. Such a thing was undreamed-of; that was all there was to it.

Jennifer sighed. "It's a trip I'd like to be making, come spring. I'd thought of investing in some cows. Darius, would you sell me a few cows?"

"I've had something of the sort in mind," Urquhart confessed.

That evening he presented her with a bill-of-sale for three hundred steers. "You'll notice I'm charging only two dollars a head," he chuckled.

"But, Darius, I could not pay even that for three hundred—"

"You're not expected to pay for them now. Your animals will make part of the herd we'll drive to Kansas. You can pay me after they're sold at Abilene." When the girl protested, he explained, "It's little enough to do, after all you did for me. I'm putting fifty cows in the herd for Albumen too. I don't know what we'd have done without him. No, I didn't give Dix a bill-of-sale for cows. Next year, if all goes well, there'll be a sizeable herd placed in his name. Meanwhile, he takes of what I have, when he needs it; it's what we've been doing for years now."

10

IN JANUARY, THE WEATHER TURNED RAW. A BLUSTERY wind roared down from the north. Corbillat and Urquhart had improvised a small forge and were engaged one afternoon in bending new tires on the wheels of the chuck-wagon. The work offered difficulties aside from the weather; tempers were short, with the two men pausing regularly to blow on stiffened fingers. Smoke from the chimneys of the three adobe houses was swept away almost the instant it emerged, and the wind tore savagely at the big oaks. Even the grandparents elected to remain within doors; their hoes lay neglected. Corbillat grunted and swore over his task. Suddenly, his hammer slipped, knocking skin from one thumb. Slamming the tool down, he cursed vehemently. Abruptly he ceased and glanced at the lowering sky. "You think it's makin' up to snow, Rius?"

Urquhart straightened his aching back. "I don't think so. We've had three days of this now. I'm looking for the weather to commence softening."

"Looks like Harnish comin' yonderly," Corbillat said, one forefinger directed across Crinolina Creek. "I wonder what that slickery bastard wants. Probably fig-urin' you'n me would be away today and he'd sweet-talk Miss Jen a spell."

Harnish's horse picked a careful way across the creek, then emerged through the willows and turned toward Jennifer's cabin. "See! What'd I tell you?" Savagely, Corbillat kicked at a tire iron lying on the ground and the sound rang sharply through the cold air. Harnish glanced over his shoulder, stiffened, then reined toward Urquhart and Corbillat.

"Thought I might find folks home on a day like this," he said easily, shoving back his sombrero. A heavy coat came down across his knees; a cigar jutted from his mouth. "It's too chill to get far from a fire." He dismounted, drew off horse-hide gloves and warmed his hands at the forge.

"What brings you out, then?" Urquhart asked quietly.

"Roove Winkler wanted to sell me his Bench-W place. I told him I'd be about today to look it over." The Bench-W Ranch lay three miles north of Urquhart Oaks. "One look was enough. I wouldn't have that desolate spread as a gift. Except a couple of pecans, there's not a tree near the house."

"It requires time to grow trees," Urquhart said mildly. "Winkler's only had that place two years. If the price was right, it would be a good—"

"Price was all right, but I don't want it at any price," Harnish said after a moment, "Is Jennifer here?"

Urquhart asked sharply, "Who?"

"Miss Keating," Harnish corrected.

"Why you asking," Urquhart's voice was dangerously quiet.

"No reason in particular," Harnish said carelessly. "I guess on a day like this she wouldn't want a visitor."

"She probably wouldn't," Corbillat said flatly.

Harnish glanced self-consciously around, his gaze taking in the oaks, the buildings, the corrals along Crinolina Creek. "Now this is the sort of layout I've got in mind," he said. "What'll you take for your place, Urquhart?"

Urquhart flushed, then turned dead white, and his eyes narrowed. He looked steadily at Harnish for a long moment, then abruptly turned his back and strode off toward his house. Harnish looked in astonishment at his retreating form. As Urquhart entered the house, Albumen emerged and headed toward the stacked firewood standing not far from the forge. The Negro passed across Harnish's line of vision without the man being aware of it, and commenced loading his arms with split chunks of oakwood.

"You God damned fool!" Amazement, anger, disgust combined to place a definite edge on Corbillat's words.

Harnish stammered, "What's wrong? What's the matter with Urquhart?"

"What's the *matter* with him?" Corbillat growled indignantly. "Personally, I'd say he had a right firm grip on himself, with you askin' him to sell you Urquhart Oaks. You, of all men! Damn your stinkin' hide, you're lucky he didn't knock your face right out from under your hat. Take my advice and light a shuck outten here as fast as that hawss will carry you."

Albumen, loaded with firewood, stood listening, with open mouth. Harnish said angrily, "Now look here, Corbillat, you can't talk that way to me."

"I already talked that way to you," Corbillat snapped. "Now you take outten here before I pitch you out, myownself." He took a step toward Harnish. Harnish made a movement with one hand within his coat. Corbillat paused. "Keep that hand away from your gun, Harnish, or let me get mine."

Harnish withdrew his hand. "You're crazy, Corbillat. I haven't a gun on me."

"I think you're a liar. Go on, fork that hawss and git!"

Muttering curses, Harnish jerked around and, crashing into Albumen sent him sprawling on the earth. Chunks of firewood went flying in all directions. "Get out of my way, nigger," Harnish snarled, reaching for his bridle-reins.

Instantly, Corbillat was on him like a tiger. "Who you callin' a nigger, you lousy, gall-sored, two-bit, spavined son-of-a-bitch? Ain't no friend of mine goin' to be insulted by no Yank bastud!" He caught furiously at Harnish's long coat as the man was setting foot in stirrup. The buttons of the garment gave way, and Harnish was swung violently about, the parted coat displaying the six-shooter at his side. "Knowed you was a liar," Corbillat exploded, one fist still clutching Harnish's coat-tail. "Now if you want trouble, you just jerk that iron and set to work—"

"Turn him loose, Dix," Urquhart's steady tones cut in, as he came striding back, his cap-and-ball pistol tucked in the waistband of trousers. Reluctantly, Corbillat released his grip on Harnish and the big man climbed to the horse's back.

"I must say," Harnish said indignantly, "this is—"

"Make your ride, Harnish," Urquhart ordered sternly. "I don't want to see you here again. Remember that!"

Harnish glared at Urquhart, then jabbed spurs violently into his mount's ribs and moved away. He traveled a short distance then turned in the saddle. "You'll live to regret this, Urquhart! I'll see that you—"

Corbillat said furiously, "You slope *pronto* now, Harnish, or *you* won't be livin' to see anythin' from here on out!"

Contemptuously, Urquhart turned away as Harnish urged his horse rapidly off. The three men stood gazing after him a minute. Albumen ruefully rubbing a bruised elbow. "Dat gemmun suah cotched he comeuppance," the Negro chuckled. "Done tooken me by' complete *suh*-prize, collisionin' inta me dat way, jus' when Ah was wukkin' 'round to de reah to lay a chunk of fiahwood 'long side he haid, casen' he mek to lift he shootin'-gun on de sahgent."

Urquhart smiled grimly. "Seems warmer than it was, Dix, I guess we can get to work again."

The Negro retrieved the scattered firewood and ambled away. Dix said, "There's Miss Jen in her doorway. Reckon she heard the commotion and is doin' some wonderin'. I'll mosey down and ease her mind—or do you want to—?"

"Go ahead," Urquhart replied. "Tell her it's nothing to be disturbed about."

Jennifer's usually placid brow was creased with concern when Corbillat explained what had happened. "The blasted fool," he concluded, "should have known better than to try to buy Urquhart Oaks."

"There's more to it than that," Jennifer said quietly. "I feared trouble."

"Trouble?" Corbillat laughed. "Wa'n't no trouble for *me*. Good for Rius to blow off steam too. Man's got to have some relaxation, now and then."

Madison rode in after supper. "What I came to see you about, Rius," he said, "Lenning Brothers, down on the Gulf, wants more beef for canning than I'd contracted for. Would you like to sell more of your old stuff? They need it early in March."

Urquhart considered. "I'd have to start a herd south before the end of February, wouldn't I? I think it could be done, Gault. That would get me back in time for calf-branding. When that's ended I want to start gathering my herd for Kansas, get 'em road-branded and on the way."

"You're got your crew all lined up, haven't you?"

Urquhart nodded. "I've had the men working for me on and off. Once we start calf-roundup I'll have a steady drain on my resources. We'll be living out of the chuck-wagon, from branding clear up to Kansas. I'll be glad to drive a herd to Lenning Brothers. It will give me that much more working capital."

"You're counting heavy on Abilene, this year, aren't you?"

"Good Lord, yes! That architect will be starting the house before long. I want to have the money to pay cash when I get back from Kansas. I'll be whipped if

164

this drive isn't successful."

"Bosh!" Madison smiled. "You don't whip that easy."

Corbillat mentioned Harnish's visit. When he had concluded, Madison said, "Served the bastard right. Personally I think one of you should have killed him."

"I've already seen too much killing," Urquhart said. "I'm wondering if Harnish will make trouble."

"Hell! There ain't a thing he can do to you and Dix."

"I'm not so sure," Urquhart denied. "Ever since Harnish left here, I've been remembering that Dix and I never did surrender, or take the Oath of Allegiance to the United States, There're records of those who did. Suppose Harnish consulted those records and didn't find our names. We'd have the Treasury Department confiscating Urquhart Oaks. Then Harnish would buy the place, to spite me if nothing else."

Madison laughed until his big frame shook. "Your names are on the records, all right, because I saw to it they were put there. I figured this might come up, so I spent a few dollars with a Yank clerk, and your monikers are entered, all proper. Done that right after you come back home. If I hadn't, the Treasury Department would have had Urquhart Oaks long ago. Those Yanks aren't that stupid—not when it comes to getting something for nothing."

A SOAKING RAIN DURING THE NEXT TWENTY-FOUR hours brought a rise in the temperature. Clouds spilled their contents and drifted away, leaving a sky of unblemished blue. A breeze blew up from the south, and the sun's rays, increasingly hotter as day followed day, penetrated deeply into the moist earth, propagating new roots and sending virile life coursing through old ones. The blossoms of redbud trees and bushes swelled to the bursting point. By mid-February the peach and apple trees began to push out small sticky buds. Almost magically, the country assumed a new, freshly-green appearance. The hides of the cattle turned sleek and shiny; small calves gambolled awkwardly through the brush, startling the birds building nests. It was a time for growing things and for making fertile all that reposed dormant, unawakened in Nature: it was the first, life-bringing, breath of Spring.

It wasn't nine o'clock one morning when Jennifer sat on the shady side of her cabin, neatly winding fresh linen thread about the band of the red carnelian ring. Sunlight streamed hotly through the leaves of Spanish oaks, scattering a dappled pattern across the dark earth. There wasn't a breeze stirring. Jennifer fanned herself with a handkerchief. The light calico dress clung moistly to her long rounded limbs, there were small beads of perspiration on her forehead. She had finished winding the ring and replaced it on her right hand, when the staccato beating of horse's hoofs sounded on the road from San Antonio.

A few minutes later, Urquhart, astride his big buckskin, came through the oak trees and turned the animal toward the corral. Jennifer rose as Urquhart reined the horse in her direction. His eyes looked weary; his shoulders and boots were covered with dust. He forced a tired smile, stepped down from the saddle and removing his sombrero, mopped at forehead with a bandanna. "Whew! It's hot!" he exclaimed. "This heat is unseasonal. On the way here I noticed redbud trees in bloom. This is just like summer."

Jennifer agreed it was hot. "I thought you'd be on the range, gathering cows for the Gulf drive, Darius. It's over a week you've been away now, isn't it?"

He nodded. "We've got that herd of canners gathered. We start tomorrow, and should be back within three weeks."

"Aren't you taking Albumen?"

Urquhart shook his head. "Madison's lending me a wagon, and I hired a cook for the drive. We'll use Albumen and our own wagon when we start calf round-up, when that's concluded we have to begin gathering the herd for Abilene. Albumen will have plenty of work ahead, so I thought I'd let him take it easy long as possible." Jennifer remarked that Urquhart had arrived from the direction of San Antonio. "I had to go into town," he explained. "Galbraith, the architect, sent word to camp he wanted to see me."

"You didn't get to bed last night?" Jennifer said.

"Sleep will have to wait. I've got to ride to Bandera.

167

There's an old Dutchman over there who's particularly good at cabiet-work. Galbraith wants him for my house, so I promised I'd ride over and see him today."

"You're starting for Bandera now?"

"Soon as I can water this horse and saddle a fresh one."

"Could you be taking me with you, Darius?" He reminded her it was hot in the sun. She pointed out it was also hot just sitting still. He nodded suddenly. "I'll be glad of your company. Maybe you can keep me awake in the saddle. Give me your rig and I'll saddle your mare while you change."

A warm breeze rose as their horses climbed among the green hills covered with laurel, cedar and live-oak. Here and there an outcropping of limestone jutted from the gravelly earth, and gradually the way became more rugged. The girl was riding slightly ahead, her heavy braids coiled beneath the old felt hat. Her erect back, sloping from trim shoulders to the neat waistband of deerskin riding skirt, reminded him, in form, of an Indian arrowhead.

The horses descended a long incline, and the riders found themselves in a shallow gulley where, at a stream lined with low cypress, they paused to eat the lunch Albumen had prepared.

It wasn't yet two o'clock when, the errand performed, Urquhart and Jennifer left the scattered collection of houses known as Bandera and headed back. Jennifer remarked, "If you didn't have me with you, you could go direct to your camp. I could get home alone, Darius. if you feel you should go. I'd not thought of this when I asked to come."

Urquhart shook his head. "I intended to return home, anyway; there are things I want to take to camp. Are you trying to drive me back to work so soon? This is the first relaxation I've had in a coon's age. I'm enjoying this." They were riding, stirrup to stirrup, across a wide stretch of open grassy country.

Jennifer said, "You need more relaxation than you're getting. Tell me, Darius, did you get more before I came?"

"What gave you that idea?"

"Sabina Madison." He asked for details. It appeared Sabina had ridden to Urquhart Oaks the previous afternoon to pay Jennifer a visit. "She's very beautiful, isn't she, Darius? But I don't see how she can feel secure on a horse, riding side-saddle. I suppose that's the way a real lady should ride."

Urquhart replied that was nonsense, and that Sabina *was* very beautiful; he agreed he didn't see how anyone could get the feel of a horse sitting side-saddle. What had given Jennifer an idea that he had less relaxation since she'd arrived at Urquhart Oaks? Jennifer answered, "I gathered something of the sort from what Sabina told me about your formerly going frequently to her house. She spoke of entertainments you had attended in San Antonio and—oh, just that you'd visited and gone riding with her. She rather hinted it was on my account that you didn't go to the Pot-Hook more often. Is it, Darius?"

"Certainly not." Urquhart continued: the truth was he'd been too busy for recreation. He admitted having spent pleasant evenings in Sabina's company, but that was sometime ago. Since she'd found other friends in town. Urquhart changed the subject: "This weather is bringing out the wildflowers. A month from now there'll be a carpet of color across this valley. There's a redbud bush." Jennifer's eyes rested on his features, then a cryptic smile curved her lips and she turned her gaze in the direction indicated by his lifted forearm.

Small spikes of ultramarine appeared here and there above the bunched grama grass. Beyond there rose the showy brilliance of the redbud. Urquhart frowned suddenly. Jennifer asked if something were wrong. He pointed off to the right where a black cloud had made its appearance above the distant hill-line and was rising swiftly, expanding as it climbed. "Thought this heat might bring rain," Urquhart said. "I know the signs, and if we don't strike out for home, *pronto,* we're going to get soaked. Come on!"

They urged the horses ahead. Behind them the cloud spread and lifted rapidly toward the sun; a low rumble of thunder growled along the horizon, followed by flashes of sheet lightning. There wasn't a breath of air now, excepting that which whipped into the riders' faces as they sped across the range. Ten minutes passed and the sun was blotted from view. Glancing skyward, Urquhart could see only an angry churning blackness closing down. They spurred the horses to greater efforts, and Jennifer's little chestnut began falling behind. Abruptly, a jagged streak of white fire ripped a momentary fissure in the murky sky, casting a strange sulphurous light over the hills. It was followed instantly by a crashing of thunder which drowned out the thudding of running hoofs.

Urquhart stole a quick glance over his shoulder. The hills to his rear were no longer visible: a dense curtain of rain had obliterated them from view and was rapidly overtaking the riders. Urquhart spurred closer to Jennifer's horse. "Maybe we can beat it, yet," he shouted. "There's a brush-shelter Dix and I threw up last fall, when we were working over here. If nothing's happened to it, perhaps we can keep dry until this has passed. Come on!"

He swerved his horse at a tangent to the right and Jennifer reined the mare to follow. The horses clattered across a winding, boulder-strewn arroyo as Urquhart indicated, with lifted arm, a point higher on the slope.

Jennifer saw first the flaming blossoms of a small redbud bush and wondered at his choosing a time like this to point it out. Then, beside the redbud, nestled within a thicket of cedar and chaparral, she saw the slanting roof of a shelter, constructed of cedar-poles, with a mud-chinked roof that sloped to the earth at the rear. There were the two triangular sides, the slanting roof and earthen floor; that was all. There was no front wall. Directly before the opening lay some remnants of old campfires. At either side was low underbrush.

The wind rose. Huge drops of rain were spattering by the time they'd urged the horses beneath the branches of a live-oak to the rear of the shelter. While Jennifer busied herself tethering the horses, Urquhart stripped off saddles. Seizing the saddle-blankets, he ran swiftly to the opening of the shelter and scrutinized carefully the earth for lurking diamondbacks before he spread the blankets. It was only toward the front that the low-sloping roof allowed him to stand upright. Jennifer entered, carrying her saddle, laughing and wiping rain-drops from her face. The deluge came with an abrupt teeming rush of wind, as Urquhart returned with the other saddle, and thrust both rigs to the rear of the shelter. "We made it!"

"Just barely," Jennifer nodded. She tore off her hat, and the heavy braids came tumbling about her shoulders.

They stood in the opening, gazing out at the rain sheeting down. Thunder like the booming of giant cannon shook the earth; jagged forked-lightning split the sky incessantly. The storm gathered in violence, driving before it dense squalls of rain which blotted out all view of the surrounding country. Water cascaded in great gusts against the roof. The branches of the live-oaks and cedars whipped furiously about.

"Will the rain run in here?" Jennifer asked.

"Not unless the wind changes. There's a trench dug around this shelter to take care of run-off. This should be over shortly. These cloudbursts don't last." As though to contradict him peal after peal of thunder crashed through the sky, with veined streaks of light-ning tearing viciously through the blackened heavens. "Reminds me of that battle at Shiloh," Urquhart con-tinued. "Does this frighten you?"

"Frighten me?" Jennifer laughed. "It's glorious! I love it! I've been told anything can happen in Texas weather. I'm beginning to believe it."

He saw her eyes were wide, her cheeks flushed with excitement. Her dark, long-limbed loveliness and the sweet soft swell of young breasts brought a choking to his throat and a sudden trembling. He tried to hold his voice steady as he said—and his tones were a trifle thick—"Yes, anything can happen . . . Jennifer . . ."

Her gaze turned toward Urquhart as he moved closer. She said softly, "Darius . . ." and her breath came a little faster, but there was no fear, no faltering, in the long-lashed smoky-gentian eyes, as she came swiftly into his arms. His lips touched her hair and the clean fragrance of orris-root in his nostrils sent a hot madness coursing through his veins. His mouth ranged lower, touching the small hollow behind one ear as he murmured incoherencies, paused a moment to brush the sweetness of her throat, and then returned to fasten ardently, clinging, upon her parted lips. Her arms tightened about his shoulders, and she was warm and close against him, and all need for words in those incomparable moments was swept away in the swiftly-rising tumult of their emotions. . . .

The fury of the storm increased, whipping the limbs of chaparral and cedar to a frenzy of wild uncontrolled movement. The torrent surged violently across the hills and grassy lowlands. Near the wall of the shelter, the redbud humbled itself beneath the savage passion of the tempest tearing through its branches. After a time, the wind abated, leaving only a steady pouring which penetrated deeper and deeper into the retentive earth. A low rumble of thunder, gathering power, crescendo-like, as it raged fiercely through the hills, burst abruptly in a final deafening blast which left the tumult spent, exhausted. Thereafter, the rain diminished, and the early wildflowers spread receptive petals to the gentle, life-bringing moisture. A faint pearly glow spread slowly throughout the western sky.

12

URQUHART STIRRED BACK TO CONSCIOUSNESS. RAINdrops spattered sporadically on the roof, and there sounded a continual dripping from branches. How long he'd slept, he wasn't certain, nor at what moment Jennifer had left his arms. He rubbed his eyes and propped himself on one elbow. Just within the shelter entrance, Jennifer sat on the floor, knees hunched beneath chin, gazing toward the distant hills. Unconscious of being watched, she removed the carnelian ring from her right hand and slipped the worn silver band with its red stone on the third finger of her left, then stretched the arm before her, hand uptilted, eyeing with grave approval the ring's new position. Presently, she settled back, her gaze ranging down the slight incline where a miniature torrent was raging through the arroyo they'd crossed in reaching the shelter.

Urquhart asked, "Has it let up?"

The girl turned and came, kneeling, to his side. "Darius, you're awake!" He drew her into his arms, his mouth against her lips. Minutes passed. He mentioned, eventually, that she should have roused him before. She protested, "You needed sleep, Darius." Urquhart replied that he had needed her still more, but she

174

gained her feet. "I think I saw someone coming, just before you spoke. You'd best come and see for yourself."

In the entrance, Urquhart peered at the moving figure in the distance. "That might be Dix," he said. "Looks like his grey pony. Dix is the only one who'd think to look for us here. Must be something amiss at camp." The sky was breaking up now; small patches of blue battled valiantly for supremacy over massed blacks and greys. "That's Dix, all right," Urquhart announced. "You wait, while I get the horses."

He made his way to the rear of the shelter, booted feet slipping across the inundated earth. The hides of the rangy dun and small chestnut mare shone cleanly wet. By the time Urquhart had rubbed them dry and cinched tight the saddles, he could hear Corbillat's voice hailing him, and Jennifer's reply. He finished with the horses and led them around to the front, just as Corbillat's pony came splashing across the newly-formed stream in the arroyo.

"Thought I might find you holed-up here," Corbillat stated, reining to a halt. Water dripped from the brim of his Stetson. A scowl darkened his features. "Sufferin' rattlers! What I been through! There was times I couldn't see a rope's length ahead, then a blast of wind and water'd strike and dang near spill me outten my saddle. All's I needed was a fin off'n a catfish, and we, could've swum—"

"Get to it, Dix, what's up," Urquhart interrupted.

"Gault's been took indisposed. Heart, I reckon. Mrs. Madison sent a *vaquero* ridin' to the camp. Albumen

175

said you'd started for Bandera."

"Has Gault got a doctor?" Jennifer asked.

"One was sent for. Prob'ly there now." Urquhart suggested that Corbillat take Jennifer back to Urquhart Oaks, but Jennifer interrupted:

"Let me go with you, Darius. I might be able to help. If this is serious, Dix will want to go too."

"Good girl," Urquhart said gratefully. He cast a quick glance about the shelter, retrieved Jennifer's hat, and they got into saddles. By the time they'd gone three miles, the sun was shining hotly at their backs and the last rain had cleared from the sky. The wet earth made fast riding difficult. Darkness had fallen by the time the Pot-Hook was reached. In the light shining through the windows, Strunk recognized the riders and hailed them. "How's Gault?" Urquhart asked anxiously, slipping down from the saddle, then turning to help Jennifer dismount.

"That back of his is sure causin' him a misery," Strunk replied, "but I reckon he'll be all right, come a couple of days."

"Back?" Urquhart said. "I'm referring to his heart."

"Nothing wrong with his heart," Strunk responded. "Go in and see for yourself. Let me take those broncs down to the corral for y'all."

They entered the house to be greeted by a tight-lipped Sabina, unable to conceal her surprise at Jennifer's appearance. "Oh, you came, too, and Dix." She turned to Urquhart. "That man! I can't do a thing with him. I thought you should be here, Darius!" She led the way into a room where Madison was propped on pillows, in bed, looking far from seriously ill. "Of all the damn' fool ideas, this knocks the cow's horns off!" Madison greeted them. "Pulling Rius and Dix off their job, right when they're busiest—hello, Jennifer, did she get you over here too? Sit down, sit down—guess we got enough chairs in here—"

"Now, Gault," Sabina interposed, "you should be quiet."

Urquhart interposed a question relative to Madison's heart.

"Nothing wrong with my heart," Madison's voice boomed through the room. "Lumbago, that's what it is. When I'm up, I can't get down, and vice-versy. There's no pain, unless I move, and so long as I keep hot irons against it. Took me hard, just before morning. For a spell I couldn't speak to any extent, and Sabina sends for the sawbones. Told her it wasn't my heart, but she knew better than me, so she sends word to your camp, Rius." Sabina said she had feared Gault was desperately ill. "All your imagination," Madison snorted. "Doc Bransome called it lumbago right off; said himself my heart wasn't affected." Sabina rose, dabbed at her eyes with a wisp of lace and left the room. Madison half rose in bed, then winced and sank back, his face white. "Y'see," he gasped, "that's how it takes me. Just a mite of a move and . . . But there's not a thing seriously wrong. I reckon I've been a trial to Sabina. That Mexican gal we had, quit yesterday, and Sabina's had to do mostly alone, with Jeff lending a hand—"

"I thought I might be able to help," Jennifer put in.

Madison nodded. "There ain't much can be done for

me, excepting change irons."

Sabina didn't return. They spoke of the storm. "Damn' nigh scared Sabina out of her senses," Madison said. "Tried to tell her there wasn't nothing to fear about a Texas storm. Might do things to your imagination, but nothing to fret about." Jennifer worked about the bed, doing what she could to make Madison comfortable. "Doc Bransome says there ain't much can be done for lumbago and that I'll just have to tough out the misery for a spell."

"The pain should leave in two or three days," Jennifer said.

"It better by God had," Madison growled, "or I'll make Doc swallow his blasted liniment. I reckon Sabina's gone to catch forty winks. She and Jeff have been kept hopping all day. Rius, you figured to start that herd for Lenning Brothers, moving for the Gulf, tomorrow, didn't you? Well, you start on schedule. Don't let this business interfere."

"I'll stay," Jennifer said, "if necessary. I don't think, Darius, this is anything to worry you. Rest is the best cure."

"That being the case," Urquhart said, "I'd better leave so you can sleep."

"Bosh! I was sleeping before you got here. Tell you what you can do: these flat-irons at my back are chilling off. If you could get me a couple of hot ones from the oven, I'd be accommodated. Sa-ay. I'll bet a pretty you two ain't had supper. Jennifer, you go along to the kitchen with Rius, and put on the coffee-pot. There's food in the larder."

"We'll get your irons fixed first." Jennifer fished beneath the blankets and produced a pair of flat-irons wrapped in towels, which she handed to Urquhart. Urquhart made his way to the kitchen. The big cookstove emanated heat from a low-burning woodfire. Urquhart unwrapped the irons, placed them on the table, then opened the oven where additional irons were heating.

He was about to remove a couple when a step caught his ear. He straightened to see Sabina, her blonde hair hanging loosely around her shoulders. Her eyes showed she had been weeping. She started past him, then stopped. "Sabina," he asked, "what's the matter?"

"What isn't?" she choked. "Nothing's right. Something has to be wrong with Gault before I can get you here—"

"Sabina, I don't understand—"

"You won't let yourself understand," she accused, eyes welling with tears. She swayed toward him, weeping silently, her arms stealing around his neck. Involuntarily, his arms closed about her shoulders. "Hush, now, hush, Sabina," he spoke soothingly. "Gault's going to be all right."

"Gault?" She spoke in low, impassioned tones. "It's not Gault worries me. Won't you realize it's you I want? You come here with that—that Cherokee girl. You can't really care for her, Darius. Tell me you don't!" She drew his head down to hers, and her lips fastened avidly on his mouth. For almost a minute he was too amazed to resist, though Sabina's action roused no response in him.

179

But in that minute, Jennifer, on her way to the kitchen to learn the reason for Urquhart's delay, paused suddenly at the far end of the hall when she saw Sabina and Urquhart, their heads forming a single pattern against the lighted opening of the kitchen doorway. For just an instant, Jennifer stood there, then her form stiffened. She turned away and returned to Madison's bedroom.

Had Jennifer waited but an instant longer, she would have seen Urquhart release himself from Sabina's arms and step back, face pale with anger. "Sabina, have you gone mad?"

Sabina faced him defiantly. "The way you've behaved toward me these past months is enough to drive any woman mad. We could go away together. It's you I want—"

"Sabina!" Urquhart stared, aghast. "Do you realize what you're saying? Gault's my best friend. He's your husband." Anger crept into his voice. "And the less you say about Jennifer, the better I'll like it." Tears commenced anew from Sabina's eyes, and her arms again started to encircle Urquhart. He seized her shoulders and shook her until the blonde hair was tumbling about her face. "You get this damn' foolishness out of your head," he spoke sternly. "You're Gault's wife. Try to make yourself useful. Now put that coffee-pot to boil and get some food on. I'm going back with Gault. Let us know when things are ready."

Sabina's eyes widened as he released her shoulders. Small spots of crimson burned in her cheeks. Quite suddenly, she lowered her eyes. "Yes, Darius," she said submissively.

Urquhart drew a long breath, and wrapped the irons in towels. He made his way back, thinking, What in the devil got into Sabina? He felt somewhat ashamed at the thought of how he had shaken her. After all, she was Gault's wife. Anger flooded through him again. By God, maybe she deserved such treatment. Anyway, what was done, was done. Maybe some women had to be handled in such fashion. The thought occurred to Urquhart that he didn't know very much about women.

Madison was lying on his side and Jennifer was massaging his back with liniment. When she had finished, Urquhart helped her return the big man to his former position. He lay back on the pillow, smiling. "Rius, I'm not surprised Jennifer pulled you through, back there in Car'lina. There's a healing in her finger-tips. Sabina don't get the hang of nursing. Doc told me I ought to have a nurse."

"I'll stay until you're on your feet," Jennifer said.

Urquhart smiled. "I know how you feel, Gault. I'm the living proof of what Jennifer's capable of accomplishing." He failed to notice Jennifer's gaze hadn't met his since he'd returned from the kitchen. Nor could he know she'd been terribly hurt by the scene she'd witnessed in the kitchen-doorway, and was resolved, at the same time, not to betray her sense of injury. The stoicism of red blood had combined with the pride of white to lend her features a mask of proud reserve.

"These irons sure feel soothing," Madison observed.

"Jennifer started out once to see what was keeping you, but changed her mind." Urquhart felt his cheeks grow warm as he explained he'd been trying to help Sabina get supper started. Madison looked surprised, but didn't comment.

Corbillat came back from the bunkhouse and dominated the conversation until Sabina called that food was ready. Jennifer insisted on staying with Madison until Urquhart and Corbillat had eaten, and when they had finished, Sabina returned to the bedroom with them, her pale-gold hair now neatly coiled. "The food's on the table, Jennifer," she said sweetly, "if Darius and Dix left anything for you."

"I'll get what I want, thank you," Jennifer replied.

When she had left for the kitchen, Urquhart suggested it was time to be getting home and thence to camp. Madison said the sooner he started his herd on the Gulf drive, the sooner he'd be back. Urquhart made his way to the kitchen where he found Jennifer sitting with an untasted plate of food and an empty coffeecup. She rose when he entered. He attempted to embrace her, but Jennifer raised a protesting hand. "Please, Darius, not now." Urquhart, puzzled, asked if anything were wrong. "I think perhaps I'm a little tired," she said quietly.

"Is this taking care of Gault going to be too much for you? I don't care to leave you here like this. You and Sabina are not what could be termed close friends."

"I'm not sure," Jennifer spoke coolly, "what that has to do with it. Gault requires a nurse. So long as he needs help, it matters not whether Sabina and I are friendly."

Urquhart frowned. "Something's wrong. Are you upset because Sabina and I were—well,"—his voice sounded lame—"because we were out here in the kitchen together? I can imagine some women being jealous of a thing like that, but you—Good Lord! you're too level-headed for that."

Jennifer managed to instil in her voice the proper amount of amused surprise. "Gracious, Darius, whatever in the world gave you an impression I might be jealous? What makes you think anything you and Sabina might do would concern me?"

"But it should concern you—you have that right—nobody more than you." Urquhart stumbled over words, a feeling of puzzled anger seized him. "Something's damnably wrong. I don't understand you." He placed his hands on her shoulders, but again she slipped away. "You were different this afternoon, Jennifer. Now it's as though we were utter strangers. What is it has gone wrong?"

She scrutinized him, grave-eyed. "Perhaps," she replied calmly, "we can blame the storm for what happened this afternoon. After all,"—a thin smile touched her lips—"Gault did say Texas storms did things to people's imaginations. Perhaps I feel differently, now; it may be you changed before I did. Once, Darius, I said you weren't sure of yourself. Then, there was a time when I thought I was mistaken. Now, I do not know what to think. I'm not even sure of myself, nor certain of what I want."

"I've not changed. Tomorrow, that herd starts for the Gulf, but I thought you and I could ride into San

Antonio and get married. I could catch up with the drive, afterward, and later, when I'd returned, we could have a real wedding."

"Married?" There was a momentary thawing in Jennifer's cold eyes, but a brittle quality edged her short laugh. "Darius, whatever made you think I'd want to marry you? I do not think you are yet ready for marriage. Think it over. Surely, an Urquhart wouldn't consider joining with Cherokee blood—"

"Jennifer! Stop it!" The girl's mocking tones sent a rush of anger through Urquhart, but before he could say more, she turned away. He caught her sleeve, refusing to let her go. When she voiced a protest, he said, "Look here, I've promised Gault I'd get that herd started tomorrow. I don't know what's happened, Jennifer, but I can only believe you're tired, tonight. I'll tell Albumen to come and get you, tomorrow, or bring you anything you want. We'll talk no more about it now, but this thing is going to be thoroughly threshed out later. May I kiss you good-bye?"

A ghost of a shrug lifted her shoulders. "If you wish. Does one kiss, more or less, mean anything in particular?"

Exasperated, troubled beyond words, he caught her roughly to him, but her lips were icy, unresponsive. "When I get back, we'll— Look here, maybe you're regretting what happened today. If so, I'm sorry. Nothing has changed my feelings. If I've hurt you—"

She made a gesture of annoyance. "Perhaps you had best not say anything more, Darius. Words seem to be getting us nowhere. Have I accused you of hurting me?

I think you are lending an undue importance to the trivial circumstances of an afternoon's—storm. It is taken for granted that men may love lightly, but it never seems to occur to you that women may have similar ideas." Her tones sounded casual. "So you see, Darius. you really have nothing to worry over, regarding this afternoon."

He stared at her, unable to believe his ears. "By God," he exclaimed, "you sound like some woman from—"

"From Drake Harnish's Dromedary, you are trying to say?" Again the mocking tones.

"I notice," he lashed out sagavely, "that Harnish's name comes mighty easily to your lips—" Instantly, he was contrite. "Jennifer, I'm sorry."

"It doesn't matter," she said coldly.

"We'll get to the bottom of this when I return," he said hoarsely, turned and walked swiftly out.

Five minutes later, Sabina entered the kitchen and found Jennifer lifting hot irons from the oven. Sabina asked: "Was Darius angry when he left? You didn't come to say good-bye to him, and he seemed so abrupt."

Jennifer raised her head and glanced coolly at Sabina. "I'm sure I don't know," she replied in a level voice. "I really know very little about Major Urquhart."

Sabina laughed softly, "In that case, I shall have to tell you about him, Jennifer. You know, I understand him quite well—and have for a long time."

PART THREE

ABILENE

1

IT NEARED THE END OF APRIL. IN A NARROW VALLEY A herd of longhorn cattle was in process of being strung out in marching order to begin the long drive to Kansas. The cattle were big, rangy, long-legged beasts with wide-spread horns and a variety of colors, though a pale dun hue predominated. To the unschooled eye all was indescribable confusion. Horsemen darted swiftly about the edges of the herd, driving back recalcitrant animals which endeavored to leave the mass. There sounded a continual clacking of horns and cracking of quirts; running hoofs thudded against the earth and an unbroken bellowing from bovine throats filled the air. Dust boiled up beneath the moving forms of horses and cattle, almost obliterating tree-studded hills; a grey haze lifted toward fleecy clouds.

On a slight rise Urquhart and Madison sat their horses, surveying the scene through the dust motes dancing in morning sunlight. "God damn!" Madison swore. "I envy you, Rius. I'm plumb sick of sitting on my rear end and doing nothing. To see my herd start north last week, and now yours getting under way—it just goes against the grain."

Urquhart said, "I'd not have been started yet, if you

hadn't sent your hands to help with branding."

"Better that than see you kill yourself with work."

Urquhart looked drawn; there were weary lines about his eyes. "I wish you were going too, Gault, but likely, Doc Bransome knows best."

Madison said, "When Doc said the rigors of such a trip would he bad for my heart, I didn't pay him no mind, but when he pointed out that I might have to tough out another attack of lumbago in a chuck-wagon, it made me think. I wouldn't have Jennifer there to make things easy for me, like—" Urquhart interrupted to remark that Madison was choosing the wiser course. "I think so," Madison agreed. "I'll reach Abilene in style—on a Mississippi sidewheeler and the steam cars. It'll make a nice trip for Sabina, too. I'll be in Abilene when Jeff arrives with the herd—be there to meet you, too."

Urquhart said, "I wanted to get started weeks earlier than this, but there's been so much to do. I've had to ride to San Antonio to see Galbraith about the house when I couldn't afford the time." Madison said he'd noticed that the carpenters had the sideboards up to the second floor already. Urquhart shrugged. "I've been too busy to notice particularly." Madison gave him a quick look, but Urquhart changed the subject: "How do these cows look, Gault?"

"As nice a gathering of prime beeves as I've seen. You've done a good job winnowin' out. Runs around three thousand head, I'd stay."

"Just under thirty-one hundred. If we graze 'em right on the way, they'll put on weight. I'm sinking practically everything I've got in this herd. It *must* reach Abilene in good shape." Madison asked if Urquhart knew Harnish had sent a herd up the trail a month previously. Urquhart nodded. "Harnish didn't go along with the herd, though. He's still hanging around San Antonio."

"Nobody seems to have much use for the crew he hired to handle the herd, either. Hard-bitten gang. Funny thing, he just put up a small herd—bought cows here and there, all from owners who had herds of their own going north. And got bills-of-sale from each one."

Urquhart scowled. "He knew better than to try any buying from me. You know, Gault, a crook could buy, say, twenty-five cows in a certain brand and get the owner's bill-of-sale. Later, he could steal some cows in that same brand, do a little fancy pen-work on the bill, and arrive in Abilene with quite a herd, if he worked the trick on several stockmen. Of course, the roadbrand would complicate a deal like that." Madison growled that no brand ever stopped a cow-thief. Urquhart laughed shortly. "Damnation! I'm allowing my dislike for Harnish to bias my thinking."

"I don't know, Rius. Maybe you've hit the nail on the head. I refused to sell to him, but I never thought—" He stopped to watch a steer that had broken away from the herd run swiftly towards the hills. Instantly, a rider took up the pursuit on a small roan pony. The pony gained rapidly on the steer which swerved suddenly to one side. showing on its ribs the Circle-U brand and freshly-healed roadbrand. Dust billowed up from the running hoofs. The pony turned with the steer, nipping at the brute's flanks. The steer bellowed frantically and swung back, seeking the security of the herd. The rider's gathered rope slapped it smartly across the rump and it quickened pace.

Madison chuckled. "Good cow-hawss. Wasn't that Tom Yeagle riding?" Urquhart nodded. Madison said, "Get Tom to tell you, sometime, about that herd he swum across the Mississippi to reach Louisiana, during the war." The *remuda* of fifty-odd saddle horses went trotting past in a colorful massed movement of rippling backs and tossing manes and tails, herded on their way by a rider in a steeple-crowned hat. "Where's your wagon?" Madison asked presently.

Urquhart pointed toward a fringe of cottonwood trees beyond the herd. "Down near the stream. Albumen's filling the water-barrel."

The herd in the valley had grown noticeably smaller by this time, but from the remaining, milling animals, a long ribbon of moving backs and tossing horns was strung out along a dusty three-quarters of a mile, as cattle were driven into trail formation. Madison said, "Well, you're started. You should be across the Cibola by tomorrow night." Urquhart said they'd planned to water the cows there, then turn north. "Rius," Madison blurted, "did you ever know that Sam Houston was married to a Cherokee woman?"

"What brought that up?" Urquhart asked casually.

Madison tugged nervously at his moustache. "Look here, this is none of my business, but you aren't letting Jennifer's blood stand between you and her, are you?" Urquhart said stiffly that he wasn't. Madison went on,

"I think she'd make you a good wife. I've watched things building between you and then—hell's-bells! Dix tells me she's gone to Seguin."

Pain showed in Urquhart's eyes. "That, I can explain," he said. "There are other things I can't. No, Jennifer's Indian blood has nothing to do with it, though looking back, I know it bothered me for a time. I've asked her to marry me, and she said no. I thought things were settled between us when you were down with lumbago. It was that night she refused me; something must have changed her suddenly. I don't know what happened and I couldn't find out. She turned cold as a norther, erecting some sort of barrier I couldn't penetrate." Urquhart added further details, trying to make the older man understand the problem he, himself, had failed to solve.

"I left the following day for the Gulf," Urquhart continued. "When I got back, Jennifer had been in Seguin some time. Her grandparents have relatives near Seguin, and one of them had broken a hip. They'd sent a Cherokee boy riding to Urquhart Oaks with the word, and Jennifer and her grandmother had immediately set out for Seguin, leaving the grandfather at Urquhart Oaks to tend the chickens and cornfield. That's the story I got from Albumen when I returned. It was natural Jennifer would stay at Seguin and help with the nursing, for a time. I managed to ride to Urquhart Oaks every so often, each time expecting to find Jennifer back. But she never returned."

A jangling of harness and quick-stepping hoofs intruded on the conversation as the big chuck-wagon, with its tarpaulin-covered bows and "cupboard" box at the rear, rumbled past, drawn by the four-mule team, with Albumen in a broad-brimmed white sombrero on the driver's seat. The Negro grinned widely and flourished a long whip at Madison and Urquhart, as he went by, the wagon lurching and jolting over the uneven earth and throwing back a cloud of dust in its wake. "That Negro," Urquhart observed, "certainly takes a powerful pride, tooling those mules. You'd think he was on the driving box of a king's carriage."

The dust settled slowly to earth. But a handful of cows remained in the valley now, and only three cowboys worked to get them strung into line and hurried on. Madison asked, "And you can't nohow figure what's gone *loco* between Jennifer and you?" Urquhart shook his head. Madison continued, "Was I you, I'd ride to Seguin, and thrash matters out with her."

"Hell's-fire! I've ridden there twice." Madison asked for details. "I lost my temper and said things I shouldn't have," Urquhart growled. "You see, Gault, I'd just reached the outskirts of Seguin when I saw Harnish riding out of town. Harnish gave me one of his smirky smiles when he passed, and for a minute I could have killed the son— By the time I found the farm where Jennifer was staying, I was still hot under the collar. I asked if Harnish had been calling on her. That's when I blew up." Urquhart sighed. "It was explained easily enough. Harnish had spotted Jennifer and her grandmother when they had driven through San Antonio, and had asked where they were going, and why. Just an ordinary, sociable question, I suppose.

Jennifer had told him. Later, he'd come out to inquire after the health of the relative with the broken hip—so he said."

"Considerate son-of-a-bitch, ain't he?"

Urquhart sighed. "That part was clear anyway. When I got to the business that'd brought me there, it didn't do any good. Jennifer said something about my not being sure what I wanted yet. Said she'd be obliged if I didn't talk about it. Finally, I left. Two weeks later I rode there again, but Jennifer wouldn't come out of the house. I talked to one of the Cherokee men on the farm—they're pretty decent people—and he told me Jennifer had been nursing the one with the broken hip. I asked about Harnish, and learned he'd called on Jennifer four times. So I gave up. If Jennifer doesn't want to see me, I won't force myself on her."

"Damn' if I understand it," Madison frowned. "There's never any telling about a woman, though. I ought to know. You don't figure Jennifer actually likes Harnish, do you?" Urquhart said fervently *he* couldn't conceive of anything of the sort. Madison said, "Jennifer wouldn't be doing it to make you jealous, would she?"

"Good God, why should she? There's no reason for that. No, Jennifer wouldn't descend to such methods. I'll just have to conclude I was mistaken—that I'm not the man for her. I'll get over it," he added, and a moment later, "I hope."

They talked a few minutes longer. Urquhart remarked that he'd best be pushing up toward the head of the herd. The cattle were strung out, now, for over a

192

mile, grazing slowly as they moved, and directed by cowboys riding on each side the undulating stream of dusty backs. Urquhart and Madison loped along until they'd reached the point where two riders were preceded a short distance by Dix Corbillat, trotting his pony at the side of the chuck-wagon. Beyond the chuck-wagon, a short distance from the herd, moved the *remuda*. Here, near the point of the moving line of cattle, the atmosphere was freer of dust, and the bright morning sunlight shone hotly on moving men and animals.

Madison drew rein and Urquhart pulled in. "Well . . ." Madison commenced reluctantly.

"It's good-bye for a spell, Gault." They clasped hands. "I appreciate your coming out to see us off."

"Pure selfishness on my part, Rius. I wish I was going all the way with you. I'll be in Abilene to greet you—Sabina and I—when you pull in, and we'll have a blow-out to celebrate." Urquhart assumed an enthusiasm he didn't feel and said that would be fine. "And, son," Madison said concernedly, "keep your hat on when you're passing through Indian country, and take care of yourself. You're worn down—body and mind. I'll ride over to Seguin some day and see what I can learn. If Jennifer says anything I can dab a rope on, I'll write you at Fort Worth." He raised one hand toward Corbillat in a farewell gesture that included the whole outfit, turned his horse and sent it loping away. Urquhart sat looking after him a moment, then spurred in the direction of the chuck-wagon.

2

Two hours later the herd was traveling at a brisker pace, the long undulating ribbon of dusty backs flowing smoothly down one slope and mounting easily the next, across rolling hill country, dotted with brush. Leaving Corbillat in charge, Urquhart had ridden ahead with the chuck-wagon, to select a site at which the riders could get noon food when they came by.

Not far behind Corbillat, and on either side of the advance steers, were the "point" riders, Tom Yeagle and Bert Hogan, both experienced men with cattle. Yeagle was tall, with leathery features. Hogan was dark, and because of a pessimistic disposition, known as Graveyard. Half a mile back of the "points," rode the "swing" men: red-haired Rusty Gates, with blue eyes, and Cordano, a chunkily built Mexican.

Still farther back, riding either side of the long line of cattle, were the "flank" riders: Shorty Weber and Zach Peters, rawhide-tough but good-natured. Three "youngsters" comprised the "drag" men, or drags: Magpie Vogel, twenty-one years of age and extremely talkative; Dave Rutson, just past twenty, with candid eyes and curly hair; and Ned Canfield, also twenty, slim-hipped, tall. These three, because they lacked the experience of the others, had drawn the most disagreeable work in the trail crew. Their job it was, not only to keep the cattle moving, but to contend against the dust kicked up by the cattle.

The crew wore wide-brimmed felt hats, spurs and

leather *chaperejos*. Their shirts were of wool. All had heavy coats on the wagon, and each was equipped, in addition to his horsehair or rawhide lariat, with a cap-and-ball six-shooter. A few had brought repeating rifles. Most of them had fought for the Confederacy. Not yet nineteen was Narcisso Revas, the *remudero,* a young Mexican with considerable horse knowledge.

Corbillat, in advance of the points, looked around to see Urquhart approaching. Urquhart swung in beside Corbillat. "Dix, the wagon's waiting about five miles farther on. I've told Albumen to have ready a handout the men can eat in the saddle. I don't want these cows pushed too hard, today, but I want to keep them going steadily until the trail habit is formed. Later, when they're trail broken, we can take it easier at noon-time."

Corbillat nodded. "Some of 'em are getting the idea too early," he scowled, jerking a thumb over his shoulder. "There's a feud started already 'tween that big black steer and that yaller line-back. The black's got his mind set on leadin' this herd, and the yaller don't like it. One of those critters is going to be minus a few steaks, if he don't learn his place."

The sun climbed. Perspiration mixed with dust formed X-shaped patterns of suspenders across toiling backs. The cattle were gradually catching the trail idea, though every so often animals tried to escape from the line of march. The riders began to look forward thirstily to the water-barrel on the chuck-wagon. Now and then one of them rode to the *remuda* moving beside, but a short distance from, the cattle, and

195

effected a change of ponies. Narcisso Revas had already learned which mounts certain riders preferred, and generally had a particular horse worked to the edge of the *remuda* by the time the rider was ready to make the change.

Mile after dusty mile rolled back beneath the hoofs of the drive. Corbillat edged his pony nearer Urquhart's buckskin. "We're stirrin' up the dust at last." Riders and cattle rounded an out-cropping of limestone shouldering a low bluff and sighted a thin spiral of smoke where the chuck-wagon waited, two miles beyond. "I'll ride back and pass the word there'll be no stop for dinner, today," Urquhart said, and turned his buckskin toward the rear of the herd.

As he swung around, Urquhart saw a rider coming fast through the haze of dust. It looked like—by God, it was! What in the devil was Gault Madison coming back for? He thrust in his spurs and hurried to meet him. A minute later, the two drew rein. Madison's horse was streaked with lather, chest heaving.

"Gault! Changed your mind? Going with us?"

Madison was breathing hard. "Wish I could," he puffed. "Say, did Jennifer know what day you were leaving?" Urquhart answered that he had known only the approximate date himself, and asked why. Madison went on, "She's come back to Urquhart Oaks. Thought I'd best let you know, Rius, in case you wanted to see her, before you got too far away."

"Did she say why she stayed away so long, or anything?"

Madison shook his head. "I didn't get to talk to her.

I was riding near your house, on the way home, when I saw that spring-wagon drive up. Jennifer and the old lady got down. I didn't go on to the house, but turned and lit out to catch you."

"Lord! I'll never be able to thank you. I do want to see her. I'll get going. You want to ride with me?"

"No, I aim to take it easier going back. I'll drop in on Jennifer tomorrow. I'll go on to your chuck-wagon now and catch a bait, before I head back."

"Wait!" Urquhart considered. "Find Dix. Tell him to make camp on Conejo Creek, tonight. I'll try to catch up to him there. If I don't, tell him to keep the cows moving and I'll overtake him later. Adios!"

3

IT WAS ONE-THIRTY WHEN URQUHART SPIED THE BUILD-ings along Crinolina Creek. In the cornfield, the ancient grandparents were bent over hoes. They paused in their labors and gaped in curiosity as Urquhart urged the foam-flecked buckskin past.

Urquhart gazed vainly for Jennifer, a sudden rage seizing him when he recognized Drake Harnish's horse standing near her doorway! Drawing near, he checked his panting mount, flung reins over its head and hit the earth, running, even before it stopped. At the same instant, Harnish, a startled expression on his face, stepped from Jennifer's doorway, and halted there, looking flustered, as Urquhart stopped ten yards distant.

"Hello, Urquhart," Harnish tried to make his voice

casual. "I thought you started for Kansas this morning."

"You know too damned much about my activities, Harnish. I warned you once to keep away from here. If you want to leave—alive—get going. Now!"

"All right, I'm going," Harnish said uneasily. "I was just pulling out anyway."

"Darius!" Jennifer appeared in the doorway. "I was afraid I'd missed you."

Urquhart was too angry to detect the glad note in her voice. "I'll talk to you in a minute," he said coldly, not removing his eyes from Harnish. "Hurry it up. Harnish! Make tracks!" Harnish dropped a comment about "Southern hospitality." Urquhart clenched and unclenched his hands, his throat thick with rage. "I've no hospitality for your kind."

Harnish doffed his hat to Jennifer. "I'll see you again, Miss Keating—under more opportune circumstances, I hope —" The words ceased as Urquhart took a step forward.

"Chances are," he told Harnish, his tones dangerously calm, "you'll not see Miss Keating, or anybody else, *under any circumstances*, unless you move away from here just as fast as God will let you." His hand moved involuntarily toward the six-shooter at his hip, then, checking the movement, Urquhart hooked one thumb into his belt, his knuckles showing white against the dark leather of *chaperejos*.

Harnish's face turned ashen. Abruptly, he kicked his horse into action and moved swiftly off. Urquhart swung back to Jennifer, features set in rigid lines. They faced each other in silence, until Jennifer spoke: "He happened to be in San Antonio, where we stopped to buy supplies. Grandmother and I had scarcely arrived here, when he came. Darius, I can't prevent him from calling."

"Have you ever tried?" Urquhart flashed jealously.

A flush colored the faint hollows below Jennifer's cheekbones. "Not exactly. But there's something—"

He heard only the first two words and interrupted angrily, "That's about what I thought."

"Darius!" Her face was white. "Surely you would not believe I care for Harnish."

"What else can you expect?"

"You must imagine I have the mind of a child."

"Older women have been fooled by Harnish's palaver," he snapped. "You need to be protected against yourself."

Jennifer's back straightened proudly, her chin came up. "I think, Darius, that you have lost your mind."

"If so, you've been the cause of it. However, I do not intend to lose anything else through Harnish. So he thinks he will see you again!" The short laugh was harsh. "I've another idea. You're trailing to Kansas with us."

Jennifer stared at him. "You're saying that *I* am going up the trail with the herd? No! You can't mean that, Darius. No—"

"I mean exactly that. You're going with us—"

"You've no right to order me about!"

He indicated the carnelian ring on her hand. "You gave me the right when you placed my ring on that finger. Do you deny that?" Jennifer was suddenly furious. "You gave me this ring, for my own. I will wear it where I wish! Or I will throw it in the dust—"

"Enough of this," he said obdurately. "Get into riding clothes at once."

"No and no and no!" Jennifer cried, her cheeks flaming.

"You'll do as I say. I've enough on my mind without you for the next few months—"

"You think I am not to be trusted?" Jennifer flared.

"I didn't say that,"—doggedly.

Quick wrath burst to the surface, as Irish blood gained the ascendancy over Cherokee breeding: "You do not have to put it into words—"

"We're wasting time, Jennifer. Get ready to leave."

"No! I refuse!"

"You can refuse from now until Doomsday," he stated harshly, "but you're going if I have to tie you into a saddle. Or come of your own accord. Make up your mind!"

The girl choked with anger. She was unable to speak for a moment. Suddenly her eyes blazed. "Darius Urquhart," she said, "you're going to regret this. I will go with you. It is not needful that you use force. Perhaps, this way is the answer—" She paused, then, "It may be this is a just payment for a time of foolishness. Yes, I'll go with you."

Urquhart was for an instant contrite. "Jennifer, I've told you, more than once, if you have any regrets for that afternoon, I'm sorry I—"

"*You* are sorry. You're a bigger fool than I think,

Darius, if you believe that was solely your doing. Heavens above! I wonder if anything on earth can be more conceited than a man!"

"Call it what you like," he said stubbornly. "The fact is you're leaving here with me." He brushed past and entered her house. She followed him and watched him fling blankets from bunk to the table. Then he gathered her saddle and bridle and stepped outside.

He led the sweat-stained buckskin down to the edge of Crinolina Creek to drink, while he removed the lariat and strode on toward the corral. Discarding Jennifer's mare in favor of the tougher mustang strain, Urquhart chose two ponies, a pinto and a dun, both good saddlers and unusually docile. Ten minutes later he was back, with the dun saddled and the pinto leading behind. He brought the buckskin from the creek, then made a quick trip to his own cabin, to return with an extra rope. By this time, the grandparents had arrived to learn the cause of the commotion. They passed Urquhart and entered the cabin. Almost instantly a babel of Cherokee broke out.

Jennifer emerged, followed by the two old people. Urquhart burst out, "I'm not taking them—"

"Nobody asked you to be taking them," Jennifer said coldly.

The elderly Indians converged on Urquhart, spouting voluble Cherokee, their wrinkled faces scowling, disturbed and pleading by turn. In all the confusion of unintelligible syllables certain words, *"agehya taluli"* and *" 'ta'hu li',"* occurred so frequently that he found them being indelibly stamped on his memory. The urgency with which the grandparents strove to make him understand the words, repeating them over and over, aroused his curiosity. "What are they trying to tell me," he demanded of Jennifer.

"It doesn't matter," the girl replied coldly. "Naturally, they do not want me to leave." She spoke rather sharply to the old Cherokees, and both fell silent, though their eyes pleaded mutely with Urquhart.

Urquhart said uncomfortably, "You don't need to worry about them. I'll send word to Gault to see—"

"My people are not your concern," Jennifer stated with cold dignity. "If I were worried about them, I'd not be leaving. Will you be putting my blankets and the small trunk on the horse, or is it for me to do?"

Urquhart strode past the girl and the grandparents and procured blankets and trunk. When he tried to help her into the saddle, she drew swiftly away and mounted without aid.

"I've no idea how many miles it is to Abilene," she said, furiously, "but the fewer words you say to me, each mile of that journey, the better I'll be liking it."

"That," he stated angrily, "is precisely as I have planned it."

They moved off, the loaded pinto following behind. Three miles passed while the horses loped along, then Urquhart said abruptly, "Look here, maybe I was wrong—" His words were checked by the cold glance the girl directed his way, as she reminded Urquhart she didn't care to have him speak to her unless absolutely necessary. Urquhart crimsoned and he fell quiet. The remainder of the journey, until they'd reached the herd, was passed in a stony-faced silence.

The setting sun was nearing distant hilltops when they mounted a rise to gaze down a long gradual slope to a point where the cattle had been checked and gathered into a loosely-held mass, not far from a stream lined with willows. Urquhart slowed the buckskin, as if reluctant to proceed, but the girl kept going, and he was forced to spur on. Even through the turmoil of his emotions, Urquhart noted that the cattle were grazing peacefully, some of the animals already lying down, contentedly chewing cuds, while two riders, on guard, slowly circled their ponies in opposite directions around the bedding ground.

A short distance from the herd, blue smoke spiraled slowly from the campfire where Albumen had prepared the supper the men were engaged in consuming. Beyond, the *remuda,* rope-hobbled for the night, cropped juicy spring grass. A number of night-horses stood, loosely saddled, near the wagon; bedrolls had been unloaded. There was a clutter of pots and Dutch ovens by the fire. The men sat on the earth, cross-legged, plates held in laps.

A coffee-cup spilled suddenly to earth. Dix got to his feet as he spied the approaching riders. Surprised comments passed from mouth to mouth; hats were swept from heads when Jennifer and Urquhart rode in and dismounted. Albumen was first to find his tongue: "Hit's Miss Jennifuh! Y'all come to eat suppeh wid we'uns? Jes' a minute, Ah fixes y'all a plate."

No one else spoke. The girl said, "Thank you, Albumen."

Corbillat said, "Howdy, Miss Jen."

Urquhart said to Jennifer, without meeting her eyes, "May I present the Circle-U crew?" He announced to the men, "This is Miss Keating. She owns three hundred Circle-U cows in our herd, and has decided to see them up the trail."

The men found their feet, with considerable bowing and scraping. Urquhart turned away and started unlashing Jennifer's blankets and the small trunk from the back of the pinto. Immediately, half a dozen men, as though anxious to leave the vicinity of the campfire, rushed to take over the job. Saddles were removed, and the horses led off by Narcisso Revas. Urquhart strode off and stopped some distance beyond the wagon. Presently, Dix caught up with him.

"Look here, Rius," Dix said wrathfully, "what sort of damn' full notion you puttin' on us? You know blasted well she can't go up the trail—"

"If it's a damned fool notion," Urquhart said tersely, "maybe it's beyond explaining. We won't argue. She's going with us. Harnish was already there when I got back."

"You should have killed the bastud. But that ain't Miss Jen's fault, is it? By Gawd, I never see such a man for seekin' out trouble the way you do. How in Gawd's name can she go to Kansas with us?" Urquhart reminded Corbillat that Jennifer was a good rider. Dix said, "You know damn' well what I mean. Trail drivin' ain't no place for a woman—not with these men around. Ain't no trail rider aimin' to mind his manners when a cow-critter gets actin' up. They'll resent her."

Urquhart's anger mounted. "Any man who gets resentful enough, can draw his pay *pronto*. And tell him to keep out of my way when he leaves."

"Don't you go to gettin' proddy with me. If there's trouble ahead, we'll face it together, like we've always done." Some of the edge left Dix's tones. "Where we goin' to sleep her?"

"In the wagon. The Negro can sleep on the ground like the rest of us. It's going to be your job to look out for her. Jennifer and I aren't on speaking terms."

Corbillat stared at him. "You ain't friendly, so you take her ridin' all the way to Kansas. Now, what you tellin' me you'd be doin' if you was friendly? Now she's my responsibility. I never heard anything to beat that!"

They walked slowly back to the campfire, to find Jennifer seated cross-legged on' the earth, eating from a tin-plate, while Albumen hovered solicitously at her shoulder. The rest of the cowhands sat in stunned silence.

4

THE STARS WERE STILL BRIGHT IN THE SKY WHEN JENnifer, fully dressed, slipped quietly out of the wagon to find Albumen placing fresh fuel on the fire. Albumen moved to a Dutch oven among the coals and inspected a batch of sourdough biscuits. The girl carried a towel and soap. Scattered about the wagon, men's forms, swathed in blankets, reminded Jennifer of rolled cocoons. Faintly, from the direction of the herd, came the off-key singing of a pair of night riders circling the bedding grounds. A cool breeze rustled the grass; the cottonwoods along the stream made whispering sounds.

The Negro glanced up as Jennifer approached. He held his voice low with a warning glance toward the sleeping men lying about. "Ya'll slumbahs tranquil?"

The girl replied softly, "Once I got to sleep. I woke only once, sometime after midnight. I heard somebody riding away; a few minutes later somebody else came in."

"De changin' of night-gua'ds. We negotiates dem in foah shifts—last paih of ridehs takes oveh 'bout two in de mawnin'. Ah didn't rouse y'all, Ah hopes, when Ah has t'reach into de wagon foah rations a spell back."

"You did, but I was glad. Wake me each morning at this time."

"Yassum, Ah does dat." The Negro frowned. "Y'all's ac'ually ridin' up de trail wid we'uns?"

"I have to look after my three hundred cows, you know."

"Ah 'spects so." Albumen puzzledly scratched his head. "Ah's got fifty crittehs in dat hud, likewise, and Ah'm goin'. And de rest b'longs to de Majuh, and he goin'. Yassum, Ah raikons dat meks sense—but Ah jist cain't believe hit."

Jennifer left the fire and walked to the stream. By the time she'd returned with her hair in freshly done braids, faint streaks of crimson were seeping into the eastern sky; the stars had started to pale. An aroma of coffee made the air fragrant. Corbillat was standing by the fire, when Jennifer came up. He said good-morning, adding, "I spoke to Revas, last night. He'll see that your pony is saddled each day before we leave—the pinto one day, the dun the next." He turned and walked among the sleeping men stretched in blankets on the earth. "Rouse out and spool them beds, cow-nurses," he bawled. "Time to stir up dust!"

The men came reluctantly awake, with the usual complaints about the miseries of a cowboy's life. Two minutes after Dix had roused them, they had scattered in the direction of the stream. They returned, water dripping from freshly combed heads, each speaking a "Good-morning," to Jennifer. Beyond that, conversation was lax. Urquhart was last to put in an appearance. He spoke to Jennifer and received a cool nod. The men got plates and pint-size tin cups, and went about forking food from the various containers, then dipped cups into the huge coffee-pot and sat down to eat. Albumen started to prepare a plate for Jennifer, but the girl insisted on waiting on herself.

Through the half-light spreading over the range, Jennifer could make out the faint outline of the herd and hear the early morning bawling of the animals. Urquhart dropped his dishes into the pan beneath the small table at the end of the wagon, and walked off to get his horse. Gradually the other men followed. The two night riders came in for breakfast, then rode off again. Gold flecked the clouds in the dawn sky; it became lighter. The herd was on its feet now, heading toward the stream. Revas, the wrangler, got the horses bunched and under weigh, leaving only the hobbled mules and two ponies. Only Jennifer, Dix and Albumen were left at the fire.

Dix said, "You'll be siding me, today, Miss Jen. We start anytime you're ready. Owners aren't supposed to work. Leastwise, not female owners."

"Do we ride off and leave Albumen?"

Dix nodded. "He'll pass us before long. He's got dishes to redd up, maybe some dough to chouse, or somethin'."

They rode in silence until the sun lifted above the eastern hill-line. "Miss Jen," Dix finally blurted, "don't you take it hard that Rius got sort of obstrep'rous. He's had a heap of worries—"

"What for instance?"

Dix swallowed hard. "We-ell, he's got into debt on that house bein' built at Urquhart Oaks, and—there's this herd. Ain't no man figures to drive cows clear to Kansas 'thout he's got plenty to fret his mind. Look at the expense. A wagon and hawsses runs into money. And wages for cowhands. Rius pays better'n most. Yeagle and Hogan are drawin' down forty a month; the rest thirty and thirty-five. I don't know what he aims to pay the Negro—generally a cook makes more than a cowhand. Was I workin' for any other outfit, I'd be gettin' likely a hundred a month. Total that up for a three months' drive, and it ain't shinplasters. Rations will crowd four hundred, includin' medicines—quinine, laudanum, carbolic, turpentine, alum, and so on—stuff like that if even you never use it, it's got to be paid for. Rius furnishes the navy plug tobacco for them that wants it. Surprisin' how much plug a man can eat in a day, when he's trailin' in dust. It's all a worrisome job, and if you're riled at Rius—"

"Dix, let's leave the Major out of our conversation, shall we? What happened is something you can't fix, so you're wasting time trying." The girl's tones were quiet. Corbillat looked miserable and nodded agreement.

The terrain across which they were passing was rolling with post-oak, cedar and mesquite. Corbillat looked uneasily back. "We're due to strike a lot of *brasada* before long. I sure hope those drags keep the cows movin' along. I don't want to chase ornery critters through mesquite tangles."

"There's no need for you to stay, if you want to go back. I can take care of myself."

"You're my job." Corbillat assumed a look of surprise. "You think I'm so *loco* I want to go back and eat dust. No, ma'am! I aim to stay in front of that herd."

Jennifer glanced over her shoulder and saw cattle streaming down a long gradual slope, the animals forming roughly a great arrowhead, as they grazed along the way. Later, the point would be narrowed as the riders got the beasts strung out in traveling formation, but this early it was best not to offer the steers too much restraint.

It was ten o'clock before Albumen caught up with Jennifer and Corbillat. The two rode ahead with the chuck-wagon to pick a spot where noon food could be prepared for the cowboys, when the herd drew abreast, though the animals would be kept marching, while the riders took turns coming in to consume hasty dinners.

"Later," Dix told Jennifer, "we'll throw the critters off the trail and take more time at noon."

The sun climbed higher as the wagon was once more left behind while Jennifer and Corbillat rode on, a mile in advance of the moving herd. The afternoon passed swiftly, and again the chuck-wagon came abreast, and the heat of the day was lessening. That evening, Jennifer watched the procedure as one point rider dropped back, while the other checked and commenced to turn the advance animals. Gradually, as the other cattle came up, the herd was resolved into a great milling mass which eventually quieted and commenced peaceful grazing. The steers had been watered at a stream two miles to the rear.

It was nearly dark when the men came in to supper, their clothing, eye-brows and unshaven features thickly coated with dust. Ned Canfield arrived with his right shirt-sleeve bloodstained. A steer had broken away and started for home, with Canfield in pursuit. It had been necessary to rope and throw the animal to prevent its escape into a thicket. Canfield's arm had become entangled in the rope tied to the saddlehorn; before he could get free the skin on wrist and forearm had been scraped raw; he was fortunate the injury wasn't more serious: cowmen often lost fingers in such accidents. Such sympathy as Canfield received carried a note of derision: he was informed he should learn to rope. How had a lenty, a greenhorn, ever wangled his name on the Circle-U payroll? Canfield accepted the raillery in good part, but Jennifer realized the injury caused him pain. It was she who washed the wound, dabbed the torn flesh with turpentine, and then bound it with clean cotton rags. Several of the men wondered aloud if Miss Keating were prepared to treat all injuries which might overtake the crew. She announced she was. That evening there was less restraint about the campfire.

5

DAY SUCCEEDED DAY WITH LITTLE TO BREAK THE monotony except the changing terrain. Such rivers as were crossed had been, fortunately, low, or provided convenient sandbars, yet had retained sufficient flow to satisfy the cattle's thirst and fill the water-barrel on the chuck-wagon. The herd had gradually become trail-broken to the daily march. One morning Urquhart remained behind when the others departed. Drawing Jennifer aside, he suggested he ride with her that day. The girl heard him in silence, then declined coldly: she and Dix, she declared, got along nicely together, unless, of course, it was necessary for Dix to resume his duties with the herd. In that event, Jennifer stated, she could get on very well by herself, or she'd remain with Albumen. She didn't, she made it clear, care to ride with Urquhart. The man flushed angrily, mounted his horse and rode off. Thereafter, he did no more than nod to her, morning and evening. If the others noted the coolness between them, nothing was openly said about it.

As the herd forged north, evidences were plain of the passage of other herds. Once, looking back from a high point of land, Jennifer could see, far behind the Circle-U cows, a long, snake-like moving brown ribbon from which blew a steady cloud of dust. Corbillat, at her side, shifted and glanced over his shoulder. "That might be the Arrow-3 outfit." Now and then, riding ahead of the Circle-U drive, she'd see other drives converging on the trail to turn north.

The Circle-U approached Austin, the Texas capital, traveling through a comparatively level country dotted with hackberry trees, oak and redbuds. Urquhart rode ahead to survey the Colorado River and judge its condition. That night he told the others: "The Colorado has been on a rampage from rains in the north. Several herds have been held up, waiting for the river to drop. There were three herds waiting when I left, but they likely got across this afternoon, or they'll make it in the morning. I checked on a point three miles below Austin and it looks best for entering the herd: an easy approach and not too steep banks on the opposite shore. Two miles or so this side of the Colorado, there's Onion Creek. We'll plan to get there before noon, water the cows, then graze 'em a while before we strike the Colorado."

Cordano nodded. "Theese ees *bueno*, Senor Major. By then, the sun is pass' overhead and ees at the back of the cows. No cattle is like to swim the reever weeth the sun in hees eyes."

"If the whole kit and caboodle of us don't have trouble," Graveyard Hogan said pessimistically, "I'll be surprised. Never swum a river yet I didn't get wet."

"That's down-right amazin'," Rusty Gates drawled.

"Must be the water has somethin' to do with it."

Laughter circled the campfire. Magpie Vogel told about a river he'd crossed, one time, that was so alkali he'd come out dry. Tom Yeagle put in. "By the way, Major, next time we kill a beef for chuck, what say we get rid of either that big black steer, or that yaller line-back. They both of 'em insist on leadin' this drive and—"

Urquhart considered. "Maybe we can profit from that feud. If they're both anxious to be out in front, neither one's going to want the other to get ahead when it comes to entering a river. Once the leaders are in, the rest generally follow. Once in, that line-back and black aren't going to have time for any feuding. They'll be too busy keeping their heads above water."

The following morning, Jennifer, Dix and the chuckwagon were already across Onion Creek when the herd arrived at ten o'clock. Jennifer heard Urquhart shout to the point riders. "Head your leaders down this creek, so the cattle that come up later won't have muddied water to drink!" He spurred along the line of march to give orders to the swing men. The cattle were held back until the advance animals had been strung out along the creek. Then these were pushed across and, when the water had cleared, the remainder of the herd was allowed to quench its thirst.

Jennifer asked Dix: "Is the Colorado River deep?"

"When it's high, like Rius says. But I reckon we'll get across all right."

She noticed he appeared troubled. "Dix, the men swim their horses across. How do they keep their clothing dry?" He replied that they wouldn't. Jennifer continued, "I've heard of men stripping to underwear and tying their clothing to their backs." That was true, but this time— "Dix, they don't have to get their clothing wet on my account. You tell them I said so. I won't be anywhere near them." "Trouble is," Dix blurted, "I got to get you across. And I'll be sticking closer than a burr to a bronc's tail."

"Look here," Jennifer said impatiently, "this is no time for foolish modesty. Remember, I learned to cross rivers on my way to Texas. We'll make out all right."

"I reckon. Rius says there's a small raft at the Colorado that somebody built to ferry supplies across. We'll work out somethin' for you." He mounted and went to consult Urquhart.

As soon as every man had eaten dinner, the chuckwagon was reloaded and sent ahead, with Jennifer and Dix riding on either side. By the time the south bank of the Colorado was reached, the previous herds Urquhart had mentioned had crossed and were out of sight. The wagon and the two riders started down the gradual slope leading toward shore. The footing beneath the horses was soggy and the wagon wheels cut deeply into turf. Corbillat signaled the Negro to stop. Jennifer eyed the wide, yellow-grey river as it flowed swiftly, though not turbulently, by. An occasional chunk of driftwood, or a broken branch, sailed past. Across the moving, light-flecked water stretched a grassy bank and trees. Jennifer glanced at Corbillat's features, heavy with concern. "Dix, if you and I started now, you could return to lend a hand with the herd."

"I was sort of considerin' that, but I dunno—"

Jennifer didn't wait. Dismounting, she climbed past Albumen and into the chuck-wagon, emerging within a few minutes in a flowing calico dress which, when she mounted astride, was voluminous enough to cover her legs. Her riding skirt, boots and other clothing made a compact bundle across her shoulders. Dix and the Negro stared. "I told you I was an old hand at crossing rivers," Jennifer smiled.

"Jehovah on the Mountain," Corbillat exploded. "I believe you're enjoyin' this business."

Jennifer sobered. "Perhaps I could, under some circumstances, Dix... Come on, time's a-wasting." Corbillat turned his horse and disappeared on the opposite side of the chuck-wagon. When he returned he was in red underwear and boots, with a blanket modestly folded across his lap and his sombrero yanked down to his eye-brows. His face was the color of his underwear. "I'm ready," he said hastily, and the two started their horses toward the river.

The Negro sat staring. He watched them urge the horses into the river. The water rose as the animals advanced, stepping gingerly. Then, quite suddenly, the horses were swimming strongly, the two riders wet to their thighs, as the swift current carried them rapidly downstream. They reached the middle of the muddy Colorado, and when beyond the force of the main center current, turned the horses upstream. A few minutes later, Albumen saw the horses climbing up the opposite bank.

"We made it!" Jennifer exclaimed, shivering a little,

as Dix dismounted. "Go ahead back any time you like." She started for a nearby brush to change into dry clothing.

Corbillat said, "Keep your eyes peeled for rattlers," then directed his pony toward the cottonwood raft he'd spied when they emerged from the water. By the time he'd dismounted, he saw three riders just entering the Colorado on the opposite side, and decided to wait. By the time the riders reached the middle of the stream, he saw they were Yeagle, Gates and Weber, all in underwear and hats. Emerging, horses and men dripping, the three lost no time discarding the bundles of clothing and helping Corbillat: tying ropes to the four corners of the raft, they sent their horses splashing into the river for the return trip.

Jennifer emerged from the brush and spread her wet things to dry in the sun. The raft was nearly across, and the first cattle were topping a rise less than a mile from the opposite shore. She shaded her eyes against the glare from the river, saw the riders drag the raft out on the opposite bank, then loosen ropes and ride to meet the cattle. The herd came steadily on, the big black steer in the lead. He hesitated only momentarily before plunging in, the yellow line-back close at his shoulders, and the other cattle followed without pause.

The cattle sank lower in the water, until only heads and wide-spread horns showed above the surface. Jennifer watched as the cattle flowed into the Colorado. The steers, as they swam, formed a great U-shaped chain of bobbing heads and horns, as the current at the middle of the Colorado bulged their normally straight line, while the riders, swimming higher above the surface on either side, pointed the beasts upstream when the current's strength had been passed. Shortly, the first cattle were emerging from the water, fifty yards below the point at which Jennifer sat.

Once all the herd had reached the northern point of the Colorado, riders crossed and recrossed: the *remuda* and chuck-wagon mules followed the cattle. While part of the crew held the steers in "loose herd," grazing along the river, others brought Albumen and other equipment, over on the raft, towing on ropes stretched to saddlehorns. In similar fashion, the wagon was floated to the near shore, hauled up on the bank and deposited. The men, in their soaking underwear hastily loosened ropes and scattered to dress.

Albumen started supper. The afternoon had passed swiftly, and the Colorado was molten gold beneath the setting sun. "Thank Moses on the Mountain!" Corbillat exclaimed. "We're across! Another seven hundred miles should see us in Kansas." Jennifer remarked that everything went well. Dix agreed, "We lost only two cows. One of the steers got panicky and tried to climb out on another critter. The two got to churnin' and both went under. Hogan headed to straighten 'em out, and in the fracas got spilled outten his saddle. He got safe, though. Cows are all right so long's they keep their heads above water. Once under, they lose hope. I saw the two that went down come up farther on, but they was both floatin' without movement. Rius says we're goin' to lay over a day. The wagon's got to go to Austin for supplies. Then, on to Abilene!"

6

THE HERD PROGRESSED STEADILY NORTHWARD, PASSING over rolling land carpeted with wildflowers. Jennifer now was accepted as one of the outfit, and when other outfits were contacted, the Circle-U hands boasted of their lady crewmember who rode and nursed when necessary. More and more herds were to be observed along the wide trail stretching to Kansas; occasionally one of them would be delayed at the side of the trail and there would be visiting between the oufits. Jennifer's appearance never failed to excite interest. Some days it rained, bringing relief from the dust of the drive. But when the mud grew heavy underfoot and the cattle bedded uneasily on damp earth, the outfit was glad to welcome hot days once more. And always, at night, there was the continual yip-yipping of coyotes along the skyline.

The weather turned dry. Creeks showed only thin trickles of moisture across sandy bottoms. A discontented bawling rose from the cattle. A thick haze of dust hovered along the trail. Throats became parched and nostrils caked. Gritty particles worked into the food. The men accepted the ordeal with a minimum of grumbling; it was part of trail-herding. Urquhart scanned the sky incessantly for rain-clouds, but though great thunder-heads were seen daily in the north and west, no rain arrived.

There came a day when the cattle had no water at all. At one stream-bed it was necessary to dig a well to procure alkali-tainted water to fill the water-barrel. The following day, the wagon was driven parallel with the herd, for the convenience of dust-encrusted riders whose trips to the wagon became ever more frequent. The *remuda* ponies tired quickly, necessitating numerous changes. Grasses lacked succulence; the cattle's ribs showed plainly through gaunt hides. Weaker animals dropped, by twos and threes, along the trail. Within a week, the Circle-U had lost a hundred head. But ever the herd crawled north, making some days but few miles, and always soaring buzzards hovered greedily above.

They passed through a series of dry arroyos. Corbillat told Jennifer, "We got to have water for these cows soon. They're losin' tallow fast."

The next day—May was three-quarters done—when they arrived at the Brazos River, they found a raging torrent, and seven herds from Texas waiting for the river to go down. The herds were being held at widely spaced points: no trail driver wanted to risk his cattle getting mixed with animals of another outfit. One of the outfits carried a big flat-bottomed scow on a wagon hauled by six oxen, for the purpose of ferrying supplies and equipment across rivers, but the scow was useless so long as the raging Brazos prevented the swimming of animals. The following day, another of the outfits, anxious to be on its way, endeavored to cross. A rider was swept from his horse and drowned and a great many cows lost before the trail-boss ordered the outfit back, deciding to wait longer.

Urquhart ordered the Circle-U a distance away from

other herds. Camp was made in a grove of tall elms, until such time as crossing could be made. A town of two thousand population, called Waco, was a few miles off.

One night, as Jennifer sat on the wagon seat, Urquhart left the fire and came around to the front of the wagon. He could see her form through the gloom and could almost feel the hostility of her eyes. He stood near one wheel, gazing up at her. "Jennifer, would it accomplish anything for me to tell you I've acted like a fool?"

"Only that you'd reached a decision I was aware of the day we left," she replied tartly.

His words were humble, "Would it do any good to ask forgiveness?" He reached for her hand, but she withdrew it. "Can't we even be friends?"

"This trouble was not of my making," the girl stated coldly.

"It's not in your nature to be cruel. I can't understand why you insist on acting like this."

"That is a very foolish thing to say. Think back; I do not believe you will have the least trouble understanding."

He drew a sigh. "I know. You swore you'd make me regret bringing you. You're having your revenge."

"I've been told," Jennifer said tersely, "that a desire for revenge is an Indian trait."

"I didn't say that," Urquhart flared.

"No, but you were thinking it," the girl said shrewdly and withdrew into the wagon.

The recent ordeals of the drive combined with the

girl's intractability brought a rush of anger to Urquhart. "You'd best return. I can place you on a stagecoach bound south from Waco and—"

"I do not wish to return," Jennifer interrupted.

"Perhaps I shall make you—" he commenced hotly.

Her short laugh was biting. "Have you learned nothing, Darius? You threatened force once before, and you see what it has brought you."

"Very well. It is understood you will continue with us."

She replied quietly, "You seem to have been the only one in doubt on that score. Now please go away. I wish to sleep."

Urquhart left the wagon and was joined by Corbillat. Corbillat said, "Well?"

Urquhart shook his head. "It's no good. She refuses to go back. I thought on account of her grand-parents—"

"Miss Jen's not worried about her kinfolks. What you got to understand, Rius, is that she's mad as hell at you. It ain't just you bringin' her with us. Can't you think of nothin' else that made her mad?"

"Nothing I care to talk about."

Two days later, the Brazos River dropped somewhat, and the other outfits got across. Urquhart wanted to wait longer, but following herds piled up at the rear. Finally, he gave orders to fell four cottonwoods and, when the logs were trimmed, two were lashed at each side of the chuck-wagon, and the vehicle floated across. The rest got over in safety, though twelve steers were drowned in the swirling currents.

The outfit picked up Aquilla Creek where it flowed into the Brazos and followed its course two days. Once more the slogan, "Stir up the dust!" resounded the length of the herd as it flowed, serpent-like, between low hills and across prairies. Nothing met the eye except fathomless sky and great stretches of level prairie, bringing to Jennifer an impression of a world so vast and wide and empty that nothing there existed except the steadily moving herd and riders. Yet she had only to shift in her saddle to see on the distant horizon the low rising dust of some following herd. There were further evidences that men and animals had come this way: crude crosses above bare mounds of black waxy earth, the skeletons of cows picked clean by coyotes; twice they had seen the charred remnants of burned chuck-wagons.

At Urquhart's suggestion Corbillat got a six-shooter from the wagon, and insisted on Jennifer wearing it. Each day he gave instructions in loading and firing the weapon. Once Texas was behind, the trail would lead through the Indian Nations country, and no man could say whether the redskins would be friendly or hostile.

It was early June when they came into the Trinity River valley and crossed the river near Fort Worth, a helter-skelter collection of low structures built along one bank. A stop was made only long enough to purchase needed supplies. In time they struck the Cross Timbers country. The prairie assumed a more undulating aspect; tree-lined creeks became numerous and there was more timber to be seen.

One morning when the herd had been less than two

hours on the trail Urquhart, riding in advance of the point men, glanced through the trees lining a creek and detected movement in the brush. He saw two horses on which Jennifer and Corbillat had left camp after breakfast, but by now the two should be well in advance. He wheeled his buckskin from the trail, calling to Hogan as he passed, "Keep 'em moving. I'll catch you before long," and directed his mount through the trees.

Minutes later he saw that his surmise had been correct. Dix and Jennifer had dismounted and were standing talking to a hollow-cheeked young Indian woman in a long soiled buckskin garment, moccasins, and some sort of beaded headband. Tethered nearby were a pair of ratty-looking ponies, and but a few yards off a low shelter had been erected of leaves and branches.

Relief crossed Corbillat's features when he saw Urquhart ride up. Jennifer continued talking to the Indian woman.

"Woman with a sick husband in that shelter," Corbillat explained. "No, it's not smallpox. Lungs. The woman hailed us when we came by. Miss Jen is aimin' to stay."

"Stay here?" Urquhart exclaimed. "I couldn't allow that. It wouldn't be safe."

Jennifer turned swiftly, "Darius, the man is sick. They've been here two weeks. Their food has given out. The woman has hailed several outfits, but no one would stop—"

"But Jennifer, we can't leave you here. The herd must keep going—"

"They're Cherokees, Darius. My own people, in a way. I can't leave them. Can't you understand?" Urquhart nodded reluctantly. He asked for more information. Jennifer continued. "They left the Indian Nations to travel to their home, near Tyler, Texas. He became ill on the way. It's nothing serious, right now. He's had some congestion of the lungs, but that's about cleared up. There's fever, of course. If that were broken and they had food, I think he'd be better in a day or so. If I could have some quinine from the wagon and some food—?"

Urquhart walked to the shelter, stooped and peered within. A gaunt Indian with flushed cheeks, lay on a pair of ragged blankets spread on the earth. Nearby lay an ancient flintlock rifle, an iron cooking pot and a bundle of some sort, wrapped in a stained section of canvas, lashed with rawhide. Urquhart straightened and turned away. The young squaw followed him with worried eyes. Jennifer spoke again, pointing to an unstrung bow and quiver of arrows hanging on a willow branch. "The woman says she shot a rabbit, four days ago, but no more small animals have come near the camp. And they've no powder or lead for the gun—"

Urquhart broke in gruffly, "Well, I guess we'll have to leave you for a day or so. You can overtake us later. We'll wait at Red River until—" He broke off. "Ask the woman what condition the Red was in when they crossed."

Jennifer addressed the woman in fluent Cherokee. The reply came accompanied by many gestures. "She says," Jennifer translated, "the river was bank-full, when they were there. A floating tree knocked her man from his horse and he was nearly drowned. That brought on the sickness."

"If we have luck, the Red will be down by the time we reach it," Urquhart remarked grimly. "All right, Jennifer, Dix will remain with you. When the Negro comes along with the wagon, get your blankets and take what medicine and food you need."

"Thank you, Darius," Jennifer replied quietly. "Could I have one of my cows to give them?"

Urquhart spoke to Corbillat. "Dix, when the drags come along, pick out one of the lame critters."

Jennifer spoke as he was getting into the saddle. "You are being very kind, Darius. I'm beholden to you."

He looked at her a long minute. "The obligation is still all on my side," he answered, and spurred his buckskin to overtake the herd.

7

TWO DAYS PASSED BEFORE URQUHART COMMENCED glancing back from time to time. He was riding in advance of the herd. The big black steer had stayed in the lead of the drive, the yellow line-back gradually acknowledging defeat by falling back. A strong wind blew from the west, the dust lifting from beneath the cattle half smothering the swing, flank and drag men on the lee side of the steers, as the long tan ribbon of horned heads moved steadily north. Now and then, when riders could no longer stand the thick hot dust, they changed sides with riders on the windward side.

It was getting on toward three o'clock when, looking back, Urquhart saw Corbillat approaching. "Glad to see you again, Dix." There was distinct relief in Urquhart's tones. "Where's Jennifer?"

"She stopped at the wagon to leave some stuff—say, you've had trouble. Peters tells me the herd run on you."

"Stampeded to beat hell,"—irritably. "The night we left you behind. We spent that night and most next day getting 'em rounded up again. I don't know what started 'em. Vogel and Weber were on night herd. Vogel swears that he heard something like somebody flapping a blanket at the rim of the bedding grounds, but you know how he is."

"Sure, Vogel talks a heap, but in a case like this—Did Weber hear anything out of the ordinary?"

"No, but he thinks he saw a rider. At the time he thought it was Vogel, but Vogel was nowhere near the spot where Shorty thought he saw him. I guess their imaginations got away from them. It's my guess a coyote got into the herd, and spooked 'em into running."

"Maybe," Corbillat said, "Vogel and Weber weren't wrong. This morning, Jennifer and I passed the Diamond-Q outfit and, later, the Ox-Yoke-A. Both have had similar trouble. They'd heard rumors about cow-thieves stampedin' herds and stealin' cows in the confusion."

"Where do these thieves dispose of the cattle they steal?"

Corbillat replied, "There's a heap of places thieves could place the critters. Stolen cows could be held to make up a herd to drive to Abilene, late in the season, after the legal owners had left for home. You ain't said how many head *we're* short."

"One hundred ninety-three." Corbillat spat an oath. Urquhart continued, "There was a bad section of broken country west of where we bedded down that night—about half erosion and timber brakes. I don't think we'd been in our blankets ten minutes, before we heard a sudden bawling and the rush of hoofs. There was a lot of yelling, but I don't know who did it. We were out of beds and into saddles almost as quick as I'm telling it. Once we caught up with the herd, we tried to head 'em north, but the cows had started west and there was no stoppin' 'em. They must have run four miles before we got 'em checked."

Through the dust boiling up at their rear came the sounds of thudding hoofs, snapping of quirt and a burst of profanity from Tom Yeagle: "Get back in step, you long-horned, slobberin,' bawlin', four-legged son-of-a-pitch-me-over-the-back-fence, or you won't never live to see Abilene." When the sounds had diminished, Corbillat asked, "Rius, you didn't see any sign indicatin' strange riders?"

"It never occurred to me to look for sign. Sure, there were plenty hoofprints about, but I never dreamed any of them might not be made by Circle-U riders. What you've told me, Dix, makes the stampede more plausible. I couldn't understand it before; this herd isn't flighty like some herds. From now on we'll have to watch that much closer." He drew a bandanna from his pocket, mopped his sweat-and-dust streaked face. "What about that sick Indian? Did he get well?"

Corbillat said admiringly, "Miss Jen should have been a doctor. From the minute she got quinine into that buck, he began to sweat and the fever quit. Toward night she fixed him some soup. In between times, she and I went off a way, and she practiced with that cap-and-ball. She can load by herself—and shoot! If we do have trouble goin' through the Nations, she'll give a good account of herself. I told her to keep it loaded at all times—" Urquhart interrupted to remind Dix he'd been talking about the sick Indian. Dix nodded. "That buck will make out, all right. He was sittin' up by the time we pulled out. I helped the squaw butcher that beef we gave 'em, so they'll be fixed for rations. At night, while Miss Jen was tendin' the sick man, me'n the squaw would sit by the fire and *habla* Cherokee. I was gettin' right rusty and it took me some diggin' to remember the right words."

Urquhart said, "Did you say Jennifer stopped at the wagon?"

Corbillat said, "Yeah, she wanted to drop the duds off." Urquhart asked what duds? "When we left the Injuns, they were right grateful. The squaw brought out a bundle which she gave to Miss Jen. When that bundle was unwrapped, I tell you, Rius, I never saw such elegant beadwork. It must have been the squaw's weddin' outfit—all made of the finest tanned doeskin I ever see, with leggin's and moccasins to match, and some beaded doodads for the braids, with feathers and fixin's, not to mention some little buffalo-horn boxes with paint in 'em—"

"Now what in the name of God," Urquhart inquired, "will Jennifer do with a costume like that?"

"I ain't the least idea and neither has she. But the squaw insisted on her takin' it, and Miss Jen didn't want to hurt her feelin's. Well, that's that. If we don't strike any more hard luck, we'll put into Abilene in prime shape. I was afraid a drive like this would whup her down, but Miss Jen seems to thrive on it. She's got brown as an Injun—even fillin' out some, seems to me."

Urquhart remarked, frowning, that he'd not seen enough of the girl to notice. "She rides off with you every morning, and turns in at night, right after supper. Dix, while you were away—did Jennifer say anything about me?"

Corbillat replied, "Your name was mentioned only once, Rius—something was said about you actin' kind to that sick man and his squaw. You didn't hurt yourself none in her eyes, only I wouldn't go pressin' the advantage. Give her time, she'll come 'round all right. There ain't no filly yet was ever gentled by rough handlin'—not pure strains, leastwise, and if Miss Jen ain't a thoroughbred, I never seen one."

"You talk," Urquhart observed dryly, "like quite an authority on the female sex, Dix. For a confirmed bachelor, you appear to know things that never occurred to me."

"That explains why I'm a confirmed bachelor," Corbillat grinned. "You mull it over, Rius. I'm goin' back and pick up Miss Jen." He reined his pony around and headed toward the rear of the trudging line of cattle.

That evening at supper Jennifer mentioned the sick Indian and thanked Urquhart for the supplies. Urquhart said quietly that he was glad to be of help. There the subject was dropped, though later he wondered if he had detected a lessening of hostility in the smoky-gentian eyes.

There were extra guards placed over both the herd and *remuda* from then on, but of stampedes and cow-thieves there came no further sign. The Circle-U outfit drew near Red River. The crew had looked forward with some apprehension to the crossing of the Red, but it was soon obvious that there would be no difficulty in negotiating the stream: its dark current flowed placidly by. The only delay in crossing was occasioned by the time required to fell logs to be lashed either side of the chuck-wagon. Then, while Jennifer and Albumen sat high and dry on the driver's seat, the wagon was towed across at the ends of ropes, drawn by riders on swimming ponies. The big black steer took the water without hesitation, and the rest of the herd followed, only nine head of stock—lame, sore-footed creatures—being lost in the crossing.

The Circle-U had at last put Texas at its rear!

8

AHEAD STRETCHED THE FIVE NATIONS COUNTRY, so-called from the five principal Indian tribes inhabiting the Territory: the Cherokee, Chicksaw, Creek, Seminole and Choctaw. Another month's travel should see the Circle-U in Kansas. Day after day, beneath blazing suns, the herd, like a great dusty serpent, moved steadily north, flowing up slopes and descending in smooth undulation, or winding around the summits of hills. Riders toiled relentlessly on either flank, unshaven features streaked with dust and sweat, while the drifting red haze rising above pounding hoofs and clacking horns of the cattle, settled thickly in the folds of bandannas drawn over mouths and nostrils, and lay a heavy powdery coating on saddle trappings. Parched throats became channels of heated sandpaper.

Jennifer and Corbillat were riding well in advance of the herd on a clear sunny morning with the dew not yet off the buffalo grass. "Dix," asked Jennifer, "do you think we'll have any trouble with Indians?"

"I don't know why we should," Dix replied evasively. "The Five Nations are friendly these days. 'Course, there's other tribes comin' into the Territory now, but they can generally be bought off with the gift of a cow or two."

Each day's travel produced fresh sights for Jennifer: prairie dog villages were passed. Jackrabbits popped suddenly from beneath tangled brush to go bouncing in zigzagging leaps across grassy stretches. A buffalo-hunters' camp, with brown pelts pegged flat on the earth to dry, was seen one day. The two men at the camp gaped open-mouthed at sight of a woman riding through this vast country. Farther along, buffalo-hunters were occasionally passed. Lean, keen-eyed men these, with long Sharps rifles and their wagons loaded with stinking hides, escorted always by a cloud of flies.

The herd followed the Washita River valley and climbed to plains. One day, Jennifer and Corbillat, a mile or more ahead of the cattle, saw approaching a small body of mounted U.S. troopers, led by an Indian scout in wide hat and fringed buckskin. The troopers pulled to a halt, while the scout and a lieutenant came to meet the riders. At sight of the hated Yankee uniforms, Corbillat stiffened. "Yank bas—bas—buzzards!" he exclaimed.

"Easy, Dix," Jennifer said. "Just remember the war's over."

The men eyed Jennifer curiously, touching fingers to their hats, as they drew to a halt. After stating they were scouting out of Fort Gibson, the officer addressed Dix. Corbillat gave the required information: they were with the Circle-U herd, traveling from south Texas to Abilene; he was Dixon Corbillat; Miss Keating owned cows in the herd; the Circle-U was operated by Darius Urquhart, who was riding with the cattle a mile to the rear. Corbillat concluded, "No reason we shouldn't pass, is there?"

"Not a reason in the world," the officer replied. His eyes went to Jennifer and he smiled. "I don't think you'll have any trouble, Corbillat."

"We're just passin' on a warnin'," the Indian scout said bluntly. "Chief Iron Wolf of the Cheyennes, broke out a few months back and raided along the Republican River, up in Kansas, then him and his braves scooted down into the Territory. Since then, he's been joined up by Tall Raven, of the Arapahoes, and Lone Cloud, of the Kiowa Tribe." The scout spat a long brown stream. "I don't reckon you people got anythin' to fear from them varmints, 'cause I cal'clate 'em to be west of here, but we got word that Yellow Drum, one of Iron Wolf's men, has cut loose on his own, with about five-score followers. Thar's a chance he might be makin' this region his stampin'-grounds."

The officer spoke again, "There's no need detaining you. I'll speak with Mr. Urquhart when we meet him." He and the scout touched fingers to their hats and the soldiers rode south amid a cloud of dust and the sounds of clattering sabers and trotting hoofs.

Corbillat and Jennifer urged their ponies on. Jennifer said quietly, "Dix, it looks as though we might see a little excitement."

Dix scowled blackly. "That fool scout hadn't no need spillin' that talk in front of you." Jennifer pointed out she wasn't disturbed. Corbillat went on, "It don't signify a thing. A lot of these scouts get the army dunces stirred up over Injun scares, so's they can make an easy livin' off'n the government."

The remainder of the day they rode close to the chuck-wagon. Albumen wasn't sent ahead to prepare camp as usual. Urquhart scouted continually in advance of the herd, though when he came into camp for supper, he admitted there hadn't been sign of an Indian to be seen. That night, Jennifer noticed the men about the campfire were unusually silent and that the guard on herd and *remuda* had been doubled.

9

THE NIGHT PASSED WITH NO DISTURBANCE. AT BREAK-fast, Jennifer saw signs of relief in the unshaven faces about the fire, though she saw as well that each man looked carefully to his six-shooter.

By the time the sun rose, all the riders except Corbillat were out with the cattle which were still peacefully grazing. Revas had driven the *remuda* to the vicinity of the herd, leaving Corbillat's grey and Jennifer's pinto saddled and waiting. Jennifer announced she was ready to ride. "No rush," Dix said. "We'll be sidin' the wagon, today, and the wagon will be stickin' to the herd. Rius wants that we stay bunched for a couple of days, and not get scattered—" He stopped abruptly, then "God-dlemighty!" burst from his lips. "Injuns!"

Jennifer heard the chorus of wild yelling on the morning air. Glancing beyond the herd of cattle she saw a band of some hundred painted warriors sweeping down the slope on loping ponies. She heard Urquhart's far-off voice, through the bawling of cattle, as he shouted orders to herd the steers into a compact mass. Corbillat had spun toward his horse, then he halted. Jennifer said quietly, "Go ahead, Dix. I'll be all right with Albumen."

Corbillat shook his head. "I'd best wait until I see what Rius wants."

The Negro scurried into the wagon and returned bearing an old Confederate cap-and-ball. "Any raid-skin comes to 'pestin' around dis fellow," Albumen stated calmly, "is li'ble get heself destructed."

Jennifer watched the proceedings. The Indians had come to a full stop and sat their ponies facing the cattle, as though to bar progress. One, apparently the chief, had halted a few paces in front of his followers. Jennifer saw the buckskin horse move out from the cattle, as Urquhart, one arm raised palm outward, rode to meet the chief. She saw the chief hand something to Urquhart, above which he bent his head, as though reading from a sheet of paper. Then he returned it. The parley continued. From time to time, the redskins raised their voices in fierce yells, as though to intimidate the whites. The sun glinted on moving lance points; feathers waved in the morning breeze. Urquhart turned and spoke over his shoulder. An instant later, Yeagle came loping swiftly toward the wagon and dismounted.

"What's Rius want?" Corbillat demanded.

"Major says for you and Miss Keating to line out fast, the minute trouble breaks—"

"You figure it's due to break, Tom?"

"Maybe yes, maybe no," Yeagle replied. Corbillat shot another question. "I ain't sure," Yeagle replied, "though judging from that divided head-dress some are wearin', I figure 'em as Cheyennes. None of 'em speak American, so the Major can't make headway. Maybe they're just pretendin'. The chief has got a paper some-body wrote—"

"What's it say?" Corbillat interrupted.

"Says he is Yellow Drum, a good Injun—"

"That's the Injun that scout warned about yes-terday—"

"—and he demands toll for crossin' his lands."

"What sort of toll?" Corbillat demanded.

"He made sign he wants a hundred cows. If we give in, he'll probably take more. What you goin' to do when you can't talk to the son-of-a-gun?"

"Maybe somebody in the band can *habla* Cherokee," Corbillat broke in. "Tom, you stay here with Miss Jen. At the first sign of shootin', you take out with her, *pronto!* That's orders!" Corbillat ran to his horse calling over one shoulder as he departed, "Albumen, catch yourself a mule, and leave when they do . . ." His voice drifted off on the wind. Jennifer, Yeagle and the Negro stood looking after Corbillat's fast-departing form. Jennifer asked, "Do you think Dix will be able to accomplish anything?"

"I misdoubt it, miss. Those Injuns've got the jump on us, and they ain't in a frame of mind to listen to no white man."

Jennifer turned impulsively and climbed into the wagon.

By this time, Corbillat had reached the herd. His gaze ran over the assembled Indians, noting first they were well mounted, with feathers and bits of colored cloth twined in the manes and tails of the ponies; few had saddles, folded blankets and buffalo-hair filled pads serving instead. They were armed with bows-and-arrows, sharp-pointed lances and round shields covered with tough hide. Some had repeating rifles, many carried coup sticks—long peeled willow wands, with feathers fastened at the small end—denoting domination of an enemy. Most of the warriors were naked, except for moccasins, breech-clouts and various ornaments; a few wore war-bonnets of crow and eagle feathers; some displayed but a single feather dangling slant-wise from scalp-lock. Remnants of old army uniforms, both Confederate and Federal, were seen. A few wore faded slouch hats with feathers jutting from crowns. All the Indians, and many ponies, were painted with slashes of red and yellow.

Corbillat reined in at Urquhart's side, facing the horde of savages. "I left Tom to look after Miss Jen. What's the situation?"

"I've tried to arrange a parley, but they either can't understand, or they refuse to. The chief gave his name, Yellow Drum; beyond that he refuses to talk. They keep yelling *'Wo-ha!'*—"

"Which means 'beef' in any Injun language."

"Yellow Drum's paper states he demands one hundred beeves. Yellow Drum has produced another paper which he got from somebody signing himself, Andy Tomkins, trail-boss of the 2-X-Slash outfit. This Tomkins writes that Yellow Drum jumped him two weeks ago, and took most of his *remuda,* in addition to cows and food. Tomkins may have given it to the redskin to warn other herds Yellow Drum means business. I don't like the looks of this."

"We're agreed. You don't figure we better fight?"

"We're outnumbered. One shot from us and we'd be smothered. I wish to God Jennifer wasn't with us. I guess we'll have to hand over a hundred beeves and feel lucky if they don't take more—"

Corbillat glanced toward the bawling cows. Hogan sat his horse a short distance away, one hand already gripping the butt of his gun. Other riders were spaced evenly around the herd, trying to hold it in check. "Those cows are gettin' uneasy. If they should take out to run—"

"What these Indians are waiting for," Urquhart deplored. "Once these cows stampeded, God only knows what might happen."

"Exactly what I was thinkin'," Corbillat nodded. "Let me see if I can remember enough Cherokee to make some of these bastuds understand what we want."

"You can try," Urquhart nodded. "Tell them we'll give ten cows as a gift, no more. A bluff might turn the trick."

Corbillat stepped his pony forward and addressed Yellow Drum in halting Cherokee. The chief was an ugly-visaged man with ponderous brown shoulders and a huge pot-belly, naked to his breech-clout. Loosely gathered about his hips was a blue blanket, from beneath which protruded bare legs and moccasined feet. Various portions of his greasy anatomy were striped in vivid green, red and yellow ochre; his heavy-lidded beady eyes, below the war-bonnet, were predatory. He listened contemptuously while Corbillat talked, and finally uttered a single derisive grunt. Immediately, there rose from the hundred throats at his rear scornful yells, and demands for *"Wo-ha!"* Corbillat asked Urquhart, "Did you try givin' 'em tobacco?"

"Yellow Drum accepted what we had on hand, but when Hogan offered his pipe, it was refused."

"I don't like it," Corbillat said, "When an Injun won't take a pipe, it spells trouble. I'll try again."

The yelling died somewhat. Corbillat raised his voice, asking if no one understood Cherokee? All he received by way of answer was more yelling, the demand for *"Wo-ha!"* rising above other sounds.

"Beef they insist on, and beef we'll have to give 'em," Urquhart said hopelessly, "and just count ourselves fortunate we're not scalped in the bargain."

"It certain looks that way."

Yellow Drum belched and shifted his bulk on the pony's back. Guttural phrases rolled from his wide mouth. There was a movement among the Indians as they made way for several scowling bucks, armed with rifles. These drew rein on either side of the chief. The big Cheyenne pounded his chest with clenched fist and spoke impatient demanding words, his ominous manner signifying far more than the actual import of: "Yellow Drum—*Wo-ha!*"

"Well," Urquhart observed with quiet resignation. "I guess that's clear enough for any man. Pass the word, Dix, to cut out a hundred beeves—"

"Wait!" Dix interrupted. Excited exclamations rose from the Indian horde, several of whom were pointing toward the chuck-wagon.

Urquhart turned his gaze toward the wagon, a frown gathering on his face, as he noted a single Indian riding slowly out from the vehicle. How in the devil, Urquhart asked himself, had that buck got 'way over there, unnoticed? As the rider drew near he saw it was no buck—

"That's Miss Jen's pinto," Corbillat exclaimed.

Urquhart groaned. "That's Jennifer in the saddle—!"

"She's wearin' those duds that sick Cherokee's squaw gave her," Corbillat interrupted excitedly.

Urquhart's voice shook. "Dix—ride like hell—tell her to get back to the wagon."

"Too late. The Injuns have seen it's a woman. Now there will be hell to pay and no pitch hot! Wait, Rius— Miss Jen's smart. She's got somethin' in mind. These bucks might listen to her."

The Indians fell silent. White men and Indians sat their horses without movement, as Jennifer slowly walked the spotted black-and-white pinto in their direction, something proud, imperious, in her manner. A knee-length doeskin garment, embroidered in colored needle-work and trimmed with polished elk-teeth and red porcupine quills, hung from her erect shoulders, and was gathered loosely at the waist with a belt of red and yellow stained horsehair. Fringe ran along the sleeves; more fringe ornamented the doeskin leggings. Jennifer's moccasins were encrusted with beadwork. Her midnight hair, braided in two thick strands, hung before her shoulders, the ends encased in small beaded sleeves, showing plumes of black hair below. A necklace of bearclaws was about her slim throat; designs in yellow and red were painted on her cheeks. A single vermilion line ran down her scalp at the parting of the hair.

"By Gawd, if that don't bring out her Injun blood," Corbillat exclaimed admiringly. "Rius, she's plumb magnificent!"

Urquhart, as though hypnotized, didn't reply. The Indians were completely silent, every eye on the approaching girl. There was the bearing of a princess in her erect form as she walked the pony within speaking distance. Her tones, when she addressed the two white men, were sharp, as though she were speaking to menials. Urquhart's jaw went slack.

Jennifer neck-reined the pony to a position slightly in advance of Corbillat and Urquhart, facing Yellow Drum and his painted braves. For a long minute she sat looking intently at the Cheyenne warrior, her figure very straight and proud, a contemptuous anger in her cold gaze. Yellow Drum managed for a few moments to meet her eyes, then commenced to blink uneasily. Abruptly, harsh, biting words in Cherokee spilled rapidly from Jennifer's lips.

Yellow Drum touched his ear and shook his head, signifying he couldn't understand. Swiftly, Jennifer touched her out-thrust tongue with one finger, then raised two fingers in the air.

"She's usin' sign-language," Corbillat said. "She says Yellow Drum speaks with two tongues. In other words, he's a liar. There she goes again." The girl was making further involved movements with her hands.

241

Yellow Drum was also using sign-language, now, but his movements were slower, as though he were being heckled and couldn't get in a word edgewise.

"Well," Urquhart demanded impatiently, "what's up?"

Corbillat shook his head. "I don't know enough sign-language to make out. You can depend on one thing, Miss Jen is sure givin' Yellow Drum hell!"

Yellow Drum realized he was being worsted. He grunted a command to someone at the rear. A greasy buck with three feathers in his stringy locks and a dirty white shirt hanging below the breech-clout, guided his pony to the chief's side and spoke to Jennifer.

"He's talkin' Cherokee," Corbillat said. "Says his name is Knife-in-the-Wind and that he will interpret. I thought it was damn' funny none of this band could *habla* Cherokee."

"Hush up. What's Jennifer saying?"

Corbillat listened intently, while the early morning sun slanted across the assemblage of Indians, whites and cattle. Feathers fluttered in the breeze and sharp glinting lights flashed briefly from moving bits of metal. Jennifer's words came clear and firm, her tones assertive, demanding. "She says," Corbillat translated slowly, "that she is *Uniskwetúgi Unega*—meanin' White May-Apple—daughter of a great medicine man and a member of the *Ani'wa'ya*—that's Wolf—Clan, of the Cherokees. The herd, Miss Jen says, belongs to her, and—my Gawd, Rius—she says you and me and the other hands are working for her, that she's payin' us wages to drive these cows to market and what does

242

Yellow Drum mean by obstructin' passage and demandin' her property?"

"Maybe we'd better go to work for her," Urquhart said. "She's making more headway than we did."

Jennifer paused to give Knife-in-the-Wind time to render her words into Cheyenne. Yellow Drum, listened, scowling, spoke at length to the interpreter and relapsed again to silence. Knife-in-the-Wind turned to Jennifer.

"Knife-in-the-Wind says," Corbillat went on, "that Yellow Drum claims toll for crossin' his land and—wait!" An expression of awe entered Corbillat's features as a sudden tirade from Jennifer interrupted the interpreter. "My Gawd, oh my Gawd!" Corbillat gasped. "Mis Jen is really tyin' into Yellow Drum now. She's tellin' him he's a liar seven ways from the deuce and a coward to boot. She says these lands never belonged to the Cheyennes, and that it is known Yellow Drum deserted his chief, Iron Wolf, leaving Iron Wolf to make war alone against the whites, while a coyote named Yellow Drum chose the less dangerous course of stealing cattle from helpless white men. The stealing from the whites, Miss Jen says, is Yellow Drum's own affair, but why should he demand toll of Cherokees, his own brothers. And so long as redskin wages war against redskin, how can Injuns ever hope to overcome the palefaces . . . ?"

Knife-in-the-Wind translated. Yellow Drum's jaw sagged. It was plain he was shaken by Jennifer's knowledge of his own and Iron Wolf's activities, though her accusation of cowardice had been but a shot in the dark. The sneer vanished from Yellow Drum's face; he slumped on his pony's back; his beady eyes shifted uneasily as though he sought escape from the biting words of this Cherokee woman. He mumbled a few words to the interpreter who relayed them to Jennifer.

"Yellow Drum says," Corbillat translated, "that the Cheyennes do not want war against the Cherokee Nation, and he wants to sit at a fire and smoke a pipe."

Jennifer again interrupted the interpreter's remarks. Corbillat went on, "She says she does not sit down to parley with cowards who lead brave Cheyenne warriors astray, and that, even now, a great band of fighting Cherokee braves are but a half-a-sleep distant, and that they will drive Yellow Drum and his men before them to the earth, as wind flattens the grass, when they learn of Yellow Drum's actions. Rius, my Gawd, did you ever hear such a bluff?" Corbillat listened while Jennifer continued, her tones cracking like a whiplash, then translated, "She says the Cherokee warriors will take many scalps, and those Yellow Drum men who might escape her revenging people, will be overpowered by the Long-Knives-in-Blue— that's U.S. troopers—who are but a short ride distant."

When Jennifer's words had been passed on to Yellow Drum, the big Cheyenne remained silent. Those at his rear commenced a troubled jabbering. Yellow Drum asked hesitantly, through Knife-in-the-Wind, what Jennifer wanted. Corbillat relayed reply: "She says Yellow Drum talks like a man who has swallowed smoke with his firewater—crazy or drunk. She says the arrow that has left the bow cannot be called back, and she feels only sorrow when she thinks of Yellow Drum's scalp dangling from the lodge-pole of a Cherokee; or perhaps his neck will be broken by the rope of the Long-Knives-in-Blue. Yes, she feels much sorrow for Yellow Drum and because she does not want him to appear in the Land of the Great Spirit with an empty belly, she will make him a gift of five cows, before her herd resumes its journey—" Corbillat broke off. "Good Gawd on the Mountain, Rius, if she puts over a bluff like this, I could die happy."

"You said it all, Dix," Urquhart replied.

The men watched to see how Yellow Drum would accept the proposal. And then, Jennifer played her trump card. Without waiting to learn Yellow Drum's reactions, as though the matter were already settled, she turned her pony away, her erect back expressing in each line the contempt a daughter of Cherokees felt for Yellow Drum. Corbillat heard the pent-up breath as it issued from her lips. He tried to speak, but his voice choked. Urquhart's mouth was working strangely. He said, "Jennifer, I—I—"

"Don't smile, either of you," the girl said fiercely. "Don't let Yellow Drum know, in any way, what I've said is untrue." Sudden pleased gabbling had arisen among the Cheyennes, as they learned the nature of Jennifer's proposal. Knife-in-the-Wind called something to the girl, which she didn't deign to answer. "It's worked," she said to Corbillat, and relaxed. "Darius, give them five cows, and send them scattering off toward the south. Then get the herd moving as quickly as possible. There are a number of things Yellow Drum may think of—when he takes time to think."

Urquhart started around the far rim of the herd, beckoning to Yellow Drum as he moved past. Meekly, the big Cheyenne and his followers trailed behind. Jennifer and Corbillat looked after them, the girl forcing a weary smile. "The Indian in me seems to come out more all the time, doesn't it, Dix? But this was the only thing I could think of. I hurried, oh, how I hurried to get changed, expecting every instant to hear shots— but maybe the Irish in me helped, too. That Yellow Drum made me so damn' mad, I just had to be giving him a piece of my mind."

"Indian or Irish," Corbillat said fervently, "you can be mighty proud of both bloods, Miss Jen. . . ." He hailed Hogan who was sitting his horse, open-mouthed. "Graveyard, you ride to the wagon with Miss Jen."

He loped his horse around the herd, passed the jabbering Indians, and caught up with Urquhart. Five steers were quickly cut out, and with ropes lashing at their hindquarters were sent fanning off toward the south. Once the animals were well started, Urquhart gave Yellow Drum a nod. Instantly, the yelling redskins scattered in wild pursuit of the frightened steers. Bows twanged and lances were poised for lethal thrusts. Sporadic reports from repeating rifles punctuated the shrill yells of *"Wo-ha!—Wo-ha!"*

Five minutes later, the steers were a quarter mile away, with Indians spread over the range. "There wa'n't a decent shot in that outfit, looks like," Corbillat commented disgustedly. "Cripes! How that Yellow Drum stunk. Don't know how Miss Jen stuck it. She sure pulled us through, Rius."

"She did that," Urquhart acknowledged. "Dix, start this herd to stirring some dust. Time's a-wasting!"

10

IT WAS NOW URQUHART SHOULD HAVE ENDEAVORED TO make his peace with the girl, the Yellow Drum incident having brought them closer together, but beyond courteously thanking her for what she had done, the man remained aloof, fearing a rebuff.

The morning after they left the Cheyennes behind, Jennifer again appeared in the Cherokee costume, minus paint and decorations. She had no intention of "going Indian" but had donned the costume in case another band of redskins were encountered. Her cheeks reddened slightly as she explained that she found the Cherokee garment loose and comfortable.

The red-banked South Canadian River, when it was reached, almost brought tragedy. The river was swirling, bankfull, and logs, lashed to the chuckwagon, were necessary to float the vehicle safely across. The herd took the water without trouble. Half of it had reached the opposite shore, with the existence of quicksands below the surface of the stream unsuspected when Weber's pony became entrapped on what he first judged to be a sandbar. Weber slipped into the water and tried to extricate his fast-sinking mount, already submerged to the saddlehorn. Too late, he yelled for help, and riders on swimming horses started to his aid.

Lacking the continual urging of these riders some of the cattle stopped to drink, and also became wedged in quicksands. The bawling of the trapped steers frightened the remaining cattle, and they commenced to mill in midstream, crowding down on Weber and sweeping him and his pony below the surface. By the time Weber had been hauled out of the water, fortunately uninjured, nearly eighty head of cattle and Weber's horse had been sucked below the surface to perish. The loss of the horse was relatively unimportant; the calamity lay in the loss of the saddle.

Jennifer stepped into the breach, with the announcement that Weber could use her saddle. She was, she stated, weary of horseback riding; the change would be welcome. From that day on, Jennifer put aside riding things and, wearing a loose calico dress, rode at the Negro's side in the chuck-wagon. Corbillat returned to herding cattle.

Leaving the South Canadian, the herd crossed a broken stretch of country, negotiated the North Canadian River without incident, and forged on toward Kansas. Since striking Chisholm's Trail more travelers were met. Now and then, herds of buffalo were seen, or a stagecoach rumbled by; horse-drawn freight-wagons, bullwhackers and muleskinners became common sights. Small bodies of U.S. troopers added their dust to that thrown up by the Circle-U cattle. Such Indians as were encountered were friendly. If Jennifer suffered discomfort from the jolting of the wagon, she failed to show it. As formerly, she disappeared within the wagon shortly after supper, but she no longer rose before the men were awake; generally she put in her appearance about the time they were ready to load bedrolls into the wagon and ride out to the herd.

The herd crossed the Cimarron and followed a hoof-chopped trail through a blackjack forest, from which it presently emerged to find the vast, slightly-undulating grasslands reaching to the northern horizon.

The long ribbon of tossing horns went steadily on, with little to break the daily monotonous regularity of heat, wind and blowing dust. Then one morning—it was the last day of June—Corbillat reined his pony beside the wagon and pointed ahead. "Miss Jen, do you see that big red butte yonderly, liftin' above the prairie? When you've passed north of that, you'll be in Kansas."

Jennifer shielded her eyes against shimmering heat waves and made out the landmark. "That means we're nearly there, doesn't it, Dix?"

"If this outfit doesn't haul into Abilene in twelve or fifteen days, I'll eat my Stet-hat. You'll be mighty glad, won't you?" Jennifer conceded she wouldn't be sorry. Corbillat scowled, noting the weary slump of the girl's shoulders. "Trail drivin's a wearisome business. *You* ain't no business here a-tall . . . though I'm danged if I know what we'd done without you."

"Don't think I regret coming," Jennifer said quickly. "It's been *something*, Dix! Once I've had a chance to bathe all over and get the dust out of my hair . . ." Her voice dwindled.

"You hang and rattle a mite longer, Miss Jen. Things will clear up in a spell." He turned the pony and loped back.

Albumen spoke through the jolting of wheels and jangling of mule harness. "That big raid rock up ahead says Kansas, huh?" His whip snaked out over the mules. "Pick up dem hoofs rapid, you fool crittehs. Git on along, now!"

The big "raid rock" was passed the following day, and the herd forged its way through broken country and queerly formed red buttes, past a lone, weatherboard shack which bore a sign proclaiming it to be the "First Chance Saloon" (liquor being prohibited in Indian Territory).

The red butte country was left behind. The cattle trudged across a great treeless plain with heat-waves quivering above the waving blue-stem grass until they entered a broad valley dotted with cottonwood and elm trees. The Arkansas River crossing was made near a settlement named Wichita, composed of a trading post, a number of grass Indian lodges and a scattering of wood structures. Two days later the cattle crossed the old Santa Fe Trail, a wide brown grassless deeply-rutted trough, tramped hard and barren by the countless hoofs and turning wheels of heavily-laden wagons. And ever present were the dust and heat and bawling of cattle as they marched nearer and nearer their destination.

Until a day came when Urquhart called a halt in mid-afternoon, and the cattle were watered at a small stream with a fringe of cottonwoods along its banks, and then put to graze in knee-high grass, while camp

250

was made a short distance off. Directly ahead, not more than five miles, lay a range of low sandy hills and the Solomon River. And just beyond the Solomon lay Abilene! Albumen was told to prepare a special supper this night; there was no further need to conserve supplies. Tomorrow, the Circle-U would be in *Abilene!* The word was on every tongue as the riders gathered about the fire for the feast the Negro had set out. And when supper was ended, smoke from smelly briar pipes and cornhusk cigarettes mingled with that curling lazily upward from the campfire. Tonight, the trail; tomorrow, Abilene! The hardships were over.

A great silver dollar of a moon was rising over the eastern horizon. The night was balmy. Jennifer sat on a saddle, her back resting against a wagon-wheel, listening to the conversation about the fire. The hobbled *remuda* ponies cropped the grass a short way off, and from some distance beyond the low singing of the night guards occasionally reached the girl. The leaping flames of the campfire made highlights in Jennifer's blue-black hair and accented the faint shadows beneath her lovely wide cheekbones. Her eyes went to Urquhart lounging on the earth beyond the rim of firelight and men, but he was taking no part in the conversation.

Down at the stream a symphony of frogs maintained a continual chorus. A nightbird practiced arpeggios on a liquid flute, among the cottonwoods. Urquhart considered he had done his best. The herd was at Abilene's gateway, and he'd brought it this long distance with no loss of human life. That, in itself, was a matter of pride;

too many outfits lost men on the long drive to Kansas. It was good to relax, now that responsibility was practically over. Almost immediately, the sense of exultation was dispelled by thought of that other responsibility not to be evaded: Jennifer.

Why, Urquhart brooded, had he been such a fool? Common-sense dictated the absence of women from trail driving. Nothing could excuse his action in bringing Jennifer on this drive. Nor would it be possible to make the girl understand what his feelings had been that day he'd ordered Harnish from Urquhart Oaks and taken Jennifer north. It would be useless, now, to beg Jennifer's forgiveness, but if he had it to do over again . . .

Urquhart's jaw set stubbornly. By God, if he had it to do over again, he'd follow the same course. Maybe Divine Providence dictated a man's doings. More than once it had been fortunate that Jennifer was with the outfit. Yes, Urquhart insisted, if he had it to do over again, he'd act the same. That was how he was built; he was forced to follow his own dictates.

Anyway, there was nothing to be done about it, now. He and Jennifer would say good-bye in Abilene, and she'd return for her grandparents . . . Urquhart's musings tarried on the two old Cherokees. They had certainly staged a strong protest the day he'd carried off Jennifer. There were those certain words that had kept recurring through their Cherokee babel of dissension. Why had those particular words been so indelibly impressed on his memory? *Agehya taluli* and *'ta 'hu li'*. What in the devil did they mean? He had intended to ask Dix for a translation, but the intention had slipped his memory.

His eyes went to Corbillat and Urquhart was about to call him, when hoof-beats sounded through the night. A minute later a rider was silhouetted against the rising moon and a hail carried to the camp fire: "Hello-o-o, the ca-a-am-m-mp!"

"Hello yourself," Dix called. "Come along and rest your saddle."

Urquhart came to a sitting position while he watched the man dismount. Though the visitor wore boots and wide hat, his clothing was definitely not that of a cowman. He stopped short upon seeing Jennifer and removed the hat from his crisp blond hair, then turned to Corbillat: "May I ask what outfit this is?"

"The Circle-U from near San Antonio. Owned by Darius Urquhart."

Urquhart came forward and introduced himself.

"My name's Purdy," said the visitor, "and I'm buying beeves for the Helmet-Speed Company, Chicago meat-packers." The men seated themselves on the earth, near the fire. Purdy continued, "It's probably bad business for me to say so, but there's considerable competition among us beef-buyers. A few of us steal a march on the others, now and then, by riding out and meeting herds before they reach Abilene. I've done business before with drovers in this fashion. Perhaps you'll care to sell to me. I can pay as high as anyone else, and more than many, if you're interested."

They talked of beeves and prices and the long trail from Texas, until Urquhart asked whether a man

253

named Drake Harnish was known in Abilene. It had been rumored that he had sent at least one herd north, but nobody knew where the beasts had come from or whether they had arrived safely. Dix began to hint darkly about cattle-thieving on the trail, but Urquhart silenced him with a frown.

Purdy's mouth opened at mention of Harnish. He admitted that he did know the man, but not in Abilene. He had, it seems, met him in New Orleans towards the end of the war. Washington would be interested to learn that Harnish was anywhere west of the Mississippi. He had been a guerrilla raider of the worst type, killing and robbing non-combatants and acting all the time on forged orders, under a forged commission. His brother had been killed in a raid on some civilian house, and Harnish had escaped after his gang had attacked a supply train which they had mistakenly thought unguarded. Then he had disappeared, despite all efforts of the Pinkerton men to trace him. Purdy could hardly conceal his excitement at the information he would be able to pass on.

A fresh relay of night riders rode out to the herd, and the ten o'clock shift came off guard, and sought beds. Finally, Purdy rose. "I've got to get back to Abilene. It's settled, then, Mr. Urquhart. I'll meet you with a crew of riders to take over, when your herd's crossed the Solomon River." They shook hands and Purdy climbed into his saddle.

11

URQUHART WAS ASTONISHED AT THE GROWTH OF ABI-
lene since his visit two years before. Gone was the scattered collection of shacks beside the Kansas Pacific
railroad; now, it was a brawling, rowdy, roistering wild-
and-woolly frontier town, a thriving rock of iniquity
almost submerged by the waves of Texas longhorns and
cowboys surging in. Streets had been laid out. Building
boomed. The single-story buildings displayed high
false fronts, with wooden awnings jutting above
uneven plank sidewalks. There were saloons, restau-
rants, general stores, dance-halls, gambling dens, red-
light houses. A continual sound of sawing and ham-
mering vied with the bedlam of noises of shunted
stock-cars and snorting engines along Railroad Street.

Urquhart guided his buckskin along a dusty thoroughfare, crowded with ponies and wagons. Cowboys
in new clothing, jostled on the walks and plunged in
and out of saloons, to the jangling of rowelled spurs.
The one article every man carried was the cap-and-ball
six-shooter. Urquhart came to the Texas District, south
of the Kansas Pacific's right-of-way, rounded a corner
and saw a double pair of tracks and railroad ties,
flanked by telegraph poles, stretching to the horizon.
Some distance down the track cattle were being herded
into a train of stock-cars; nearer at hand the locomotive
of a second train awaited its turn, chuffing impatiently.
Facing the railroad stood Abilene's first hotel, the
Drovers' Cottage, a large, three-storied clapboard

building with green shutters at the windows, and a slanting-roofed gallery running the width of the first floor. North of the tracks were more buildings, some of log construction, of a more sedate appearance than found in the Texas District.

Behind the Drovers' Cottage was a livery stable. A long fence jutted from one front corner of the hotel, the top board of which was lined with cowboys who appeared to have nothing better to do than sit and talk, gesticulate, smoke, spit and sun themselves. The gallery of the Drovers' Cottage was jammed with stockmen and cattle-buyers; horses, wagons and buggies stood in scattered confusion. As Urquhart neared the hotel, Corbillat came to meet him. "Thought you was never comin'," Corbillat scowled. Urquhart asked if anything were wrong. "Nothing wrong, but I'm sick of answerin' the same question, over and over. Half this town is interested in findin' out if a female really come up the trail with us."

"You got her fixed up, all right, didn't you?"

"Gault Madison's around town someplace. He had rooms saved for you and me and Miss Jen, at this hotel. Miss Jen's all right. The lady who runs this hotel, Mrs. Lou Gore, took Miss Jen in charge right off. I heard the two of 'em makin' *habla* about hot water for a bath. Don't you fret, she'll be perky as a broomtail once she gets rested."

Urquhart relaxed. "What happened to our crew?"

"What do you think happened, with wages burnin' holes in their pockets? They've scattered to get new duds, drinks, a barber-shop." Urquhart asked regarding

Albumen. "He took the wagon and went to buy rations and clothes. Did you get settled with Purdy?" Urquhart nodded. Corbillat hesitated. "Just after I left Miss Jen, I saw Sabina Madison, and she wanted to know about that rumor a woman come up the trail with us. She dropped insinuations no lady would do such a thing. Then started fishin' around to find out how friendly you and Miss Jen was on the trip. I told her you and Miss Jen hardly spoke to each other all the way." Urquhart smiled wryly. Corbillat said, "Sabina wants you should come up to her room, the instant you get here. She's got somethin' important to tell, she allowed. No, her and Miss Jen didn't meet. I was just leavin' the lobby, when Mrs. Madison hailed me."

Urquhart ran his fingers along his unshaven jaw. "I don't think I'm presentable at the moment. I'd like to find clean clothing and a barber-shop—"

"Let's get started."

Two hours later, fed and barbered, the two men were riding along crowded Texas Street, looking for Albumen. They had already located the wagon, standing in front of Dalzell's Drovers' Supply Store, but of the Negro there was no sign. "Dammit," Corbillat growled, "it ain't like him to stay away from his wagon so long. If anybody's been devilin' him—"

"Rius! Dix!" The booming voice reached them from a saloon, as Gault Madison came barging through the swinging doors. Corbillat and. Urquhart reined in their ponies and climbed down, all three men talking at once. Madison smelled strongly of bay-rum, hair-tonic and whisky; there was a curl to the ends of his heavy moustache. His nose was a network of tiny purple veins; his eyes were bloodshot. He wore a fancy vest, wide white sombrero and black string tie over a white shirt; one leg of his trousers dangled at the ankle, the other was tucked sloppily into a boot-top. "When'd you two curly wolves get in?" Madison beamed.

"We crossed the Solomon between six and seven this morning," Urquhart replied. "It's good to see you, Gault."

"And you!" Madison sobered and added, "You utter damn' fool!"

"Now what's wrong?" Urquhart asked cautiously.

"Bringing Jennifer on a drive like that," Madison growled. "God damn it! You act like you got no more sense than a baby with a big navel. Of all the fool—"

"How'd you know?" Urquhart asked uncomfortably.

"How'd I know?" Madison stared. "That day you started I went to Urquhart Oaks to see if you and Jennifer had come to any agreement, and she was gone! Those two old folks spouted at me faster than I could understand, even if I savvied Cherokee. So I rode to San 'Tonio and brought back a feller that *habla-ed* the language. Then I got the story. And when I got here, I talked to men who'd met the Circle-U on trail. You and her make things up?"

"Let's get a drink," Urquhart evaded.

"You said something! C'mon!" Urquhart asked how long Madison had been in Abilene. "Mite over three weeks," Madison said. "I've been havin' myself a time! Never saw such a town. It's got everything a man needs—whisky, women, entertainment, new clothes.

And fighting! There's been six or seven men killed since I been here. Nobody knows how many wounded. Gunfights! The town's full of hard-cases drawn here by Texan money."

"Ain't they got any law in Abilene?" Corbillat asked.

"Nothing that's enforced. God knows how many town marshals Abilene has had. Several local men tried, but things are too tough. Got one here now, named Ryskoff. He's holding down the job because he doesn't interfere with anybody. Got a jail, but you could butt your way out with your head. They're figuring to build a brick jail and court-house next season, and get a law officer with guts, but damned if I know where they'll find one to control this town."

They turned north at the first corner. Madison continued, "Something's got to be done, the way Abilene is growing. Right now it's got three hotels and a fourth a-building." Urquhart interrupted to thank Madison for reserving rooms at the Drovers' Cottage. "Don't mention it, Rius. Mrs. Gore could only hold the two rooms. There's a woman for you, Mrs. Lou Gore! Regular angel. Abilene's going to have to put up more places. There's going to be close to four hundred thousand cows reach here, this season. Two years from now, they figure it will hit three-quarter million. Texas has found an outlet for its cows, and we can thank Joseph McCoy for that. Some of these other Kansas towns will soon start offerin' inducements to draw trade away from Abilene. That means railroads will have to build farther west. This whole damn' country will get opened up, and all due to McCoy and Texas cattle."

Madison ceased talking to usher his companions into a frame building with three wide double-doored entrances, above which were painted the words, ALAMO SALOON. The long bar was jammed with cowboys; stacks of polished glasses and bottles were reflected in a mirror. Faro dealers did a brisk business in one corner; there was a clicking of poker chips at green-felt-covered tables. An odor of unwashed humanity, stale liquor and tobacco permeated the atmosphere.

Madison procured a bottle and three glasses from a bartender and led the way to chairs standing near one wall. "This is where wages go. Fool cowhands break their backs working up the trail, only to fling their money away in places like this. Few have sense enough to quit before their money's gone. I started my boys back soon's they blowed off their first steam—"

"Your herd got in all right, then?" Urquhart said.

"Jeff Strunk pulled in ten days ago, and I found buyers immediately. I've just been waiting until you got here. What about your cows, Rius?"

"All delivered and paid for." Urquhart told him about Purdy. "He wants to buy our *remuda* too. I'm going to let him have it."

Madison said, "What shape did your cows arrive in?"

"First rate. We lost about four hundred on the way, though. Two hundred of that might have been stolen, one night when our cows stampeded." He gave Madison the story.

Madison said, "Several outfits have pulled in with

260

similar stories. There's been so many complaints that Washington has sent troops out looking for cow-thieves." He lifted the bottle. "Talking is dry business." Urquhart noticed that Madison's hand shook slightly.

Corbillat said, "Gault, Rius ain't told you about Drake Harnish. The bastud was a guerrilla durin' the war. Now we know why he shied clear of trouble with Rius."

"The hell you say!" Madison looked startled. Urquhart relayed the information Purdy had given him. Madison said slowly, "The low-down son-of-a-bitch. He was one reason—" He broke off and abruptly changed the subject: "Rius, that architect has done a bang-up job on your house. It'll be all done by the time you get back."

Corbillat rose and guessed he'd step out and look around. "See you later," he said, and strode out to the street.

12

WHEN CORBILLAT LEFT, URQUHART SAID, "DIX IS worried about our Negro. Albumen dropped out of sight, shortly after we got here."

"Pshaw! Ain't nobody going to hurt him in this town. What about your trip? I'm waiting to hear." Urquhart related the various adventures of the Circle-U on its way north. When he told of the meeting with Yellow Drum Madison's eyes bulged. "By God, Rius, there's a girl to tie to. If you let her get away from you—"

"I'm afraid that's all finished," Urquhart said

soberly, and concluded, "That's the yarn. I've made around seventeen thousand clear, but it's not what I hoped for. By the time I pay for the house I'll not have the money I counted on. I wanted to get some blooded bulls—some Herefords and Polled Angus—and see what could be done about improving the Circle-U strain. I'd like to experiment and see if I can't get the stringiness out of those longhorns. I won't be able to do it this year. A drive next year might put me on my feet."

"It's an idea, son. I'd like to try some of that experimenting with you." He asked abruptly, "Did you see Sabina, at the hotel?" Urquhart said he hadn't; he'd not been presentable enough. Madison frowned. "Sabina and I are finished, Rius. No,"—as Urquhart began to voice the usual expression of surprised regret—"don't say it. You know, well's I do, we wasn't mated. Maybe I'm not the mating kind but I feel Sabina hasn't done all she could, neither. After you started up the trail, I fooled around San 'Tonio a lot. Then a few afternoons when I got home, I'd find three or four Yank officers hanging around listening to Sabina play the piano. That griped me, but I didn't say anything. Then it got so Harnish started making calls regular. He pretended he came to visit me, but I wasn't whelped yesterday."

Feeling embarrassed, Urquhart interrupted to ask if Harnish's herd had reached Abilene. Madison shook his head. "No, and it left a month before you. I figure it to pull in toward the end of the season, with two-thirds of its critters stolen stock. Like I say, Harnish's visits continued to rile me, so I suggested that he don't come to visit any more. We argued and he got nasty—made a remark that Sabina and you had been carrying on, right under my nose—"

Urquhart swore angrily. "That's a damned lie!"

"I know, son, I know. Keep your shirt on. Though I'm surprised Sabina didn't try. She's made a play for so many young males— To make a long story short, I shoved my gun against Harnish's guts and told him to get out. And he got! Sabina and I quarreled some more. I figured it might be a prime idea to get her out of Texas for a spell. We took a boat to St. Louie and then the steam-cars to here. But coming up on the boat, Sabina got to flittin' around with a Yank officer. Then we had words again, and she never let up until we got to the Drovers' Cottage. And she must have figured me for a gelding, because she insisted we have separate rooms. Just like she was the only woman in Abilene, and for God's sake, I can think of at least two, right now, that's got it all over her for looks, and are a heap more sociable—"

Urquhart interrupted. "Is it necessary to tell me this? Some day, things will be ironed out and you'll regret telling me—"

"I'll regret nothing!" Madison pounded one knee with a clenched fist. "Maybe she's my wife yet, but not for long. After we got here, she wouldn't be friendly. At the same time she wanted me to stay around the hotel 'with the other *gentlemen* stock-owners and their wives.'" Madison's imitation of Sabina would have been laughable under other circumstances. "I couldn't stand it any longer. Last week I put it up to her, would she take all the money I got in Texas banks and we'd call it quits, me keeping only the Pot-Hook, some bonds and such, and the cash I received for my herd. She fair jumped at the offer! So I hired an attorney-at-law in Abilene to draw up the papers, and we signed 'em. I made me a new will too. So that's how things are. Sabina received about nine-tenths of what I owned; now she's got all the money she needs. I can't call myself wealthy any longer, but it's worth it. She's going to Alexandria to get the divorce. She's been waiting in Abilene until you arrived. Said she wanted to say good-bye."

Urquhart said soberly, "You may not like it, Gault, but sometimes I think you've been a bit hard on Sabina." That, Madison admitted readily, was more or less true, though he insisted it was not solely his fault. Urquhart continued, "Maybe it doesn't sound like I've both your interests at heart, but I think you've done the best thing."

"It's just hawss-sense and we both know it. Now let's not talk any more about Sabina. I'm going over to see Jennifer now. I've got to tell Jennifer exactly what I think of her, and what a damned fool you are—"

"Look here," Urquhart said seriously, "you visit all you like, but leave me out of it. I mean that. There's something you can do for me." He took a check and a small canvas sack of coins from a pants' pocket. "Give her this money. It's the profit from her three hundred cows. She won't want to take it, but you make her see she's entitled to it. Lord above! Jennifer earned that and more when she put the quietus on Yellow Drum."

Madison promised to see that Jennifer took the money. Urquhart went on, "How about you and Dix and me having supper later on?"

Madison said sheepishly, "Cripes! There's nothing I'd like better, Rius, but I've got a previous engagement. I'll see you first thing in the morning." He rose heavily from his chair, eyes averted, cast a longing look at the bottle, and went on, "We'll be able to talk all the way back to San 'Tonio."

He paused when Corbillat entered the Alamo Saloon. "I can't find hide nor hair of the Negro," Corbillat said worriedly, "and my legs feel like they were wore down to the hocks. If some bastud's gone to harmin' that Negro, he's going to have me to deal with."

"I'll be right with you, Dix," Urquhart said. "Gault's just leaving to see Jennifer." They parted on the sidewalk, Urquhart and Corbillat starting at a brisk walk toward Texas Street, while Madison headed the other way.

The sun was below the horizon now; the crowd on the street had increased. "By jeez!" Corbillat complained bitterly. "I blame myself. That poor little Negro ain't scarcely been outten our sight since we had him, and like a damn' fool I turn him loose in a town like this." Urquhart tried to quiet Corbillat's nameless fears, as they pursued their way along the sidewalk, streaming with cowboys.

They reached the tie-rail where they had left their horses and rode to the Drovers' Cottage, but there was no sign of Albumen. It had grown dark by the time they once more returned to the Texas District, now

265

ablaze with the illumination of oil lamps. A house with a closed door and a red-globed railroad lantern suspended from one jamb, seemed to be receiving considerable attention from a knot of cowboys clustered about the entrance. "Ain't no Negro got a right to be frettin' me in this fashion," Corbillat bemoaned, reining his horse close to Urquhart's. "Few hours back, I swore I'd take a hame-trace to him for disappearin'. Now dam'd if he couldn't give me the floggin', if he'd only show up." Urquhart too was commencing to feel concern over the Negro. To distract Corbillat's mind, Urquhart told him of Sabina and Madison's split-up. Beyond remarking it was "probably a good thing for both of 'em," Corbillat scarcely gave the matter a thought.

"I think we'd best go back to the hotel," Urquhart said finally. "Albumen knows we're staying there, if he's in trouble." Corbillat agreed, adding dismally, "provided he's able to send word."

Lights were streaming from the windows of the Drovers' Cottage by the time they returned. Corbillat almost immediately spied the Circle-U chuck-wagon. "There's our wagon, anyway. Maybe the Negro's there."

Without waiting for Urquhart, he spurred to the side of the wagon and thrust his head inside, then drew back in astonishment. A female voice, like slowly-poured honey, warned him off: "Y'all keep away from dis heah vehicle, cowboy. Dis Cucle-U prop'ty."

Corbillat backed his horse. "Rius! You'd best come look into this."

Albumen came hurrying from the hotel entrance, resplendent in a new suit. "Majur Ukhart! Sahgent! Ah's bin travailin' dis hull town tryin' to locate y'all—"

"Look at that fellow," Corbillat gasped, in relief, "rigged out like a church window, and him so black he'd make a head-lamp in a snow blizzard." He raised his voice, "Where in the name of the seven bald steers you been, Albumen? I got me a mind to—"

"Majuh! Sahgent!" The Negro's upturned face shone, as he halted before the two horses. "Ah's done found Dicey Nell. Some scrabble-brain done told she Ah was daid. And den she gettin' a job wid a woman whut come to Kansas, and now Dicey Nell's wukkin' rat heah in dis heah Droveh's Hotel. Dicey Nell, come along down and confabulate wid de Majuh and de Sahgent." He pivoted back to Urquhart. "Ah done tells she 'bout dat big white house we's 'structin' at Ukhart Oaks, and she 'lows it be mighty satisfactual to wuk dar foah y'all."

While Urquhart and Corbillat gazed in speechless amazement, a slim Negro woman in her twenties, in a patterned cotton dress and a bandanna wound turban-wise about her head, descended from the wagon and bowed, with dignity, to the two white men. "Albumen's allowed dey ain't nobody to compare to you gemmuns and de young Miss Jennifuh who Ah ain't yit had de pleasuah of bowin' to. Ah supplicates y'all dat Ah gits de opp'tunity of suhven' yo' to de best of mah 'bility, suhs." The woman had very white teeth, comely features, and stood nearly a head taller than Albumen, who was bowing pridefully at her side.

"Thank you, Dicey Nell," Urquhart replied. "Albumen, you take Dicey Nell to see Miss Jennifer, sometime. How did you happen to find Dicey Nell?"

"Quincedunce," Albumen explained. "Ah was jist leavin' de Giniral Stoah when Ah sees Dicey Nell sashigatin' in, and foah a minute we jist stands dar and looks at de otheh. Den we both stahts talkin'." His voice took on an apologetic tone. "Ah'd liked a-plenty could y'all come to de ma'iage suhvice, but Ah figgered Ah betteh not take no moah chances of losin' she. So Ah locates de Justice of de Peace, and we gits us ma'ied t'once, and den Ah stahts seekin' y'all—"

"You what?" Corbillat exploded.

"We gits us ma'ied, sahgent, joined in de holy bonds of wedlock."

"It's incest," Urquhart muttered.

"You—you *married* Dicey Nell?" Corbillat's voice held shocked amazement. "Why, you old ram! Look here, Albumen, you ain't tellin' me you've married your own daughter!"

Albumen looked puzzled. "Dicey Nell ain't no datter t'me. Wheah-at y'all git dat idee, sahgent, suh?"

"Blast it, man, you told me yourownself," Corbillat fumed. "Back there in Car'lina, you told me—"

"Never told you Dicey Nell was mah datter," Albumen maintained stubbornly. "All's Ah ever told you was Dicey Nell had always been lak a datter t'me. Dicey Nell was datter to old Ephraim White befoah he died of de lung misery. Ah'd give Ephraim mah solemn promise to always look afteh she, ontil she come of de ma'yin' age, and den de wah comes along and we done got sep'rated lak Ah told you befoah—"

"But—but both your names is White."

"Cehtain dey is. All us slaves taken de name from Cunnel Bu'lette White of Ve'de Groves Plantation. Ah hopes dis is sats'factory to y'all."

Urquhart chuckled. "It's more than satisfactory, Albumen. I congratulate you and wish your bride much happiness."

<h1 style="text-align:center">13</h1>

IT WAS CLOSE TO TEN THAT EVENING BEFORE URQUHART and Corbillat left their horses at the stable and made their way around to the hotel entrance. "Dam'd if I ain't ready to hit the hay," Corbillat commented. "It's been a long day, Rius. But we got here, by Gawd, and that's somethin' to brag on."

They passed into the brightly-lighted lobby where drovers and stock-buyers, and a sprinkling of modishly-dressed wives, stood talking. At one side was an arched doorway, with hanging drapes, leading to what was known as the Ladies' Parlour; a carpeted staircase led to the second floor. It was the first time Urquhart had been within the Drovers' Cottage. Corbillat led the way to the desk, behind which was the motherly-looking Mrs. Lou Gore. "You want your key, I suppose," Mrs. Gore smiled. "Here it is, Mr. Corbillat— Oh, and this is Mr. Urquhart? I'm pleased to make your acquaintance, sir." Urquhart bowed and said something about being honored. Mrs. Gore continued, "Mr. Madison came this afternoon to visit Miss Keating. I put her in No. 25, thinking she might like to be near Mrs. Madison's room, but I believe she's hardly been out. She's a brave girl, Mr. Urquhart." Urquhart agreed courteously, then he and Corbillat started toward the stairway.

"Darius! Darius Urquhart!"

The two men paused. Corbillat grunted, "It's Gault's wife. I'll go up to our room, Rius."

Sabina in a satin dress of ultramarine blue, with arms bare to the elbow, had just emerged from the Ladies' Parlour, and was threading a rustling course across the lobby. Her hair of pale gold was parted in the center, swirled at her nape and brought forward in a full curl to dangle over one shoulder. She was laughing excitedly as she moved toward Urquhart, cheeks flushed, velvety-brown eyes bright. "Darius! It's *so* good to see you again."

He bowed and took her hand, flushing self-consciously, intensely aware of a certain remembered fragrance, feeling again the definite attraction this woman held for him. "Sabina, you're looking extremely well," He complimented her. "I should say beautiful—more beautiful than ever before."

She smiled confidently, glancing quickly around the lobby. "No one," she said softly, "at all, says such things quite as well as you, Darius. You're mortal flattering." The smile faded. "Why didn't you come to see me when you first arrived? But you've talked to Gault, of course. You've had only his side of the story. You must hear mine. You will, won't you?" Before he could answer she continued, "I have Room 24. Give me five

270

minutes, then come up."

His eyes widened. "To your room?" Sabina Gault told him tersely not to be stupid; where else but her room? "I hardly think that's the thing, Sabina," he stammered. "Suppose we meet in the morning? I've had a long day." Mistaking his attitude, Sabina assured him Gault wouldn't return to the hotel before morning, if then. Urquhart felt his face growing warm.

He tried to explain to Sabina he'd scarcely had an opportunity to, wash off the trail dust; he'd been continually occupied since reaching Abilene.

An annoyed flush seeped into Sabina's cheeks. She was about to protest when a door was banged open and a hatless individual in shirt sleeves rushed to the desk, demanding to know if Mr. Urquhart was in the hotel. Urquhart excused himself and hastened to the desk. "I'm Urquhart. What's the trouble?"

"You're wanted right away. Gault Madison has been shot in Belle Silk's parlour-house—"

Urquhart clapped one hand over the fellow's mouth. "Hush it, you fool. Mrs. Madison is standing over there." The man stated sullenly that he couldn't be expected to know that. Conversation in the lobby had ceased. Urquhart swore under his breath. Had Sabina heard? He couldn't be sure. He was conscious of Madison's pressing need and the thought that he must hurry to Gault's side immediately. He went swiftly to Sabina and said quietly, "There was nothing for that fellow to be excited about. A matter of business. That is all. I must leave at once. I'll see you in the morning." An instant later he had crossed the hotel gallery and stepped into the full flood of moonlight, the man who had brought the message trying to accommodate his shorter legs to Urquhart's long strides.

Urquhart demanded, "Who shot him?"

"I don't know much," the man said cautiously. "Some ruckus with a couple of the girls. Marshal Ryskoff was called in, and Doc Newell. Madison asked for you, and Ryskoff sent me to find you." Urquhart asked if Madison were badly wounded. "I don't know anything about that. I'm just Belle Silk's professor."

"Professor? You mean you play the piano in this Belle Silk's place?" The man said that was his job, adding his name was Keg McKunnel. Urquhart glanced at him as they turned a corner, taking in McKunnel's slicked-down hair, pasty complexion and silk sleeve-garters. "How much farther is it?" he demanded impatiently.

"We'll be there in a few minutes," McKunnel panted, trying to keep up. "Belle's house is just t'other side of Texas Street." They had reached the Texas District by this time. Cowboys were milling like cattle along the street, spurs jangling. Lights blazed. Swinging doors of saloons continually fanned the night air. Soon McKunnel stopped before a large two-story frame building, with a red-globed lamp in a window; shades were drawn at the other windows. "This is it," McKunnel panted. He opened the door and Urquhart passed into a long hall stretching toward the rear. A single hanging lamp was suspended from the ceiling, and at the far end, a carpeted stairway rose to the second floor. Just before Urquhart reached it a door to his right opened and a full-bosomed' woman in a cerise dress, stuck a head of frizzy hair through the opening. McKunnel said, "Here he is, Belle."

"Mr. Urquhart?" Belle Silk's voice had a whisky-induced husky quality. "Thank God, you got here. This business has got me upset." One plump be-diamonded hand waved helplessly. "Mr. Madison is the most generous visitor we got. My, he's popular. Small wonder he comes here, though. I've always kept the highest-toned house in Abilene." An ugly note crept into her tones. "If I don't send those two bitches packing out of town, first thing in the morning! It's things like this give a stylish house a bad reputation—" Urquhart, his hands clenching and unclenching, interrupted to ask where Gault Madison was.

Before Belle Silk could reply, a raw-boned man with his hat cocked to one side of his dark head, appeared at the top of the stairs. He wore a six-shooter and marshal's badge. "You Darius Urquhart? . . . Mr. Madison's up here. You'd better hurry, Mr. Urquhart. He ain't got much longer."

From somewhere above, Urquhart could hear a woman's convulsive sobbing as he hastened up the stairs.

14

IT WAS PAST THREE IN THE MORNING WHEN URQUHART'S steps carried him to the Drovers' Cottage. Moonlight glistened on the rails stretching along the Kansas Pacific right-of-way. There were noises from the cattle-yards, but no sound at all from the train of stock-cars, near the pens, awaiting the coming of daylight and the resumption of loading; only a thin column of grey smoke drifted steadily from the funnel-shaped stack of the silent locomotive. Across Railroad Street, in Abilene's respectable neighborhood, no lights were visible. Somewhere over there, a minister of the gospel, Calvin Huneker, was to be found. He'd see him in the morning. Meanwhile there was this business of breaking the news to Sabina. Not that Sabina would "take it hard." Still, any woman would experience shock at the news her husband had been shot dead. Even those two girls at Belle Silk's house had carried on considerably. Urquhart swore and quickened his steps.

He crossed the deserted gallery and stepped into the lobby. Only two men were in sight: a male clerk behind the desk and a man with whiskers and a derby hat. The clerk glanced up. "A sad happening, Mr. Urquhart."

"It's all of that," Urquhart agreed in a tired voice. He added he hoped Mrs. Madison hadn't heard that fellow who brought the news. "But she did, Mr. Urquhart. She fainted after you left, and had to be carried to her room. We sent a man to ascertain the extent of Mr. Madison's injury. When Mrs. Madison was able to bear up, Mrs. Gore broke the news to her."

"Thank God for Mrs. Gore," Urquhart said fervently.

"She thought she could take that much off your shoulders. She also told Miss Keating. Hang the luck—I don't think anyone remembered to tell Mr. Corbillat."

"It doesn't matter," Urquhart. said. "You've been very accommodating." He started to turn away when the man with whiskers spoke, "May I introduce myself, Mr. Urquhart, and express sympathy? I'm Phineas Aikman, Attorney-at-Law. Perhaps Mr. Madison spoke of me." Urquhart shook hands. "I drew up some papers for him and Mrs. Madison to sign."

Urquhart said, "Gault told me about that." Aikman continued, "If I can be of service, please call on me." Urquhart thanked him, and turned toward the stairway. His hand was on the bannister when Aikman said, "A minute more, Mr. Urquhart."

"What is it now?"—wearily.

Aikman lowered his voice, "Please understand, Mr. Urquhart, I don't want to detain you longer than necessary, but did Mr. Madison mention I'd drawn a new will for him? I don't think Mrs. Madison knew about it." Urquhart stated Gault had mentioned a new will. "Apparently, you are not aware," Aikman continued, "that Madison made you his heir, aside from certain sums of money to be paid men who worked for him."

Urquhart said wearily, "Are you trying to tell me Gault left me his Pot-Hook and other holdings in Texas?" The attorney said that was exactly what he meant. Urquhart stared at him. "No," he said finally, "I didn't know that." He swallowed hard. "I never dreamed of anything of the sort, Mr. Aikman. I—" He faltered, seeing the sympathy in the lawyer's eyes.

"I wanted to be certain you knew, Mr. Urquhart. I'll wait on you, tomorrow, when the shock has passed somewhat. I bid you good-night, sir."

The long wearisome day and night, the blow induced by Madison's death, the news the attorney had given, reduced Urquhart to bewilderment. He reached the dimly-lighted second floor and proceeded along a corridor of closed doors, scarcely conscious of the snores issuing from transom openings. When he glanced at a number, on the nearest door, he realized he was on the wrong side of the building. Retracing his steps, he had rounded a corner of the corridor when he heard a door open and a whispered voice called his name.

Turning, he saw Sabina, a blue-silk wrapper clutched about her, the pale-gold hair piled high on her head. She beckoned him in and when, after a moment's hesitation he entered, hat in hand, softly closed the door at his back. His gaze ran over the room, taking in the array of feminine apparel scattered about. A lamp with a half-globe stood on a table near a dresser cluttered with hair-pins, combs and brushes. Sabina said, a trifle self-consciously, "I seem to have acquired a habit of waiting for you at doorways. You're shocked, of course." It wasn't quite what he'd expected. He watched her anxiously as she crossed the room and seated herself on the side of the bed, after motioning him to a chair. There were slippers with pom-poms on her bare feet, and an edge of gossamery material peeped from beneath the hem of her wrapper. Urquhart asked if she were all right. "Of course, I'm all right," she replied tartly.

"They told me you'd fainted after I left."

"Gracious, Darius, I had to do something. It was mortal embarrassing. So I just closed my eyes and let myself wilt." The corners of her mouth twitched. "There were several men ready to catch me. I don't take it kindly that you hurried off—"

"Look here, Sabina," he interrupted, "do you realize that Gault is dead? Can't you understand it, or didn't they make it clear?"

"Heavens, Darius, you can depend on that Mrs. Gore to make things clear. I thought I never would get rid of her. She wanted to bring Jennifer Keating to stay with me. You'll never know what I've been through. I must say, Gault didn't show me much consideration, getting himself killed in a house of ill-fame. Whatever could he see in such women? I'll not be able to face a soul in this hotel, so long as I'm here."

He stared, scarcely able to believe his ears. Sabina went on, "Don't take this too much to heart, Darius. Really, you must understand it's the best thing could have happened. If I'd divorced Gault and married you, there'd been no end to the gossip. Now, you'll simply be marrying the widow of your old friend and taking her home to Urquhart Oaks. It will be splendid, Darius, with the great white house you've built—oh, we'll be envied. Gault really settled a great deal of money on me, you know. The whole situation is— Darius, what is wrong?"

Quite suddenly he averted his shocked gaze as he might have from something shameful. "You're wrong, Sabina, terribly wrong." Urquhart rose to his feet. "I think I'd best be leaving now, but there's something to be settled first. I've no intention of marrying you. I've said no word to lead you to believe that. It's something you've conjured up in your own vain, selfish imagination—"

"Darius, no!" Sabina whipped up from the bed and across the room in a single cat-like movement to hurl herself against him. She locked her hands about his neck to draw his head down to her mouth. "Darling, you don't know what you're saying. You know Gault meant nothing to me—never has. It has been only your foolish sense of honor that kept us apart."

Deliberately, Urquhart disengaged her hands and held her, by the wrists. "If it was a sense of honor that kept us apart, I thank God. But there was something else, Sabina, beyond your comprehension. Gault Madison was the truest friend a man ever had. He would have been a great deal more to you, if you had let him. He had his faults. But you did make a compact, a bargain, when you married him, and you were the first to break it. You asked what Gault could find in 'such women.' I believe he found forgetfulness of the wounds you'd given him. You'll find it difficult to believe, but those women had a genuine liking for Gault, and not because of his money. One of them was even ready to kill to retain his affection. That is something your kind of woman could never understand. No, Sabina, it's not all been your fault; I realize Gault's actions did furnish you justification. But it was in your power to change that, and you wouldn't even make the effort."

She had been struggling while he talked, and now he released her wrists. She stood back, panting, facing him defiantly. "What you are telling me, Darius," she insisted hotly, "is extremely ridiculous. You're letting this business of Gault's death shake your best judgment. You speak of compacts and bargains. Well,"— she drew herself up confidently, a provocative challenge in the sloe-brown eyes—"look at me. Where will you find better than I have to offer. Right now, if you like. You and I belong together." Her voice softened. "Last night, Darius, you told me I was beautiful. Have I changed so greatly since then, that you take this absurd attitude, or am I still beautiful?"

He surveyed her almost impersonally, taking in the chiseled perfection of blond features, noting with a momentary fascination a throbbing in Sabina's slim throat and the faint blue tracery of a vein where it followed the satiny texture of white skin to vanish in the tumultuous rise and fall of rounded breasts cradled in the frothy lace showing above the loosely-gathered edges of silk wrapper. For a second he closed his eyes and drew a sudden breath as though in pain, and there was almost a wistful note in his tones when he spoke. "Yes," he said at last, "you are beautiful, Sabina. But your beauty is all on the surface, and I can see beyond that now. Inside, you are ugly as sin."

Sabina's eyes widened and the lovely mouth went loose and repulsive; an incredulous frown furrowed her forehead. "No, no, Darius," she insisted in a hoarse whisper, "you can't mean that. You loved me, you did, you did—!"

"Believing that, is one more trick your vain imagination played you," he said evenly. "I've never loved you. An attraction, good God, yes! A kind of sickness, of which I've been entirely cured for some time." She backed away from him, trembling, then flung herself on the bed and began to sob, the pale-gold hair tumbling about her shaking shoulders. He stood looking at her, stony-faced. "That won't work, either, Sabina. You'd best quit pretending, before you lose even your surface beauty."

She sat up, face suffused with anger. "You're a fool, Darius Urquhart. The day will come when you'll regret not accepting me. It's all that Keating girl's fault. She must have you hypnotized. Go to your Cherokee squaw, and much good may it do you. She won't even have you. I fixed that! I talked to Corbillat. He said she wasn't even friendly, coming from Texas—"

"Sabina, exactly what do you mean?" Urquhart demanded. "You fixed what?"

"You fool! Can't you understand? I fixed it so you and your squaw . . ." Sabina's voice trailed off at the look in his eyes. "Don't pay attention to me, Darius. I'm distraught. Gault's death has me so upset, I'm out of my mind . . ." She cowered as he crossed to the bed. "Don't, Darius. I haven't done anything. What's the matter with you?" He seized her shoulder, demanding sternly what she'd been hinting at. "Please, Darius, you're hurting my arm."

"Be thankful if I don't break your neck," he said savagely. "Now you talk, Sabina! What did you fix? And how? And when?" His grip tightened.

She commenced weeping, but he was inexorable. "I—I just wanted to save you from her. I told her you'd been my lover, since we first met—"

"God almighty," Urquhart breathed.

"—it wasn't hard to convince her, after she saw me in your arms, that night in our kitchen." Sabina looked anxiously up at him.

He released her and stood back from the bed. "Tonight," he said harshly, "Belle Silk applied a certain name to those girls who were concerned in Gault's death. I think that name is far more applicable to you, Sabina." He started toward the door. With one hand on the knob, he turned. "Gault's to be buried tomorrow at eight o'clock. There'll be a hired rig waiting at the hotel to drive you to the funeral."

Sabina's back stiffened. "I refuse to attend his funeral. I couldn't stand the shame. I'm going to pack and take the first train—"

"After the funeral, you can leave as soon as you choose, but you owe Gault's memory this much. You'll attend, or by God, I'll spend every dollar I own to deprive you of money Gault made over to you. That shouldn't be difficult, if I make public what has passed here, tonight."

Sabina was aghast. "You—you wouldn't dare, Darius. You're a gentleman."

He shook his head. "Not where you're concerned. Not after tonight. Remember, the funeral will be at

281

eight." He opened the door and quietly closed it after him, an instant before a slipper, hurled by Sabina's hand, crashed against the panel.

He walked to his room, opened the door. A faint light from the moon came through the wide-open window where the curtain waved gently in the soft early morning breeze across the Kansas prairies. Corbillat lay in bed, snoring rhythmically. Urquhart tossed his hat on the dresser and walked to the window. His vision blurred, but he stood there, without movement. Corbillat opened his eyes. "You, Rius?" he grunted. "What time is it?"

"Getting on toward four o'clock." Urquhart's voice wasn't steady.

"I drifted off instanter, once I'd settled on this mattress. You been talkin' to Sabina Madison all this time?"

"Not all this time, Dix," Urquhart answered wearily.

"Something wrong with you, Rius?" Urquhart didn't reply. He quit looking through the window and walked to a chair. He removed one boot, placed it carefully on the floor, and then sat staring toward the window again. "What's the matter with you, Rius?" Corbillat asked, sitting up in bed.

Urquhart groped for words. "It's happened almost too suddenly for comprehension, Dix," he began in a monotonous murmur. "There's this house run by a madam named Belle Silk, and two of the girls there, Babe and Dolly. They thought a lot of Gault, Dix. You've got to believe that. I talked to them. It wasn't just Gault's money. All women aren't like some Gault has known—"

"You tryin' to tell me somethin's happened to Gault?"

"I'd doing my best to make it clear, Dix, only the words won't come right. At first, Gault favored Babe, and then he commenced making his play with Dolly. Something about Dolly's eyes reminded him of Texas—they were like bluebonnets, Gault said. But favoring the two girls that way didn't work out. It made for jealousy. At least on Babe's part, and she's hardly old enough to know better. And last night when Gault was in Dolly's room, Babe rushed in and got Gault's six-shooter—"

"And shot Gault?"

"Not intentionally, Dix. She was trying to shoot Dolly, and while Gault was struggling with her to get the gun, it went off, and—and Gault's dead—"

"Gawd A'mighty!" Corbillat's feet made padding sounds across the floor and he stood over Urquhart. "Why'n't you send for me?"

"There wasn't a thing you could have done. If I'd waited for you, I might not have got there before he died. Yes, he was conscious. He talked right up to the end, insisting it was an accident. He was even able to make a joke of it. Gault said he couldn't hold one woman, in Texas, but after traveling clear to Kansas he'd found two who wanted him, and maybe that was worth dying for."

Corbillat said, after a time, "There's nothing here, Rius. You want I should go bring you a drink?"

Urquhart said no; this was something a drink couldn't help. Dix recrossed the room, found the "makin's," and rolled two cornhusk cigarettes which he lighted, sticking one between Urquhart's lips. "And then," Urquhart resumed after a time, "I waited for the undertaker to come, and we went down to his place and made arrangements, and—and—well, Gault's dead—"

"Seems like," Corbillat said in a troubled tone, "an arrest should have been made."

"The town-marshal had been called in—fellow named Ryskoff. But Gault had requested especially that the girl not be arrested. He swore it was an accident. Anyway, making arrests for shooting doesn't seem to be the custom here. Ryskoff did make Belle Silk close her place for the night, though. And the two girls who made the trouble—I suppose Gault was responsible too—patched up their differences, and were crying in each other's arms when I left. What are you going to do with women like that."

"What you going to do with women?" Dix asked dully.

15

LIFE, CORBILLAT CONSIDERED, AS HE SAT ON THE gallery of the Drovers' Cottage, was a queer proposition. Gault Madison, just laid in his grave yesterday mornin', and to judge by the activity you'd think he wasn't only not dead, but maybe hadn't even ever been to Abilene. It seemed that the death of a man like Gault would give life a pause and everything would be hushed for a spell, 'specially after that big turn-out at the funeral. There was no difference in the bawlin' of the cows, and the stock trains kept shuntin' back and forth, with the engine sendin' up clouds of smoke and steam. And all along this gallery the cattle-buyers were augerin' prices with stockmen, and ponies and buggies and wagons milled about the front, stirring up dust motes to float lazy in the mornin' sunshine beyond the shadow of the gallery overhang.

There had been one odd thing happened though, and that was the way Sabina caught the first train available when the funeral was over. And why had it been his job to help her on with valises at that little clapboard shanty Abilene called its depot? You'd thought Rius would have been on hand to see her off. Rius hadn't even said good-bye, and Sabina hadn't mentioned Rius. Sabina'd looked kind of subdued when she got on that little old train. Maybe she'd realized what she'd lost, after Gault was dead. She hadn't given any sign at the funeral she cared about Gault. Any fool could tell that Miss Jen felt far worse'n Sabina. Not that Miss Jen shed tears, but a man could tell she felt bad about the business. Yes, there was a heap of things to ask Rius. It was high time him and Miss Jen got back to friendly terms. No sense in 'em actin' like a couple of strange houn'-dawgs with the hair bristlin' along their spines.

The door of the hotel opened and Urquhart and Phineas Aikman stepped to the gallery. The two men stood talking, then shook hands before Aikman departed. Urquhart glanced about, and seeing Dix, took the empty chair at his side. He produced two cigars, handed one to Dix and lighted the other.

Urquhart said, "You know, Dix, I think Gault had a premonition of death when he started for Kansas. He brought all his valuable papers with him, and it's taken time for Aikman to go through his things and find how matters stand."

"Say, if you're in the mood for talkin', will you please explain just why it was me had to see Mrs. Madison off on the train?"

Urquhart's lips tightened. "I was too busy."

"If that's an answer," Corbillat growled, "I'll eat my Stet-hat. All right, let it go. If you don't want to talk, don't." Urquhart remarked quietly that Dix seemed full of questions this morning. "Maybe so," Corbillat admitted. "I'll ask you another. When we goin' to start home? I'd like to get our boys started before they spend all their money, or get killed in a gun-fight. Anythin' can happen in this town."

"Do you know what the men are doing?"

"Oh, Gawd, do I have to go through that again? They're around town, spendin' their money on liquor and gambling and—well, you can guess that part. Meanwhile, Albumen is maintainin' a camp for them, and every mornin' he drives Dicey Nell to her job at the hotel, where she stays on to be near Miss Jen. And Miss Jen is all right—I beat you to that question, didn't I? Yesterday, Mrs. Gore took her store-buyin' and she got a new dress. I can't tell you what she had for breakfast," his voice turned sarcastic—"because I ain't asked. And why it should be me instead of you keepin' an eye on Miss Jen, I don't know, when you're—"

Urquhart cut in meekly, "I guess I've put more than your share of the burden on you, but I've had my hands full. I'm sorry. I'm as anxious to get back to Texas as you are. I'd leave today, except—well, I've been waiting for Jennifer to start first. She can go back, pick up her grandparents and then—I don't know what she plans to do. I thought it might be more pleasant for her, if I wasn't there—"

"Buffalo-chips!" Corbillat said inelegantly. "Why'n't you go up to Miss Jen's room and thrash out your differences? I can't square that business whatever it is, 'cause she won't talk when I mention your name."

"I tried, and I won't try again. After all, a man has his pride, and if she could doubt me once . . ."

"What you talkin' about?" Corbillat frowned. "Who said anythin' about her doubtin' you?"

Urquhart shook his head. "I've already said too much. It's not a thing I want to go into. I'll take it as a favor if you say no more."

Corbillat shrugged. "Just as you say. It's sure goin' to be good to get to Texas again, and see trees. I'm mighty sick of lookin' at buffalo-grass, far's a man can see. It's gettin' hot down there about now, but that little old Gulf breeze will be along to cool things off, and there's the big oaks for shade and Crinolina Creek flowin' past. And I suppose Miss Jen's kinfolks are out workin' their cornfield same as always."

Urquhart frowned. "Speaking of Cherokees, Dix, there're a couple of words, I've been intending to ask you to translate. Let's see, if I can get it straight. Oh, yes,"—trying to enunciate slowly and carefully—

"what do *agehya taluli* and *'ta'hu li'* signify in the Cherokee language?"

Corbillat's head furrowed in thought. "Ain't certain I ever did hear those words before, Rius. Say 'em again." Urquhart repeated the syllables. The lines in Corbillat's brow deepened, then suddenly cleared. "Oh, you mean *agehya taluli* and *'ta'hu li'*. Let's see . . . long spell since I've heard those words . . . well, *'ta'hu li'* means 'she carries it'. That's close enough. Now, *agehya taluli* . . . *agehya* is a woman, and *taluli* is . . . is . . . why, *taluli* means pregnant. They both mean practically the same thing, Rius. Whoever said that, was tellin' you about some woman going to have a baby. Does that make sense to you?"

Urquhart scowled. "I don't recollect now where I heard 'em," he commenced evasively, and then as though to himself, "I can't see exactly what—" The cigar dropped suddenly from his mouth to the gallery floor. In swift succession, his wide-eyed gaze reflected shock, skepticism, incredulity. "Good God, no!" he exclaimed. "No! It couldn't be!" He was on his feet now.

"What's wrong with you, Rius? You gone *loco?*"

Urquhart began backing away. "I'll see you later, Dix," he said hoarsely. "I've—I've got to get away and think something out . . ." He stepped hastily from the gallery and started pushing his way between men, vehicles and horses standing before the hotel.

Corbillat stared after him.

16

URQUHART WAS SOME DISTANCE FROM THE HOTEL, HIS mind a turmoil of complex emotion, when he heard his name called: "Majuh Ukhart!" Albumen appeared from nowhere. "Whut's do matteh, Majuh, suh? Y'all sashigatin' 'long lak a steeah wid de blin' staggehs."

The appearance of the Negro provided a welcome diversion for Urquhart's seething thoughts. Glancing around, he became aware he'd been heading in the direction of the Texas District. He noticed for the first time, the Negro's dusty, rumpled clothing, and the smear of blood on one cheekbone. "What happened to you?"

"Hit ain't nuthin', suh. Ah jist took me a tumble; tripped oveh mah own two clumsy feets. It ain't nuthin' foah you go frettin' 'bout."

"Albumen, you're lying to me."

Albumen shuffled his feet uneasily, and started to back away. Urquhart seized him by the arm and insisted on learning the truth. Eventually, the Negro yielded: "Hit's lak dis, suh,"—reluctantly, "Ah don't aim cause you no trouble, you a'ready gotten a hatfull wid de killin' of Mistuh Madison, so Ah jist figgehs . . ."

"Damn it, Albumen, get on with your story."

The Negro's eyes rolled whitely. "Well, t'tell de exact truth, Majuh, suh, one of mah mules taken a gall-soah, so Ah hies me to Mistuh Gayla'd's Twin Livery t'see did dey got any tuppentine-sulphah ointment, and dey's the usual gemmun standin' 'round mekkin' talk, and den Ah sees Mistuh Hawnish, and de gemmun is—"

"Harnish!" Urquhart's mouth went hard. "In Abilene?"

"Yassuh. Ah heahs he say he gits in on de mawnin' train, and puts up at de Mulbe'y Hotel, an' he's tellin' how he gots de hud comin' up de trail, and him has come to de Twin Livery to arrange foah de rentin' of a hawss, so's to ride out and meet he hud. And—and Ah raikons dat's all, Majuh, suh."

"You know damned well that's not all, Albumen," Urquhart said sternly. "Now tell me exactly what happened."

Albumen looked miserable. " 'Peahs lak you got you mind made up t'dreen it outten me," he sighed. "Well, one gemmun mentions 'bout de Cucle-U whut pulled in wid a lady trail-driveh along. And Mistuh Hawnish boasts how he knows de lady and de owneh of de Cucle-U and dat de lady had been livin' wid you, suh, at Ukhart Oaks, and dat you brung she long foah you pleasuah—"

An oath broke from Urquhart's lips. His face was set in rigid lines. "What else happened?"

"Ah cain't take kindly to dat kind of talk, so Ah intrudes in de convehsation and tells de gemmun dat Mistuh Hawnish ain't got he facts right, and dat Ah knowed y'all and Miss Jennifuh a long time and dat Ah was present when y'all ma'ied she, back in No'th Ca'lina—"

"You told those men that we were married in North Carolina?"

"Yassuh. Ah couldn't figgeh nothin' betteh to say. Ah hopes dat don't meet wid you dis'proval, suh."

290

"Probably the best thing to say, under the circumstances."

"And wid dat," Albumen went on, "Mistuh Hawnish asks whut in hell rat a 'man's' got int'ruptin' white folks. And he fetches me a clout on de haid, and Ah finds mahself stirrin' de dust on de ground. Dat Hawnish man shouldn't go 'round spraidin' scan'lous gossip 'bout Miss Jennifuh—"

"All right, Albumen," Urquhart interrupted. "I'll take care of this. You go on back to your mule, and stay away from Dix. You hear?—I don't want him messing into this. This is my concern." Without waiting for a reply, Urquhart strode off, failing to notice that the Negro was following him, a discreet distance to the rear.

Gaylard's Twin Livery, off Railroad Street, was two immense peaked-roof structures, connected by a flat-roofed runway with a wide arched entrance. From within the stables came sounds of industry, but the exterior presented a scene of indolence, with eight or nine loafers seated on bales of straw near the entrance, exchanging smutty stories. Among the men was Drake Harnish in wide hat and coat, his striped trousers tucked into knee-length boots and a flowing necktie against a white shirt. A stable attendant had just led out a horse, and Harnish was preparing to set foot in stirrup when Urquhart called, "One minute, Harnish!"

The sharp tones caught the attention of the other men. They glanced at Harnish and saw the uneasy look that crossed his face. This had the appearance of trouble, the idlers concluded, noting Urquhart's bleak gaze and tight mouth. They stood watching while

Urquhart drew near. Harnish forced a tentative smile. "Well, if it isn't Urquhart! I understand your herd got up the trail all right—"

"You've already talked too much regarding my activities, Harnish," Urquhart said coldly. "You're going to retract everything you've said. Now!" He stood squarely before Harnish, his right thumb hooked in his gunbelt.

The smile died from Harnish's face; beads of perspiration formed on his forehead. One hand tugged uncertainly at his moustache. "I haven't the least idea what you're talking about. If you'll explain—"

"You know. My Negro tells me you've been making some free talk before these gentlemen." Urquhart's ironical glance swept over the loafers.

Harnish managed a short laugh. 'Was that your 'nigger' I knocked down? You wouldn't expect me to recognize a 'nigger,' would you? When he misunderstood some remarks I made and contradicted me, I put him in his place. I said nothing about you—"

"You're a liar, Harnish." Urquhart's voice had the bite of a frozen whiplash. "There'll be no names mentioned, but you will now inform these gentlemen that you lied in your remarks concerning the Circle-U outfit and anyone connected with it."

"By God!" Harnish blustered, "you can't ride roughshod over me. I refuse to—"

"Refuse and be damned," Urquhart snapped. "You'll do as I say, or I'm going to kill you. Here and now!"

Harnish's eyes fell before the fury blazing in Urquhart's gaze, shifted nervously to the holstered gun at Urquhart's hip, then slid sidewise as though seeking escape. His tongue licked at dry lips as he drew apart the lapels of his black coat. "Why, Urquhart, you can see I'm not armed. You wouldn't dare shoot me. These gentlemen will be witnesses to any attempt——"

"Talk fast, Harnish," Urquhart's voice was relentless.

Harnish's face turned a sickly yellow hue. "Now, look here, Urquhart," he began apprehensively, "you wouldn't dare try this if I were armed. You're taking an unfair advantage——"

Urquhart's harsh laugh interrupted: "Exactly so, Harnish," he conceded, "as you and your guerrillas took an unfair advantage of many helpless people during the war." Harnish's eyes bulged. "Yes, Harnish, I know about that. Talk fast."

A trembling seized on Harnish's limbs. A maze of confused speculation occupied his agitated mind. Where had Urquhart learned of the guerrilla activities? How much did he know? He fought to get his nerves under control. It was imperative that he get away until he'd had an opportunity to think. Once he had a gun, he could deal on equal terms with Urquhart. Perhaps better than equal terms. Brains still counted, when backed with the force of powder and lead. The most urgent need was to extricate himself from this present difficulty. Given time, ten minutes, even five minutes, this situation could be reversed. . . . As from far away, he heard Urquhart's chill inflexible demands:

"Make up your mind, Harnish. I won't wait much longer."

A crafty smile curved Harnish's lips, and he turned to the idlers. "You gentlemen know I am unarmed. Under the circumstances, Mr. Urquhart leaves me no alternative, if I have any consideration for my life. So there's nothing left—except to say that I lied in any statement I have made regarding the Circle-U outfit and anyone connected with it." Disappointed sighs arose from the onlookers. Harnish turned to Urquhart. "That satisfy you?"

"Only partially," Urquhart said coldly. "Now, get armed, or leave Abilene. At once! I won't be able to stand the sight of you, again, Harnish." His contemptuous gaze ranged briefly over the assembled idlers, standing silent and abashed, then came back to Harnish. "I prefer that you get armed," he concluded, and strode rapidly away.

17

JENNIFER, THE MIDNIGHT-BLACK BRAIDS COILED ABOUT her head, sat sewing in a small cane rocker, where the occasional breeze, fluttering the curtain, alleviated somewhat the heat of Kansas midday. She bit through the thread and put down the white cotton-flannel on which she'd been stitching. She leaned back in the rocker, considering the vase of lupine blossoms Dicey Nell had brought that morning. The wildflowers carried her thoughts to Texas; her mind strayed over the long trail north, eventually coming to rest on the little scuffed-leather trunk standing near the wash-stand; from the trunk, her eyes went to the red carnelian ring on her hand. It was imperative, Jennifer concluded, that she talk to Darius. Had not the shooting of Gault and consequent proceedings interfered, various matters might have been settled by this time. She must see Darius before another day passed; this afternoon, if possible.

A knock sounded and, rising, Jennifer shook out the folds of her full loose skirt, and opened the door. Dicey Nell stood before the doorway, bearing a large tray which held covered dishes. "Shuah regretful Ah's late fetchin' you dinneh, Miss Jennifuh, but we pow'ful busy in de dinin'-room dis noontime. Ah done brung you some buffalo-meat, but could be you don't fancy hit, so Ah adds a suhvin' of roas'-pohk."

"Gracious, Dicey Nell! Dix would say you were trying to put tallow on me."

"You comin' 'long all rat. Ah notes you eats all Ah fetches. With you appetite, was you ma'ied, Ah'd cal'-clate you was eatin' foah two." A flush crept up Jennifer's cheekbones. The Negro girl rattled on, "Beggin' youah pahdon, Miss Jennifuh, but could you be predictin' when we's haidin' foah Taixus? All dat Albumen chattehs 'bout, is Ukhart Oaks, ontil him got me nigh loony to see de place."

"We'll be leaving Abilene shortly, I hope. Do you know where the Major is at present?"

"No'm, not at de present. De sahgent in de dinin'-room, rat now, eatin' he buffalo-meat. Does you want he?"

Jennifer shook her head. "You might tell him, when he's finished dinner, that I'd like to see Major Urquhart."

"Yassum, Ah tells he." Dicey Nell departed.

Jennifer stood thoughtfully, looking from her window. Below, flanking Railroad Street, a long four-board fence jutted from the front corner of the Drovers' Cottage, and tethered to the top-rail were a number of saddled ponies and several horse-drawn vehicles, waiting while their owners finished dinner. Beyond the far end of the fence, commenced a rough board sidewalk which fronted a saloon, a two-story hotel, a pair of frame buildings with false fronts, and another saloon located on a corner that turned in the direction of the Texas District.

While Jennifer stood in the window, a rider trotted into view from the opposite side of the hotel, and reined his mount into the fence, next to a four-wheeled surrey. Something about the man touched a reminiscent chord in Jennifer. When he dismounted, fifty-odd feet distant from her window, the girl recognized, with some feeling of disquiet, the figure of Drake Harnish.

What on earth was Harnish doing in Abilene? When had he arrived? Was Darius aware of his arrival? The girl drew back watching Harnish's movements. It was natural to assume Harnish had come to Drovers' Cottage for dinner, but after dismounting he moved only slightly beyond the bay horse's hind-quarters, and stood peering out, from time to time, past the rear ends of the vehicles ranged along the fence. Apparently, Harnish was waiting for someone to put in an appearance. But why did he skulk in such fashion?

A feeling of trepidation possessed Jennifer. Farther along Railroad Street, she saw Urquhart approaching on the plank sidewalk. For an instant Jennifer stood paralyzed. Urquhart came steadily on, walking slowly with deliberate steps. The distance of half a city block to his rear, Jennifer saw Albumen, but why the Negro was following Urquhart she had no idea, nor was this the time to ponder such a question.

She lifted her voice to cry a warning to Urquhart, but a train of stock-cars rumbling past combined with the snorting of the locomotive to drown out her tones. Jennifer hesitated an instant longer, then turned swiftly to the little leather trunk. With steady fingers she unfastened the straps and released the catch. The lid was thrown back. Clothing within the trunk was flung aside, while Jennifer's hand reached for the Colt's revolver which Dix had given her. Thank heaven, she had followed Dix's admonishment to keep the gun always loaded. She quickly inspected the weapon, then cocked it.

When she returned to the open window Darius was much closer. Harnish was crouched behind one rear wheel of a surrey, his right thumb already curling about the hammer of his gun. "Come out of there, Drake Harnish!" Jennifer cried sharply, and at the same instant felt the heavy cap-and-ball reverberate in her hand. Through the haze of powder smoke she saw an abrupt scattering of sand and gravel spray over Harnish, as the bullet ploughed into earth near his crouching figure. Harnish's head jerked around, his startled gaze changing to alarm as his eyes ranged up the side of the building to Jennifer, gun in hand, leaning from the window. He ducked, scrambling frantically, beneath

the wheels of the surrey, and sought the shelter of saddled ponies tied beyond the vehicle.

Urquhart by this time had halted. Whether or not he
had heard the shot, Jennifer couldn't determine; the
train of stock-cars rumbling past may have smothered
the sound. He stood a moment, frowning, then spying
the girl, pistol in hand, in the window, he raised one
arm in a puzzled, uncertain greeting, and started on
again, still unaware of Harnish lurking in the shadow
of the ponies.

Again, Jennifer drew back the hammer of her gun
and tightened one finger about the trigger. A sudden
raw yellow of splintered pine appeared, as her shot
chamfered the top board of the fence, almost beneath
the noses of the tethered ponies. Instantly, the animals
took fright, jerking back their heads and snorting in
terror. One horse started bucking; the other two struggled wildly to release themselves.

The sharp, plunging hoofs proved more than Harnish could face. He burst precipitately into the open,
not thirty feet from Urquhart, a streak of white fire and
black powdersmoke bursting from his gun-muzzle.
Jennifer saw dust spurt, a short distance beyond
Urquhart and realized, thankfully, that Harnish had
missed aim. The man was in the act of recocking his
weapon when Urquhart drew and fired, the impact of
the heavy-caliber bullet knocking Harnish to earth,
and sending the gun flying from his hand. He was
trying to struggle to his feet, when Urquhart fired a
second time.

Instantly men appeared, running, to converge upon

the two antagonists, one of whom now lay huddled, face down, in the Kansas dust. Jennifer saw Albumen rush to join the crowd and push his way to Urquhart's side. Corbillat came plunging into view, followed by an excited throng from the Drovers' Cottage. A trembling seized on the girl's limbs, as she stood watching the commotion below, but soon her heart resumed its normal beating and the weakness passed. She turned away from the window, and after placing the cap-and-ball on the dresser, seated herself on the bed to wait.

After a time, Dicey Nell came running to her door. "Is you all rat, Miss Jennifuh!" Jennifer said of course she was all right. "De Majuh sent Albumen to say he be up, jist's soon as he gits done wid de formalties wid Ma'shal Ryskoff. Albumen say dat man, name Hawnish, was mekkin' some scan'lous talk, and Majuh o'dehs he git outten Ab'lene, and t'was dat leadin' to de contentionin' wid de pistols . . . Yuah suah you is all rat?" Jennifer said again she was all right, and Dicey Nell went away.

18

WHEN JENNIFER HEARD HIS STEP, SHE WENT TO THE door before Urquhart could knock. He came hesitantly through the doorway, hat in hand, and crossed to the window while she closed the door. His gaze fell on the cap-and-ball on the dresser, then returned to the girl and there was a definite awe in his grey eyes when he saw her unshaken poise. Abruptly, the great sense of responsibility he owed Jennifer swept over him, and there was a choking sensation in his throat. He said, at last, "Well, Jennifer. . . ."

She said gravely, "Well, Darius?"

She could scarcely hear him when he began, "Jennifer!—I—" He paused, then went on, "You've put me still further in your debt." That, Jennifer assured him quietly, was a matter of no concern. "But, Jennifer, I had no idea he was there, waiting for me. If it had not been for your warning—" His final words came with a rush, "Jennifer, I had to kill Harnish."

She replied calmly, "I'd probably have done it, if you hadn't, Darius. It was Drake Harnish who killed my father, that day in Carolina when you and Dix arrived to drive off the guerrillas."

Urquhart stared at her, unbelieving. Comprehension abruptly swept over him. "Good Lord, of course it was Harnish! Now I realize why he looked familiar the next time I saw him. Jennifer! Do you suppose he recognized us?"

"That is a thing I do not know," Jennifer said slowly. "Dix said he was running away, that day when you came to the cabin. He may not have seen your face. He should have remembered me, but perhaps he had seen so many other frightened girls . . ." She paused, then, "That day I met him in San Antonio, I knew it was not the first time, but for long I could not remember where I'd encountered him before. That day at the cabin, he wore a heavy black beard, and it was almost like a disguise for his features, and a hat pulled low. And that day there was a terror in me that blotted a great deal from my thoughts. The more I saw of the man, the more it all began to come back, until I was almost certain—but not quite. And you couldn't understand, Darius,"—she was very earnest about this—"but I just had to keep seeing him at every opportunity, until I could be very sure. And you misunderstood my motives. But when Purdy told you Harnish had been a guerrilla, there was no more doubt in my mind it was he you had driven from our cabin that day."

A wave of self-condemnation possessed Urquhart, but at last he found his voice. "Jennifer," he said, and the tones were not at all steady, "I've told you before I was a fool. I never realized I could be so cruel. I think I must have been insane—yes, and jealous, too—"

"Ah, jealousy," she said swiftly. "I, too, have learned what that is, Darius. And if you were a fool, I was a greater one. I thought I knew so much of men and their way with women. And when Sabina Madison told me a great many lies, which only an idiot could believe, I was that idiot—"

"The night Gault was shot," Urquhart broke in, "I went to Sabina's room. We talked and—well, she lost her head and said things that explained much."

Jennifer said, "I overheard your talk with Sabina. Sabina's room was directly across the corridor. Her transom was open, as was mine. I could not help hearing all that was said." A smile touched her lovely mouth. "That wasn't lady-like, was it, eavesdropping in such fashion?"

"Thank God you did hear us! I'd hoped to make you understand I cared nothing for her, nothing at all, and now you must know—"

"I was very sure of that," Jennifer interrupted, "even before we started north. While I was at Seguin I did a deal of thinking on things Sabina had told me and I decided they could not be true. There was so much that was not like you. Even for the evidence of my eyes— a thing I saw that night at Gault's, I knew there must be an explanation. And Sabina had told me so many lies, I concluded nothing she said could be true. I returned to Urquhart Oaks, ready to admit I had been wrong. And then you came, and Harnish was there, and you acted like a madman. Your suspicions made me angry, and we both said things we shouldn't have. I think for a time I lost my senses, when I consented to go north with you, for I was very wicked—"

"Ah, no, Jennifer, not wicked—not you—"

"There is no other word for it, Darius. I hoped something would happen on that journey north that would make you suffer a great deal and would remember all your life. It was the Irish in me was to blame for that, but the Cherokee blood has bred me stronger than I knew—"

"Good Lord!" he burst in. "I—Jennifer! Dix translated for me those Cherokee words your grandparents kept repeating that day I took you away—Jennifer, even if you won't forgive me, you must marry me now. You must!"

The girl stood very straight and splendid, and there was a shining in the smoky-gentian eyes. "I knew it was but a matter of time before you discovered it, Darius—"

"But why didn't you tell me—?"

"After Sabina had made that trouble between us? I didn't want you to know, then, for fear . . ."

"When, Jennifer, when?" he interrupted excitedly. She mentioned something about the third or fourth week of November, and added, as though she were very certain, he would be named after her father and Darius Urquhart. Words tumbled in a confused torrent from Urquhart's lips and he scarcely knew what he was saying. "There's that parson, Calvin Huneker. I'll go get him. At once!" He crossed the room and his hand was on the door-knob when he turned. "Wait," he said, and his voice was hoarse with emotion, "wait right here for me."

"Darius!" Her soft laughter made music in his ears, and he saw a mischievous light in the long-lashed eyes. "Is it so urgent that you make me an honest woman, that you cannot first hold me in your arms a little, before you leave? Dear God! I've been waiting all too long, Darius Urquhart."

He turned slowly back from the door as she came to him, very straight and proud, and he was conscious of a loveliness in her, more poignant than he'd ever known before. And there was an aching in his heart and in his arms that could be eased only by her sweet touch, and a misty fragrance in his head that sent the blood surging hotly through his veins. But there still remained in him a certain awe of the girl, and at first his hand reached tentatively to one shoulder, as though she were some fragile, ethereal being who might suddenly vanish beneath his fingers, then feeling the warm flesh through her garment, he swiftly gathered her

303

close, and felt her arms tighten about his neck, and her mouth was soft and warm under his own. His lips moved down to the sweet hollow of her throat, and he was saying over and over, "Oh, Jennifer, Jennifer," and again, "Jennifer . . ." the words, with her soft endearments, making a kind of litany to rise, golden-winged and forever, above the dust of all defeats that had been, or all that could ever be again.

Center Point Publishing
600 Brooks Road ● PO Box 1
Thorndike ME 04986-0001 USA

(207) 568-3717

**US & Canada:
1 800 929-9108**